SEATTLE SCORPIO

BOARDED
Hearts

RUTH STILLING

TRIGGER/ CONTENT WARNINGS

You should be aware that while this book is a work of fiction and is, of course, a happily ever after, Boarded Hearts does contain themes of the following:

Sexually explicit content, strong language, emotionally manipulative behavior from a former spouse (not the main characters), off-page death of parents (which took place years before the book being set), reference to cheating (not between the main characters), themes of anxiety and depression (for the male main character) with off-page therapy.

For those who bravely face a silent battle with themselves each day.
You are never alone.

PLAYLIST

You can find Jon and Felicity's playlist on Spotify.

Adore You – Harry Styles
Midnight Sky – Miley Cyrus
Style – Taylor Swift
Iris – The Goo Goo Dolls
Ready For Your Love – Gorgon City, MNEK
Tidal Wave – Sub Focus, Alpines
Dangerous Woman – Ariana Grande
Hands To Myself – Selena Gomez
Call It What You Want – Taylor Swift
Bloodstream – Ed Sheeran
Keeping Your Head Up – Birdy
Better – Khalid

PROLOGUE

Two years ago

OXFORD, ENGLAND

FELICITY

"Consider this your notice then, Felicity."

I can't do this. I can't even process the words as Elliott says, well, barks at me.

We're moving? To Seattle.

I shake my head and grip the kitchen counter hard, trying to steady myself, or maybe trying not to blow a gasket at my husband.

He went right ahead and signed the contract without a second thought for me, my job, or the life we've built here. Not to mention our two teenage children, Darcy and Jack. Sixteen years of this, the Elliott Show.

"I can't believe you didn't discuss it with me first. Two years. You expect us to just uproot our lives for that long? What about my job and Darcy and Jack's schooling?" A cold shiver trickles down my spine. Darcy's long-term boyfriend and childhood sweetheart, Liam, is here. At fifteen, it will feel like her world is

1

imploding. I shake my head and take another sip of wine. "You can break it to Darcy."

Elliott waves a dismissive hand in the air. "It's young love; it's trivial and will never last anyway. This is an opportunity for her to see the world."

I quirk a brow in surprise at his admission. "We were young when we met. We didn't think it was *trivial* then, and I doubt she does now." My heart breaks for her—Liam isn't only her boyfriend but her best friend too. She has a close relationship with her dad, but this is likely to put a significant strain on that.

Jack, I'm less worried about. He's a keen ice hockey player and plays for the Oxford Giants. At sixteen and very outgoing, he'll likely see this as an opportunity to play in America and maybe one day live out his dream in the big leagues. He's talented, but ice hockey isn't big in the UK. That said, we will be moving during his finals at secondary school, and he's always struggled academically, so this could set him back permanently.

"What about my job? I was on for a promotion. I have dreams too."

Elliott scoffs and rises from the dining stool where he's casually sat for most of the evening, his leg crossed over the other at the knee, like this conversation isn't totally life-changing and gut-wrenching for most of his family. Stepping toward me, he places his palm over the top of my hand, but I snatch it out from underneath; I can barely look at him, let alone touch him. And that feeling isn't just isolated to tonight and this news. Our marriage has been failing for years, and as I look up into his cold blue eyes, I see very little affection there. I wonder if he sees the same when he looks at me.

"You earn £27,000 a year Felicity. I earn over eight times your salary. You don't need to keep pushing this 'dream career' of yours in law." In a condescending tone, he repeats the words I've said to him more times than I can count. "I can take care of all of us. It's a two-year contract to help establish and oversee the

US equity fund and if it works out, the bonus on offer has the potential to change our lives."

Frustration emanates from me in waves. He never listens. Throwing my hands up in the air, my voice several octaves higher than before, I say, "Change our lives? Elliott, we have enough money! Look around, we have everything we need. I'm not interested in wealth or social status. I want to be happy; I want our children to be happy. I want to feel like a part of this marriage." I sound angry but really, I'm desperate, trapped in an unhappy cycle of yielding to what my husband wants.

I draw in a steady breath and try to hold back the tears I'm not prepared for him to see, but my eyes are glassy. Swallowing past the lump forming in my throat, I try once more for him to see reason. "This isn't what I want."

He shrugs an unaffected shoulder. "Yeah, well when you're the main breadwinner in the house, when you pay the bills and provide solely for a household, you kind of get to call the shots."

I don't say a word. What's the point anymore?

Elliott furrows his brows at me. "You know, I'm kind of disappointed in you Felicity. I thought as my wife you'd be celebrating with me tonight. Instead, all I see are tears when *I* should be the one upset by your behavior."

I suppose I shouldn't be surprised at his parting comment. It was only a matter of time before the gaslighting began.

CHAPTER ONE

Two years later - September

JON

ZACH

Come on. Couple bars, no clubs. The guys want you out.

ME

I'm gonna skip this one.

Just an hour? They're asking where you are.

I toss my phone onto the comforter. "Fuck."

Resigned to my fate and dressed in only my boxer briefs, I stand from the bed and make my way to the bathroom to grab a shower. Leaning forward, I rest my hands against the marble tiles and find some relief from the jets of warm water as they soothe my tired and aching muscles. It's only pre-season, but my body feels like it's halfway through the playoffs.

Fifteen minutes later, I'm dressed and make my way down the few short steps from the hotel lobby and out into the Vancouver night air. I can think of a million other places I'd rather be right now, but I can't keep letting my teammates down, and they're counting on me as their center and captain to set an example, especially to the rookies. Team nights out are as important as practices when it comes to our form on the ice.

I've been to this bar before, many times, and each time I recall leaving with a different girl. *Not like the media would let me forget.*

Over the years when it comes to women, I've refined the art of narrowing down my best option. Preferably a busty brunette looking for one night, and by one night, I mean back to my hotel to fuck before she's out the door by sunrise. I *do not* do sleepovers. I make it clear before they leave with me but largely, they know what they're getting, and they only need to read the press to know what my deal is. I've never had a girlfriend. Hell, I don't think I've slept with the same girl more than twice. After multiple bad experiences in my rookie years, I have strict rules and I stick to them. They never come back to my place and if I can help it, not to my hotel. I never give out my number, and I don't go on dates.

Pushing through the door of Hugo's, a borderline seedy bar in downtown Vancouver, I keep my head down as I nod at the barman who instantly recognizes me, and I make my way to the back booths to find Zach and the boys. We're particular about where we go in each city and have a shortlist of places we hit up on the road. Bars where the owners and patrons treat us like anyone else and don't tag our whereabouts on social media the first chance they get. I like my privacy, and as I've gotten older, it's become even more important. Trouble is, it's hard to escape the spotlight, no matter how hard I try.

"Jon, get your ass over here, I've got an IPA with your name on it," Zach shouts on my approach.

Dumping myself down in the huge booth, I pull my cap off and run a hand through my hair. "Yeah, and I bet it's room temperature now."

"Probably, you took your time getting over here," Zach counters with a low chuckle.

I roll the sleeves up on my white button-down shirt; it's stuffy in this bar and overflowing with people.

"Two more goals tonight. What's your secret old man?" I hear Jessie ask.

Jessie Callaghan, our latest trade from Chicago, is only twenty-three, and with one season in the NHL, he transferred to Seattle under, let's just say, questionable circumstances. He was a first-round draft pick, so I very much doubt they wanted to trade him due to his lack of sporting prowess. Rumor is a scandal forced him out of the team. Jessie doesn't talk about it, and we don't ask. I get the feeling the less I know, the better. He's an awesome winger though; I've never seen anything move so quickly across the ice and even more frightening, he has the stick skills to match.

I pin Jessie with a cocky grin. "Just pure talent, and drop the old man, or I'll drop you."

"That blonde can't stop eye-fucking you." Jessie changes course and tips his head in the direction of the bar.

He's not lying, and she's hot as hell. I'm trying to break the cycle of hookups, knowing they do nothing for me, only serving to temporarily fill a void. Where maybe a relationship could be a permanent solution, but realistically, who could I trust to be in it for more than the fame and money? Plus, I've never met anyone who "knocks me on my ass," as my mom keeps telling me will happen.

"Maybe I should grab a refill on my beer," I say, looking at my half-empty glass.

"I'm sure she can help you with that." Zach shakes his head, all too aware of my routine.

"And I thought you were into brunettes," Jensen adds.

Zach Evans, my assistant captain and hard-as-nails defense-man, is my closest friend these days, having spent the last six years together playing for the Seattle Scorpions. Jensen Jones is our goalie, Canadian, and an absolute lunatic. Wild nights are plentiful when in his company but despite his crazy ass, he's one of the best I've seen in the crease.

I shrug. "Hair color doesn't matter when it's wrapped around my fist," I retort, which draws a few laughs.

But the thing is, I'm not an asshole to women. I look after them during our time together. If they don't get off, neither do I. I was raised to respect women and while I enjoy fucking, shortly followed by alone time in bed to chill with a movie, I always make sure they leave satisfied. There's more than one way to rock a chick's world.

Changing the subject, I turn to Zach. "So how are things going with Amie? Gotta be six months now, right?"

Zach and Amie met at the start of spring at his thirtieth birthday party. The night started innocently enough; I'd reserved one of our favorite Italian restaurants and invited his friends and family with the promise I'd foot the bill. Things started to wrap up when Jensen, *always fucking Jensen,* suggested we take the party to a club, one well-known to the puck bunnies. Within minutes, Jensen starts inviting girls to get cozy.

Enter Amie, smoking-hot with legs for days, blonde, athletic, and smart too, having built up a successful business as a fitness influencer. She gets to travel and often spends time with Zach on the road. On the face of it, she's the perfect woman. Only I don't get that "perfect" vibe from her. In fact, I get a vibe that makes my skin crawl. That night, she moved with a little too much purpose toward Zach. She took on this cute persona, laughing at everything he said, a little try-too-hard if you ask me. Disingenuous would be a good description, but Zach, well, he thinks he's found *the one,* and I think Amie has found her sugar daddy. She's eight years his junior and frankly, it shows. She's petty, bitchy, and needy as hell. Funny thing is, the eyes she gives me when she thinks no one is looking, tell me she wouldn't abstain from other athletes given half a chance. Zach deserves better.

A fond smile traces Zach's lips. "Yeah, going well, I told her I loved her last night."

My eyes ricochet to his as I try to look pleased with his admission. He doesn't buy it though. It's obvious Zach knows my feelings about Amie and even though we're close, we haven't discussed my concerns out loud.

Say something, Jon.

"Oh...cool. Sounds like you're err...making...progress buddy. Happy for you."

He shuffles in his seat, his arms folded across his chest in a protective manner. "Ha, yeah sounds like it. Cheers, man."

I want to push it and ask him why the sarcastic response, if only to drag this god-awful tension forward and have it out with him once and for all, but I'm tired and the team is here. This is a conversation for a private moment. The Zach-Amie saga will have to wait.

I need a release from the pent-up adrenaline, following the game and the frustration from tonight.

Stepping out of the booth, I inject a well-refined amount of swagger into my stride as I make my way to the bar before setting my almost-empty glass down and leaning over on my forearms.

"After another, sweetheart?" the blonde who's been eye-fucking me for the last hour asks in a faux sweet tone.

Standing up straight, I fix her eyes with mine. "A drink isn't really what I'm after."

"Oh, no?" she replies in a coy voice, and it's clear this is a well-practiced routine.

But I'm not after a drawn-out, soul-searching night, so I decide to cut to the chase; we're both only interested in one thing after all. "What time do you finish?"

A smile slowly pulls at her full lips. "Half hour."

Soon. Good. "How about finishing your evening with me?"

Her smile grows as she quickly scribbles on her order pad before handing me her number.

"I don't do numbers sweetheart, but I could probably make my next beer last thirty minutes."

She smiles and gets back to re-filling my glass, serving other customers and occasionally I throw her the odd wink.

But despite my physical attraction to this girl, the thought of heading back to her place to fuck has lost its appeal. I want something more from my life besides big moments on the ice. I want someone to share my life with. That feeling has been growing within me for a long time, leaving internal chaos and at times resentment of hockey and my lifestyle in its wake.

My head screams at me to get up and walk out of this bar, not looking back, but habit keeps my feet firmly planted where they are, unable and unsure of how I'll break the cycle of meaningless hookups.

CHAPTER TWO

FELICITY

These past two years have both flown by and dragged.

In many ways, Seattle has started to feel like home. A feeling of comfort has crept into my everyday life despite the initial upheaval.

Things started to turn a corner for me around six months ago when I finally bit the bullet and left Elliott. I moved out of our temporary rental paid for by his firm and got myself a one-bedroom apartment downtown. Finally, I have some freedom and autonomy over my life. I can go out and make friends and just be myself. I was with Elliott since my early twenties. We met at university; he was studying economics, and I was reading law. Elliott was my first and only, having been wrapped in cotton wool my whole life by my parents. I had next to no experience in the guy department back then. Hell, I still don't today. Elliott, on the other hand, had more than enough experience to go around, but that still didn't stop us from falling pregnant at university.

My twenties came and went in a whirlwind of marriage and babies, and while I never wished for anything other than Jack and Darcy, I would wish for a different start to my adulthood. At thirty-nine, I feel like I'm re-starting my life and I finally have a chance to work out who I am, alone and free of a man's influence.

The rain beats against the twelfth-floor window of my office, and I'm broken out of my trance by the bloody awful ringtone Darcy set last week on my phone.

"Mum, I'm downstairs in the lobby waiting, can we get going?"

"I'll be right down; shall we grab a coffee too?" I look at the stack of files on my desk; lord only knows I need caffeine today.

"Yeah sure, just bring your umbrella. It's absolutely chucking it down out here and I've just done my hair. Damn, this city!" Darcy lets out a frustrated groan.

"On my way, sweetheart," I reply and end the call.

Darcy has never taken to Seattle; from the outset, she was determined to hate it. For the past two years since Elliott broke the news, she's been clock-watching, waiting to get back to Liam and her friends in Oxford. In contrast, Jack has thrived, making more friends than I've achieved in my thirty-nine years on this earth, and at nearly eighteen, he has a steadfast plan—go to college, study sports, and make it in the big leagues.

The Grind café has become my and Darcy's regular meet-up spot, and we tend to catch up a couple of times a week at least. But today, she seems preoccupied. We grab our chai lattes, something I've become totally obsessed with since moving out here, and take a seat side by side on our favorite plush pink sofa.

One scolding sip later, Darcy's frown still hasn't lifted. "So, Jack dropped the bomb last night. He's not coming home; he's chosen to take an offer from the University of Seattle and study Kinesiology."

You know that expectant look someone gives you as if they've rehearsed this conversation over again in their minds and fully anticipate a certain response? Well, that's *the look* I'm getting right now. On this occasion though, I can't pacify Darcy because I'm not heading back either. There's nothing there for me. The friends I made back in the UK were all affiliated with Elliott in some way, and those who weren't haven't kept in touch. My boss seems to value me more than my ex-husband ever did, securing me an employer-sponsored green card, allowing me to stay and work in Seattle.

In three weeks, Darcy and Elliott will board a plane back to Heathrow, and right now, she thinks I have a ticket. It's getting to crunch time, and I *need* to tell her.

I take a bite of my salad, wishing I ordered a panini instead because this rabbit food really isn't cutting it. "Yeah, we need to talk about that."

Darcy straightens, her frown turning into a full-blown scowl. "What do you mean?"

"The thing is, well..."

"You aren't coming home either are you?"

I feel every muscle in my body tense. "No."

"Yeah, I figured as much."

I continue pushing the salad around my plate, any remnants of my appetite now completely depleted. "You guessed?"

She shrugs nonchalantly, but I can see the sadness in her bright blue eyes, and it breaks my heart. "With you and Dad splitting, and Jack staying here, I guess the UK hasn't got much left to offer you."

I balk. "Other than my beautiful daughter."

She chuckles softly. "No, seriously though Mum, I get why you're staying. I just feel like my world is flipped upside down."

I scoot across the sofa and pull her into my side, wrapping my arm around her slender frame, her long honey-colored hair falling over my shoulder. Darcy has her dad's height just like Jack, and despite being twenty-two years older, my small five-three frame feels tiny compared to hers.

"I know, sweetheart. The thing is, life, it sometimes deals you a hand you least expect, but it's what we do with those cards that matters. We can either fold or make the best of what we have.

Me and your dad should've split years ago, but I guess I held out for you and Jack. Now though, you're both growing up, and you'll be off to college with Liam next year. I promise I'll be back to visit you as much as I can." My voice is thick with emotion and trepidation, hoping desperately she'll understand. But the way Darcy nods along tells me at seventeen, she is far beyond her years; still, it doesn't stop the overwhelming sense of guilt.

We finish our lunch and Darcy updates me on her plans for finishing high school and applying to university with Liam. I love her take on life, her romantic heart, falling in love with Liam at such a young age, and both so fiercely loyal to one another. As her mum, I fully support their relationship, but I can't say I understand it. For me, true love has been elusive, and at times, it's hard not to inwardly project, wondering why it hasn't happened to me.

Then at thirty-one I also lost my parents to cancer; Mum went first closely followed by Dad, and that was the last straw. I've boarded up my numb heart, only prepared to feel for my children. Lending out my heart for romantic purposes, yeah, that's a solid no from me. Been there, tried that. Failed.

The rain has stopped as we step out into the mid-September air. A comfortable sixty-eight degrees has me wearing a dusky-pink dress and black sandals. I don't live far from work, so I like to walk each day. At my age and post two children, I find it harder to stay in shape despite an array of gym classes filling my schedule. I miss the twenties body I had and God, I can't remember the last pair of size four jeans I could fit into without contorting my body like a pretzel to do up the zip. So, these days I opt for comfort, confident in my body and curves.

I turn to Darcy. "Let's meet up as much as we can between now and when you leave, okay?"

"Okay, but just don't shut Dad out completely, yeah. He's been different since you left. I don't think he's doing that great."

I haven't shared half of what went on between Elliott and me with Darcy and Jack. They don't need to know everything, and they're already trying to process our divorce. Darcy and her dad remain close, even after the forced move to Seattle, and the last thing I want to do is rock their relationship. But Elliott as a father and Elliott as a husband are two very different people.

I tuck a lock of hair behind her ear. "I won't, sweetheart." Truthfully, I'm not sure how good I'll be at keeping that promise, but I know I need to try.

BEING a PA for hotshot defense attorney, Mark Preston, is honestly not what I dreamed of when I enrolled at university. Don't get me wrong, it's a good, solid, and respectable job, and Mark is great to work for. But I wanted to become a lawyer and change the world, one human rights court after the next. Elliott always thought he was smarter than me academically, and I let myself drift into his shadow. I was a straight-A student, and even taking my finals while pregnant didn't deter me from being awarded top student in my class.

"I still think you should set up that profile." My colleague and best friend, Kate Monroe, comes to stand next to me at my desk, watching me scroll absentmindedly through Instagram.

"I've told you. I'm not dating. I don't need a man."

Kate bends down to my height as I'm seated at my desk and whispers softly, "Maybe not, but we all know Tinder is really for hookups. I think you could use a bit of the d."

I flush but don't respond. I've never had a one-night stand, but a girl has needs, and there's only so much a toy can do.

"I mean, how long has it been?"

I balk at her, my eyes scanning the room to make sure no one hears. "A while."

"How long?"

"Not since Elliott, but why does it matter?"

Kate almost drops her coffee. "What?!" She attempts to whisper but it's more of a low-key shout. "Six months?!"

I flush again and quickly rush out, "More like a year, but I *don't* need a man."

"Girl, you could give Saint Mary a run for her money."

Unlike me, Kate is super confident around men. I suppose when you're thirty-two and look like a supermodel it always helps. She eats up men like she does her litigation cases and takes no prisoners. She's had a few short-term boyfriends but nothing serious. Honestly, I wish I could be more like her, but I don't know how I could have a casual thing with someone.

"Yeah well, I'm still waiting for Tom Hardy to sweep me off my feet," I joke.

Kate looks off dreamily as she takes another sip of coffee. "Damn, he is fine, gorgeous, talented, rich, and famous..."

"And lives in the UK," I finish.

"Maybe you made the wrong decision staying here after all."

I click on Tom Hardy's profile, unabashedly stalking him.

"Kate, your three o'clock is here," someone announces from behind us, and I quickly close our swooning session.

"Catch you in a bit, babe." Kate takes off, her fitted black suit and patent heels turning heads as she goes.

It's GONE eight when I finally get home. I managed to squeeze in a quick yoga class after work. But now, my sofa is calling me, along with ice cream and Ed Sheeran.

My eyes are drifting closed when my phone pings with a text.

JACK

Mum, some of the boys want to go to
Vancouver for my eighteenth. Is that okay
with you?

ME

Is this with Will, Dan, and Max?

Yeah, Garrett too.

Ah, well that means there will be girls.

And will there be girls?

Hopefully.

Jack Thompson!

I dunno, maybe, why does that matter?

Just be safe, you know what I'm saying...

So that's a yes?

He's not your baby anymore, Felicity.

Yes. But we need to meet up soon, so I can give you your present. I think you'll like this one this year.

Okay. But can we skip the Batman socks this time?

Trust me, I'm about to become your new favorite person.

Unlikely, unless you play for the Scorpions.

I smile to myself, smug mode well and truly activated.

CHAPTER THREE

FELICITY

Stepping off the monorail, I arrive at the Scorpions' stadium. Time to collect Jack's present, ice-level season tickets. Prepare to officially become his favorite person, Felicity.

I've been here a couple of times with Jack over the last eighteen months, but we always ended up in less-than-great seats.

Checking my watch, I realize I'm late to meet Kate for lunch and totally lost in the maze of corridors. *Where is the box office?* I reach for my bag and pull out my phone, typing a message to Kate, letting her know I'm going to be late because, apparently, I can't follow signs effectively, when I hit a wall. A very muscular wall.

On impact, I fumble backward as my phone flies across the room meeting its end with a *crack*. Dammit. I'm about to hit the ground when I feel a strong arm loop around my waist, hauling me back to my feet.

"Hey, whoa there, you okay?" a deep and sensual, almost not-of-this-world voice permeates my shocked state as I'm stood the right way up.

Gathering myself and pulling my dress down to a respectable

length from where it had gathered, let's just say to higher than mid-thigh, I begin my visual ascent.

Holy mother.

Have I died and gone to heaven or suffered some sort of severe concussion because this can only be a hallucination? The man standing with his arm wrapped around my waist must be at least six-four, and although he's wearing a hoodie, his corded arms are plain to see *and feel*. He presses me close to his warm solid body and I feel dizzy, his presence is so overwhelming. His steely-gray eyes are the first thing I notice as they pin me in place with his stare. His nose is strong and sits perfectly with a smattering of light freckles across the bridge, almost like beauty spots. His high cheekbones are enviable, and as I move down further, I'm met with full, kissable lips.

The things I could do with that mouth. *The things that mouth could do to me.*

It's surely not legal to look that good. But then, he bloody smiles, and *sweet baby Jesus,* he has dimples for days.

Yep, I've definitely suffered a head injury.

JON

"Great practice, Morgan, you're looking in good shape."

Yeah, if only I felt it.

But I'll take the rare compliment from Coach Burrows. He's a hard-ass, ex-pro player from the days when the NHL was even tougher than it is today. He rides us hard and isn't afraid to bench you on the first signs of weakness. He made me captain three seasons back when Jameson, our previous starting center, suffered a career-ending injury on the ice. A day etched into my memory forever. It's easy to take your time as a player for granted, and I'm lucky to have enjoyed a long and illustrious career with only a few light injuries and blows along the way.

"Thanks, Coach, I feel good." White lies never hurt anyone.

Coach nods and swings the locker room door open, headed for his office. As I turn back to the bench, I pull out my phone and see the overdue reminder I set earlier. Shit. I forgot to pick up opening night tickets for Mom, Dad, and my brother, Adam. Granted, I could have them waiting at the stadium on game day, but I plan to drive home to Bellevue this weekend. Sure, my schedule is stacked over the next couple of weeks ahead of the season starting, but I want to see my parents, and I can't miss Adam's face when he sees the box tickets I got him.

Usually, my parents prefer to sit close to the ice. My dad, James, is an avid hockey fan and although I'm the only player in my family, he can't get enough of the NHL. His passion for it is part of the reason I started playing. We lived and breathed hockey when I was younger, and they always found the money to help me pursue my dreams. My mom, Jennie, would stay at home with Adam because we couldn't afford box seats, and quieter seats are the only option to safely get Adam to games.

Adam's autistic and has sensory processing disorders. His ear defenders do a lot to block out the noise, but sitting in a box means we can control his surroundings. Things haven't always been easy for my parents; they're the best a child could hope for, but earning mediocre wages, juggling two boys, and fighting for Adam's future, it's a lot to take on and there's no denying the impact it's had on them. Adam lives in his own place across town during the week and generally comes home on the weekends, and from time to time, I surprise him and my parents with tickets.

I take a left at the end of the hallway when a flash of green crosses my path. I slam on the brakes but it's too late; I'm body-checking the tiny frame to the ground and practically fall on my own ass as a squeal reverberates off the walls.

Because I'm Jon Morgan and highly inappropriate, my first

thought is how I'd like to hear that scream under different circumstances. My second thought as I maneuver the tiny frame the right way up and check she's okay is, yeah, I'd definitely like to hear that scream under different circumstances. Preferably involving a bed, her naked, and a whole different kind of body check.

Well, fuck me.

All I can see is green, two big pools of emerald to be exact, which match a cute jacket thrown over a flowing black summer dress, which has ridden higher than it should on impact. But hey, I'm not complaining. The view I get of her creamy thighs makes my dick twitch. She smells insane too; a wave of coconut overtakes my senses, not too strong, but sweet and addictive. I need to calm down, or I'll find myself revealing far more than I should in this hallway. She's petite but oh so curvy in the right places. This woman clearly works out. I could feel her tight body tense against me as I held her to my side.

I want to hold her again. Now.

"Hey, whoa there, you okay?" Is all my floundering brain can manage as I reach down and hand her the tote she was carrying.

Placing it back on her shoulder, she tucks a silky chocolate wave behind her ear, and flushes, *full-on flushes.* If I wasn't so enamored, I would appreciate in more detail the way her eyes glide over my body, but all I can do is stare wildly at the woman in front of me.

"Sorry for uh...bashing into you. I uh, was rushing to grab my tickets and not looking where I was going." Her first sentence to me is the most fumbled and disjointed string of words I think I've ever heard, yet somehow, I could listen to it on repeat. Her voice envelops me in warmth and comfort. Cheesy as it is, it feels like coming home.

Clearing my throat and trying to rekindle a modicum of self-control, I smile. "No problem, I was rushing, too. You picking up tickets?"

Of course she's picking up tickets, you dope, why else is she standing outside the box office?

My idiocy is clearly not lost on her when she snorts, making it sound way cuter than a snort ever should. "Nah, I was just taking my dog for a walk."

Ah, so it's like that—feisty, sarcastic, and witty...

Wait, is that a British accent? Sure as shit doesn't sound American to me. I playfully smile and narrow my eyes at her as she uncomfortably shifts from one foot to the other, thumbing over her shoulder.

"So yeah, I need to grab these tickets before I miss my ride home, but thanks for picking me up off the uh...floor."

I stand waiting for her to finish up, desperate to hear what she's ordering, so I can work out when I'll see her again. Are the tickets for her? Damn, I never thought they might not be. Karen, who works the stand, keeps her voice hushed as she hands the mystery woman an envelope before peeking to the left and spotting me.

"Mr. Morgan, what are you doing here? This is a public access area you know."

Yes, Karen, thank you for reminding me. "Yeah, I just need to grab the tickets for my parents and brother for the opener. Should be in the back. Chrissie said she'd put some to the side."

Karen stiffly nods and turns on her heel, heading in search of the tickets.

Standing at the booth, I glance to my left to see my emerald angel, hovering as she puts the envelope in her bag and inspects her phone, which thankfully looks like it's survived our incident unscathed.

Still, I can't help the next words that leave my mouth. "Does it need testing?" I point at her phone, a playful smile back on my lips.

Her head whips up, pinning me with those intense eyes once again. "Testing?" she replies in confusion.

Seizing my opportunity, I reply. "Yeah, I can test it for you.

Text you to make sure it's not damaged, give you a call maybe." I know it's a cheesy pick-up line, but apparently, I'm all sorts of crazy around this girl. Once she walks out those doors, I'll likely never see her again, which cuts me with a foreign sense of unease.

"But how would you..." At the realization, her eyes shoot to mine and instead of a playful look in them, they fucking roll. An unimpressed expression is written right across her pretty face. Okay, I wasn't expecting that. I don't think I've ever seen a woman roll her eyes at me, especially when I'm making a play for them. Damn, is my game slipping?

"Ha!" she scoffs. "Yeah I don't give my number out to strangers, but top marks for effort, hun."

This time, I'm flushing. It's safe to say I've crashed and burned.

Wait. *Strangers?*

She doesn't recognize me. Well, shit. She's clearly not a hockey fan which means those tickets are even less likely to be for her. Yeah, I've well and truly blown this.

I open my mouth to try and save what's left of my dignity right as Karen returns. "Here you go, Mr. Morgan. I have three box tickets for you for next Saturday." She pauses. "You do know players don't need to collect tickets, don't you? I could have these sent directly to security."

Well, if she didn't know before, she sure as shit does now.

I grab the envelope and stuff it in my pocket before glancing up to find my newfound obsession slack-jawed and slowly backing away. She clearly heard my exchange with Karen as the rosy tint previously painting the apple of her cheeks has returned.

I open my mouth to say something, *anything*.

But it's too late. She lifts her left hand and supplies me with something close to an awkward British royal wave and then she's gone, out the double doors and probably from my life forever.

CHAPTER FOUR

FELICITY

J ack is poised on the edge of my sofa, staring down at the
open envelope.

For several beats he says nothing, simply studies the
tickets before him. It finally seems to sink in when a whopping
smile spreads across his face, mirroring mine. Suddenly he
launches himself toward me, arms outstretched as he lifts me
into the biggest bear hug. For a moment, he forgets it's not cool
for an eighteen-year-old to hug his mum and dance around like
an excitable puppy, and just as quickly, he's setting me back down
on my feet before clearing his throat. "These are awesome Mum,
and the seats, they are immense."

"You're welcome, honey; I'm glad you like them."

Jack reverts to giddy mode. "Like them? Zach Evans up close
and watching *the* hockey genius Jon Morgan at work...*Yeah, I like
them.*"

My stomach clenches at *that name.*

Before I can stop myself, my brain seizes a chance to inquire
further about the man who not so-subtly asked me for my
number a couple of weeks ago. After all, I can pass this off as

pre-season research. "So, why is this Jon Morgan a 'hockey genius'?"

That earns me an eye roll. "Mum, *seriously*." Jack elongates the seriously. "He's a hockey legend, he scores for fun, and I swear the man practically dances across the ice. He's just awesome."

I've never been into sports, so I don't know why hearing my son gush over a hockey player I met for less than three minutes is having such an effect on me. But the truth is, I don't need to hear Jack fanboy over Jon Morgan to elicit my physical response. I've been doing some fangirling of my own over the last few days, lost in those steely-gray eyes and how waves of thick dark hair fell over them. I'm tempted to tell Jack that I quite literally bumped into his hero when collecting the tickets, but something holds me back from spilling, a need to internalize the private moment we shared. It felt intimate and intense. Far more intense than a chance meeting like that should. So, I shove down my words and bury the feelings.

"Well, clear your schedule because the first game is next Saturday."

I JUST NEED to get out and face the music. Sitting in the airport car park is neither comforting nor productive.

Just the other side of the departure entrance is Elliott and Darcy. I've barely seen Elliott since we separated, and I moved into my apartment six months ago, but the hardest part in all this is by far saying a temporary goodbye to my daughter. It cuts deep to be so far away from her but in my heart, I know this is the right decision for her and for me. Darcy has always been close to her dad and when back with Liam, she will bloom once again. Jack is pleased to have me close by in Seattle, and I'll be flying back to see Darcy as many times as I can.

Swinging open the door to my Mini Cooper, I head inside

the airport and look for them both. Jack said his farewells yesterday as he has tryouts today for the college hockey team which he couldn't miss. I find them sitting with coffees, Darcy's head thrown back in laughter. She seems happy, and it warms my heart. I've got a bet with myself that says $100 she'll be in Liam's arms within thirty minutes of touchdown in London.

"Hey, you two," I say as I approach their table, a fake smile plastered on my face.

Elliott snaps up from his seat when he hears me. "Felicity! Nice to see you. Can I get you a drink?"

I'm shocked by my ex-husband's chivalry, but I shake my head. "No thank you, I need to head straight to work after this, so I don't have much time." Which is the truth.

We make polite chatter as I take the remaining seat at their table, and all the while I can see Darcy texting Liam to confirm their flight details and that they are on time. A few minutes later, glancing up at the clock, it's time for me to leave. "I'd better let you both get through security and to the gate."

With that, Darcy pockets her phone and pulls me into the sweetest hug. "I'll miss you, Mummy, but I'll come see you as soon as possible."

I squeeze my eyes shut as they form a dam to my tears. "Yes, darling, Christmas. I'll be back for Christmas."

She smiles and kisses me on the cheek and then grabs her bag, whipping off to check the departure board for the thousandth time.

Once out of earshot, Elliot turns to me, his eyes looking a little glassy which takes me by surprise. During our marriage, I saw little to no emotion from him, which is part of the reason why our relationship felt so devoid of love. Yet here we are, divorced and going our separate ways, and he's now getting emotional? My inner cynical side tells me he's uncomfortable with his sudden lack of control over my life, that I'm finally forging my own path without his supervision, and it dents his ego. Or could it be that he will miss me? That I meant something to him after all and the imminent separation across different continents has finally brought it home.

Who knows, *and why does it matter?* I'm almost annoyed at myself for spending so much emotional energy on him, us, or what was an us.

"So, you'll keep me in touch about Jack then? I doubt he'll contact me when he heads off to university—you know how he is."

I smile weakly, and I can tell Elliott is every bit as uncomfortable with this as I am.

"Yes, I take him to watch the Scorpions tomorrow night, first game of the season, so I'll remind him to keep in touch with you, let you know how his tryouts went."

Elliott nods and extends the handle on his carry-on bag, kicking it out onto two wheels. I stand there, arms crossed, ready to back away when he lurches forward and plants a kiss on my cheek, catching me completely off guard. I stumble backward but steady myself on the table with a firm hand.

"Take care of yourself, Felicity. I... yeah... just, be careful okay."

Be careful? I'm tempted to ask why he thinks I can't look after myself, but it's not worth it. I, too, want Elliott to provide me with updates on Darcy, so I think better than to start an argument. "Yeah, I will. You too."

His lips pinch together in another awkward smile and then he takes off toward Darcy, throwing his arm across her shoulders. She turns around and sends one last wave my way before disappearing into a crowd of people.

Well, shit. I think I will take that coffee.

CHAPTER FIVE

JON

I've missed this.

The pre-game buzz. There's something about the first match of the season that just hits differently. I've won the Stanley Cup twice, and while that was mad, *and I mean mad,* the feeling when my blades hit the ice for the first period of the NHL season is unbeatable. Heading through the player entrance and toward the locker room, I can already feel the crowd reverberating through the stadium. There's still well over an hour before the puck drop, but the first game excitement doesn't disappoint. The fans are hungry and so am I.

I suppose that's why I take care of my body like I do, to extend my career for as long as possible. I feed off this feeling; it's in my DNA. We had a light practice this morning, and I was sharp. Good, I need to be feeling this way against New York.

Entering the locker room, I find Zach already at his bench, inspecting his blades. We're always the first to arrive. Zach has a specific routine with his skates and carefully re-laces them before every game. I, on the other hand, re-tape my stick in a manner that can only be described as OCD in nature. We often sit in comfortable silence focusing, lacing, taping, the noise of each routine filling the room. It's therapeutic, and I can't ever imagine my pre-match prep without him by my side.

"Hey, man," Zach says without lifting his head.

"Alright, buddy. Blades, okay?" I reply in a relaxed tone.

He lifts a shoulder in a slight shrug. "Yeah, I think so, I sent them off for sharpening after practice; they look on point."

Zach still hasn't looked at me. I sit down next to him with a thud, resting my forearms on my thighs, and turn my head to look at him. "We good, man? You know I got your back, right? Always have, always will."

His lip tips up at the corner. "Yeah, I know, I just...I know how you feel about Amie, but she's good for me, you know? She makes me happy."

I've never been very good at poker, mostly because I wear my thoughts firmly on my sleeve, but for the sake of our friendship and the game tonight, I forcibly swallow my concerns and pat him lightly on the back. "As long as you're happy, bro, then I'm happy."

With that, I stand and quickly change the subject. "New York is going to come at us tonight, so we've got to be on top of our game."

Zach's face hardens as he rips a lace from his skate and looks me dead in the eye. "Bring it."

I'm always last to be called out onto the ice, and as I stand at the edge of the tunnel, stick in hand, ready to hit the ice for warm-up, my blood surges through my body.

"And welcoming back to the ice we have a future hall of famer, NHL top goal scorer, Stanley Cup winner, and your captain...Jon Morgan!"

The crowd erupts as I glide out on the ice, lights flashing, music blaring. Yeah, this is why I do this. I take a lap with my stick in the air, acknowledging the crowd as I always do. As I pass by my box, my eyes flick up, they're a distance away, but I can just about make out the figures of Mom and Dad with their hands above their heads, clapping. Adam is waving his arms around in excitement, his blue ear defenders on to help with the noise, but the lights are sending him wild. He seems happy tonight though, and I point at him with my stick and wink, sending the jumbotron to his face. The crowd cheers at that, knowing Adam's story. I've spent a lot of time using my position to raise as much awareness of autism as I can. I love that he's here. I may be earning millions and living my dream, but Adam's my hero. The way he takes everything in his stride and faces challenges every day of his life. He's dealt with his fair share of discrimination and sometimes cruelty, especially during high school. Yet, he never let the bullies win. His inner strength, along with the help of my fists, meant they never stood a chance.

I make my way to center ice and collect a puck, ready to take a few warmup shots at Jensen. At this point before a game, I'd normally be fully focused, locked in, with the crowd and everyone else around me a mere blur. Yet tonight, hockey shares a place in my mind with something else. Since I laid eyes on her, she's rented a space in my brain, my every thought. I have no idea if those tickets she collected were for her, but there's a growing feeling in my chest that hopes she's here, somewhere, watching me. I find myself scanning the crowd for wavy choco-late hair and emerald eyes, but I come up empty and disap-pointed. Still, thoughts that she might be watching give me added motivation to bring my best.

The game is as tough as expected. New York is dirty; they play dirty, fight dirty, and talk shit constantly. Top of my shit list is their alternate captain, Alex Schneider. He's a dickhead, plain and simple. Also thirty-four, he played with me at college in Michigan. Born in Germany and raised in the US, he's a top player in the league. Trouble is, his attitude stinks. He's respon-sible for a string of career-ending injuries, and for all the money he's made, he's probably paid out half in fines. I hate him, he hates me, and let's just say, there's no love lost between Schneider, Zach, and every other player in this league. Hell, even his own teammates think he's an asshole.

The buzzer goes, indicating the end of the second period, and we're two points up thanks to a thunderous early lead from me and a great slap shot from Jessie. Jensen is on fire, and we're on for a shut-out if we can hold them in the third.

"Morgan! Is your family here?" A snide smile traces Schneider's lips as he shoulders past me, skating backward on his way off the ice. I know what he's trying to say; he's always talked shit about my mom but never dared to bring Adam into it. My mom though? She's a good-looking woman, and he takes full advantage of this to try and crawl under my skin.

"Out in full force," I retort in an unaffected tone, and turn away to congratulate Jessie on his screamer, when it happens...

The birthday messages begin to flash over the jumbotron, and I look up right when the camera lands on a young kid, red-faced and wearing an oversized "I'm eighteen" pin on his chest. Honestly, he looks mortified, and I'm mortified for him. But it's not the pin that steals my attention—it's the beauty to his right, my emerald angel. Kissing the boy's cheek, she giggles and ruffles his hair with her dainty hand. It's this sight that almost has my skates giving out underneath me.

Fuck me. She's stunning. She's the sort of stunning only the most talented artists can create, and it's right there and then, I know I'm totally fucked.

As if she senses my gaze, she looks up at the screen and flushes that adorable deep shade of magenta. Casting her eyes out to where I stand on the ice, I can see her, watching me while I stand rooted to the spot, watching her on the screen, and I swear, a wave of sweet coconut hits my senses from all angles. I can see the plexiglass in front of her, so I know she's near the ice, but I just need to work out where. Time stands still as the ice clears around me.

A gloved hand lands on my shoulder as Zach pulls up alongside me. "Who's the girl?"

I don't answer immediately as I'm still too mesmerized, but slowly, I open my mouth. "My angel."

Zach puffs out a humored breath. "Okay, buddy. Come on, we need to head off."

He tugs at my arm, eventually tearing my gaze away, but in a last-minute plea, I raise my glove and point at the screen. If I can't locate her then sure as shit the twenty thousand people in this stadium can. With that simple action, the crowd goes wild. I wink in response, taking it up a decibel or two before turning to skate off the ice.

Striding toward the locker room, I can't wipe the shit eating grin off my face. She's here.

FELICITY

Right now, that great big slab of ice looks very appealing.

What I wouldn't give to lie my cheeks flat on the freezing surface to ease the burning. I look like a tomato; I don't need a mirror to know that my entire face and neck are brighter than the surface of the sun. How had I not expected to appear on the jumbotron when I forced Jack to wear that ridiculous badge? I howled in his face when he opened it on the way here. Turns out, jokes on me.

"Does he know you, Mum?!" A once again giddy Jack asks in between bites of his hot dog. I compensated him for his badge-related devastation by buying him all the snacks he wanted during the break, and I think he's just about forgiven me, plus he's now too distracted with curiosity over attention from a certain hockey player to care.

"Nope, he must have us confused with someone else, honey." Lame response, I know, one Jack doesn't believe, and neither do I.

"Yeah, okay, the way he looked at you. He definitely knows you."

I don't reply. Instead, I'm saved by the start of the third period. The players skate out onto the ice, and I bury my face beneath my favorite green scarf. But while it keeps me warm, it makes a terrible disguise as Jon rejoins the ice and heads straight over to us.

My heart rate picks up as he approaches and removes one of his gloves, pointing at us through the glass. I can feel his steely-gray eyes burn right through me as I keep mine trained on the floor.

"Happy Birthday..."

"Jack!" My son screams back over the noise of the crowd.

I chance a quick glance up at the towering hockey player. He looks even bigger in his skates, pads, and helmet. He exudes a warrior-like vibe, and it's so freaking sexy.

"Is your phone still working?"

I take it out of my pocket and wave it in front of me. "Just fine, thanks."

He tips his chin in my direction, and a cocky smile spreads across his face. "Good to know."

He taps the glass in front of me a couple of times with his knuckles before skating off to join the rest of his team.

And I'm left there, fully melting in the middle of a freezing stadium, mentally preparing myself for Jack's inevitable inquisition on the way home.

CHAPTER SIX

FELICITY

KATE

I'll be at your place in an hour. Prepare for
questions!

ME

I have no idea what you're talking about.

Of course not. It's almost like a tall, dark,
handsome, and super famous NHL star,
swooning over a fan happens every day of the
week.

He wasn't swooning. He wished Jack a happy
birthday.

Uh-huh. I'll be there soon. Oh, and wear that
black figure-hugging dress. You look so hot in
that.

I'm starting to think you have ulterior motives
for inviting me out tonight...

You'd be right :) XOXO

I close out the text conversation with Kate but quickly divert to Instagram. Jon's profile to be precise. He doesn't post much on there, and when he does, it's rarely personal, mostly roundups of games and thanking fans. But when I search for Jon Morgan via Explore, there's plenty more revealed.

Photos of him with a different woman each time, and they could all be supermodels. Mostly they're brunettes with big boobs, amazing figures, and legs at least twice as long as mine. They say comparison is the thief of all joy, and this is without a doubt stealing mine.

I knew he had a reputation as a playboy, but seeing it in the flesh, or through a screen, brings me back down to reality with a thud. He clearly doesn't take women seriously and besides, I have no interest in being another one of his "puck bunnies" as the comments underneath each photo keep repeating.

Jon Morgan is bad news for women. Plain and simple.

I finish the last sip of my Pinot Grigio, just as my door buzzes, and I press the speaker.

"Hey! I'm downstairs, and I've managed to flag a taxi. You ready?"

"Yep, coming down now!"

On first sight of me, Kate low whistles. "Damn, girl, you're giving me a toothache," she croons.

"Oh, this old thing?" I point to my dress. "Yeah, some bossy bitch told me to wear it tonight." I playfully wink back at her.

"Love the shoes—they look like Jimmy Choo."

I scoff, "Yeah, because my excessive salary and monthly clothing budget definitely stretch to high-end designer shoes."

Kate looks stunning in a red halter dress and black ankle strap heels; her blonde hair is wavy and falls around her shoulders.

The ride to our first bar is a short five-minute drive, but I can already feel the weight of Kate's intrigue. I brace for impact.

"Okay, I can't wait any longer. Spill."

I turn to her in the back seat. "Spill what?"

"Don't deny me the tea, babe, tell me!"

I chew nervously on the side of my thumb. "Honestly, there's nothing to tell. He saw the birthday message on the jumbotron, and when they came out for the third period, he skated over to wish Jack a happy birthday. It was sweet."

"Except even from the angle on the TV, I could tell he wasn't looking at Jack. He was one hundred percent eye-fucking you."

I puff out a disbelieving breath. "I find that very hard to believe."

"Well, yeah, you wouldn't have noticed, since you kept your head down the entire time."

I'm not surprised Kate saw the footage. She's an avid Scorpions fan. What she doesn't know about the team and players you could write on the back of a postage stamp.

"Yeah, well, he's a playboy. I'm sure he does that with every fan."

"Yes, he's the biggest man-whore ever. But I've never seen him, or any other player, do that. Like, ever."

I wave a dismissive hand in front of my face. "You're making something out of nothing."

We pull up outside the new cocktail bar Kate wanted to try. It's packed with barely any space at the bar, but we find a gap in the bodies and squeeze our way in. I order my number one cocktail, a Cosmo, and Kate tries the mojito.

"Oh my god, that's sooo good." My best friend throws her head back. "I needed this after the week at work I've had."

"Tell me about it," I agree.

We find a spare high-top table surrounded by stools and take a seat.

"He's supposed to be amazing in bed, you know."

I almost spray my cocktail across the table. "I'm sure he is. Sounds like he's had enough practice."

"Oh, he definitely has." She wiggles her eyebrows.

"Wait, you know someone who's been with him?"

She eyes me over the rim of her glass. "Not exactly, no. But there are plenty of women who have, and they say he goes all night."

"Does he, really?" I reply in a semi-sarcastic tone.

"I can't believe you're not even the least bit curious."

Oh, I'm curious. But I'm not about to have my face plastered across social media and labeled as a puck bunny.

"We bumped into each other when I went to collect Jack's tickets. We sent each other flying across the corridor, and I almost broke my phone. I think he kind of feels bad about it."

"Ohmygod. So, you didn't think to tell me that you've had physical contact with him?"

"No, Kate, I didn't. It was like a three-minute interaction."

"Three minutes! What did you say?"

"Let's just change the subject," I say, knowing this whole conversation is utterly pointless. I'll likely never see or speak to him again beyond watching his games.

"I just think it's strange how he looked at you, that's all." Kate shrugs a shoulder.

"Well, whether it was strange or not, I know what his terms are when it comes to women, and they aren't going to fly with me."

But I might as well be talking to myself because Kate has clearly tuned out and is now staring right past me and over my shoulder toward the bar. Her eyes are wide and her mouth is agape.

Her gaze eventually returns to mine, but it's now replaced with a hint of smugness. "Tell me again how I'm making something out of nothing." She brings her glass to her lips as she nods in the direction she was staring as if inviting me to turn around and see the source of her satisfaction for myself.

I freeze, not daring to turn around, and in all honesty, I don't need to. I know what's behind me—no, *who's* behind me— because I feel him. Right down to my toes. It's unmistakable. The same zing of electricity that's only zapped through me when he's been in my presence. I clench my thighs together as my body betrays me, an aching throb deep in my core begins to build, and I haven't even laid eyes on him yet.

"Jesus, Felicity, he can't take his eyes off you." I hear Kate's voice just above the heavy pulsing of my heart rate.

I down the rest of my drink in one gulp and set my glass on the table before slowly turning to look at him.

JON

Despite our strong start to the season, I haven't been any more inclined to go out with the boys. If anything, I've been less concerned with nights out and more interested in relaxing in my apartment with a beer and feeding my *Breaking Bad* habit because, man, that's a good show.

Tonight though, I've been forced to come out by Jensen as he practically ripped me from my apartment, insisting we "try that new cocktail bar attracting all the hot pussy."

All night I've been pissy and grumpy as hell. Convinced my days of going out post-game and practices are way behind me.

But as of around three minutes ago, my annoyance has completely dissipated, replaced with the need to kiss Jensen full-on and in public for dragging my sorry ass out. Because sitting about twenty feet away from me, in a figure-hugging, hot-as-hell, little black dress, with come-to-bed silver strappy heels wrapped around dainty ankles, is my angel.

Fucking hell. She is other-worldly.

There's got to be a hundred other females in here, yet she's the only woman I see, *want* to see. At first sight of her, I crossed my ankles and leaned back on the bar, if only to disguise the tent setting up residence in the front of my pants. Sure, I've been aroused by other women before, and I've fucked nearly all of them too. But this, this isn't arousal—this is feral need.

"Take a picture; it'll last longer." Jensen sidles up to me, handing me a beer. We've only just gotten here and immediately when I walked through the door, I felt her presence dance across my skin.

"Huh?" It's all I can manage; I'm tongue-tied like a pre-teen.

"That's her, right, the girl you freaked out with your intense staring through the jumbotron last home game?" Jensen points to her.

"Don't fucking point to her. *Christ*, I'm trying to act cool about this. I wasn't expecting to see her."

His shoulders start to shake and then the bastard doubles over in laughter, "Cool? You must be joking, Jon. Cool left the building the moment you stared at her through the jumbotron for like an hour. Add to that, you haven't been interested in any other females. Don't think we haven't noticed. Usually, if it has brown hair, big boobs, and a pulse, you're leaving with it, but since you laid eyes on her?" He fucking points *again*. "You've become all pussywhipped."

I scoff, "Pussywhipped?! I haven't even formally met her; how can I possibly be pussywhipped?"

Jensen's laughter returns with vengeance, "No, no, you're right, you're not pussywhipped; you're absolutely fucked."

"It's true, Jon—you are fucked." I hadn't noticed Kyle Johnson make an appearance, but here he is, putting his two cents in, a rookie forward getting a little too comfortable at his captain's expense if you ask me.

But I *am* fucked. I barely recognize myself right now. Jon of old would be sitting in one of those big booths at the back with a lady of his choice sucking at his neck while considering which is closer, her place or a hotel room. My privacy is golden, and aside from my teammates, agent, and close family, no one knows where I live. I've even managed to keep my place secret from the press.

However, this Jon, he can't stop staring, borderline pining for a girl he barely knows.

"Oh, wait, bro, she's turning around! *Shit,* that is one *fine* piece of a—" My glare bitch slaps Kyle into submission.

But if he's thinking it, then every single guy in this bar is too, and I can't have that. I'm tempted to rip off my jacket, stride across, and cover her over, so no one will ever lay eyes on her again. For my eyes only. And yet I am striding over, but not to cover her with my jacket. That's too much, *for now*. Instead, I'm flanked by Jensen, and for all his annoyances, he makes an awesome wingman, ready to entertain and distract her blonde friend. I've been desperate for a chance to make my move, and tonight is too good an opportunity to pass up.

CHAPTER SEVEN

FELICITY

J on Morgan is walking toward me. *I repeat, Jon Morgan is walking toward me!*

The eyes I haven't been able to stop thinking about since I first saw them, fixing me frozen on the spot. He's joined by one of his teammates, by the looks of him. I can't look away, and neither do I want to; he's a sight to behold. Trying to act relaxed, I casually cross my legs over at the knee, and I don't miss the way Jon's eyes travel as my dress rides slightly higher up my thigh.

"Oh, holy hell. He's bringing Jensen Jones with him too," Kate squeaks out.

But just as they get a few steps away, he and his friend are stopped in their tracks as a stunning brunette jumps out in front of Jon. She wastes no time in bringing him into a hug, her perfectly round tits pressing against his chest.

"Oh, for God's sake," Kate drawls, and I can practically feel her eye roll without even looking at her face.

The girl wrapped around Jon is scintillating, just like the photos I saw on social media. Long legs, tiny model-like frame,

41

and perfectly silky straight hair stopping just above her pert, round ass. I haven't seen her face, but I'm willing to bet that's not bad either. The fact that a girl like this is hanging off him, like he's her last meal, does not shock me in the slightest, and it's likely they've been well acquainted with each other before. Am I being incredibly judgy? Yes. But I can't stop the slither of jealousy from rising within me, and I don't like that I'm feeling it. What does surprise me, however, is that despite Jon's new accessory, he hasn't looked at her once. She's clearly doing her best to divert his attention, but her valiant efforts are falling more than flat. It's kind of embarrassing, to be honest.

I decide I've had enough and turn back around to Kate, who arches an unimpressed brow at me. "C'est la vie," I say and wave a hand in the air before standing up from my stool and grabbing my jacket. "I need another drink, in *another* bar."

Kate nods, understanding completely why I want to get out of here, but before I can pull on my coat, it's whipped from my hands, and an imposing figure comes to sit on the empty stool next to me.

"Why are you leaving? I was on my way to say hi."

Jon towers over me and leans forward on the table, bringing his eye level a little closer to mine as he fixes me with a stern yet playful glare. "I've been replaying in my mind the moment we'd cross paths again, and none of those scenarios winds up with you running out on me so, please, take a seat."

What can I possibly say to that? All I can do is swallow thickly and inwardly curse myself for getting off this stool in the first place because now I must "gracefully" lift myself back on it. After a moment and once safely seated, I take a steadying breath and fight back the outbreak of butterflies unleashed in my stomach.

"Actually, I was going to get another drink." *Sort of true*, just from a different bar.

Jon smiles at my response, although I know he doesn't buy it. "Cosmo, right?"

I blink. "Uh, yeah."

He turns to look at the heaving bodies all lined up vying for space at the bar. "I've got it."

I press my lips together; he can't wait in that crazy line for me. "Oh no, it's fine; there's no need to queue up for me."

But he simply lifts his arm, empty Cosmo glass in hand, and tips his chin toward a man standing at the other end of the room. In response, the man nods his head and makes his way over to the barman. With a small smirk tracing his lips, Jon turns back to me. "No problem, Angel."

Angel?

I fight to maintain my composure. "Thank you, but I was going to get one for my friend too." I look across the table to find Jensen, returning with a beer for himself and you guessed it, a cocktail for Kate. *Smooth.*

"So, tell me, what's a British lady like you doing in Seattle?"

I quirk a brow. "I live here."

Jon seems pleased with my response. "I see, and have you been over here long?"

"No, well, sort of. I moved to Seattle just over a year and a half ago, and it was going to be a temporary thing, but I've since decided to stay."

That smirk instantly grows wider. "Wow, you work fast."

I throw him a puzzled look.

"I mean, we've barely spoken beyond sharing a few heated glances, and you're already applying for permanent residence."

I can't help it; I blow out a hard laugh. "Nice try, but I work at Preston & Preston in town, and they offered me a green card to stay and work for them."

I've got to hand it to him though, he sees an opportunity and goes for it. Watching me chuckle, his smile now meets his eyes, and I can confirm, it's award-winning. At that moment, a Cosmo is placed in front of me, along with a beer for Jon, and I reach for my purse, but he's already beaten me to it.

"Put it on my tab, please."

"No problem, Mr. Morgan."

I'm guessing this is the owner by the suit he's wearing and the authoritative way he's been moving around the bar.

I turn back to Jon. "Does everyone do what you want?"

He cocks his head, eyelids slightly hooded. "I don't know, Angel, do they?"

I flush, hard. The heat from my cheeks traveling down to my core as I descend into a puddle. I'm thirty-nine years old, not eighteen, and I feel instantly annoyed at my uncontrollable physical reaction to this man.

Get it together, Felicity.

I re-group, taking a sip of my drink to buy me a couple of seconds.

We continue to talk, the conversation flowing with total ease, something I never experienced with Elliott, even in our strongest moments together.

Jon continues to order me drinks, which I accept but feel uncomfortable taking and frequently try to pay for, without success. He asks about my presence at the games, and I tell him about Jack and the season ticket I bought him for his birthday. At the mention of me being a mum and having an older child, he doesn't flinch, almost like he'd considered that I might be a few, *or maybe a good ten,* years older than his usual type.

"This all seems a little unfair," he says as another cocktail is set down in front of me.

"Well, I have offered to buy the last three rounds."

He throws his head back and laughs. "You're funny. No, that's not what I'm referring to."

"I've stayed and talked to you, haven't I?"

He places his hand over his heart, feigning hurt. "Wow, low blow, Angel." Leaning closer, his spicy cologne wafts over me, and it's intoxicating. "First you won't give me your number, and now we've been sitting here talking for hours, yet you still haven't told me your name."

Shit. I guess I haven't. You kind of skip over introductions when it comes to Jon Morgan. Everyone knows him.

"Felicity," I burst out. "It's Felicity."

He leans back in his stool and brings his bottom lip between his teeth. "That's a really pretty name."

"It means happiness."

Jon's dimples pop as he releases his lip and smiles. "I'd say your parents did a great job of choosing the perfect name."

At the mention of my parents, I look down at the table. Eight years since their death and it's still just as raw.

"Do you have family here in Seattle?"

I shake my head. "Only my son, Jack."

"I'm relieved to hear that was your son at the game. I was worried it might be your boyfriend or something."

I laugh. "Yeah I don't go for toyboys."

He arches a brow. "How old do you think I am?"

"It's kind of pointless guessing facts about you when every detail's plastered all over the internet."

I notice he frowns slightly when he says, "Not every detail."

I wonder what he means by that; the statement felt loaded. "You're thirty-four," I respond.

"Been doing some research on me, have you, Felicity?"

The way my name sounds coming from his mouth sends me into a spin and the aching need that's been simmering within me all night returns tenfold.

I playfully pat his shoulder. "You wish."

"Babe, we should head out soon. I have an early Pilates class tomorrow, and it's already past midnight," Kate chimes from across the table.

I look at Jon, and I wonder if that's a hint of disappointment across his face.

"Unless you want to stay and head back later..." Kate's eyes dart between me and Jon.

Tempting as it is to stay, I discipline and remind myself that if I stay here with him, there will likely be only one outcome: a one-night stand. And there's no way that's happening.

"Yeah, let's get going, it's pretty late for me too," I reply, pushing myself off the stool, realizing quickly just how much those cocktails have gone to my head.

Jon is busy looking at his phone before he pockets it and stands along with Jensen, with whom Kate has been getting cozy all night.

"Let me walk you out to the car," Jon says.

I turn to Kate, asking, "Have you ordered a cab, or do you want me to get it?"

But before she can answer, Jon places his hand on my lower back and hovers his mouth over the top of my head. "Already sorted, Angel."

"What do you mean?"

He doesn't answer, instead guiding me toward the door, saying bye to the owner on the way out.

Oh fuckety-fuck, does he think he's leaving with me?

I feel panic rise, and blurt out, "I'm not going home with you."

Jon glances down, offering me a sweet smile before taking my hand in his and interlacing our fingers. It's the first time our skin has properly touched, and a static charge surges through me, while I wonder if he felt it, too.

"I know, Felicity, but since you're leaving, I have no reason to stay either."

I can't help but gush a little at that. He's forward and confident with me, but it doesn't make me uncomfortable.

As we step out into the night air, Jon lets go of my hand and reaches across for the door of an executive black SUV. I guess this is where we part ways, and he heads home.

But he doesn't get in, instead, opening the door and waving his hand inside. "Your Royal Highness," he says, putting on his best British accent. "Just let the driver know where you need to go."

For the hundredth time tonight, my jaw hangs open. "You booked this for us?"

He shrugs like it's no big deal. "Just wanted to make sure you get home safe."

I look like a codfish; I'm sure I do.

"Oh my god! That's so sweet!" Kate gasps before she says her goodbyes and climbs in.

"Um, well, thank you." I step forward to get into the car, but Jon puts a hand gently on my elbow.

"You're welcome. But please, don't make me ask for your number again. Since your phone has survived our second encounter, I think it's only fair I get to text or call it from time to time."

Giving him my number is probably a bad idea; I barely know the guy. Yet something inside me trusts him. "Okay, but you need to know, I don't respond to booty calls."

His eyebrows shoot up as he hands me his phone, and I type my number in.

"I didn't have you pinned as a booty-call kind of girl. I promise to be on my best behavior."

With that, I quickly step into the car before I'm tempted to do something totally crazy like stick my tongue down his throat. "Goodnight, Jon. Thank you for the drinks and ride."

He rests his forearms on the door frame above my head as he casts a discrete glance over my body and face. "Sweet dreams, Angel."

And with that, he shuts the door, leaving me a hot mess and debating which toy is going to be summoned when I get home.

47

CHAPTER EIGHT

JON

I t's been four days since Felicity took off down the street from the bar in the SUV I arranged for her and her friend.

It was a foreign feeling leaving on my own. I'd been on my absolute best behavior, only flirting with her here and there, because it quickly became very clear that Felicity isn't like any other woman I've met. Sure, I've spent nights with plenty of gorgeous, smart, and self-respecting women, but Felicity? She's on another level entirely, the complete package, a goddess— from the way she looks to how she carries herself. She's totally out of my league, and I'm not ashamed to admit that I'm a bit intimidated, and I have absolutely *no idea* what I'm doing.

All I know for sure is I want to be around her; I want to impress her, and I want her to give me a shot at taking her out. When Jemma wrapped herself around me in the bar on Friday night and Felicity turned to leave, I couldn't unravel myself quickly enough. Jemma is a supermodel and a handful in bed— every guy's dream. But she nearly wrecked my chance with Felicity, and that thought alone left me regretting my past playboy behaviors even more.

We've been on an away series in New Orleans for three days now. Last night we secured our third win of the season, taking the game five to two. I played okay but there's no doubting my mind has been elsewhere, trying to figure out how to see her again. Right now, I should be throwing on a pair of jeans and a shirt, ready to head out with my team to sink a few beers. Instead, I'm lying on my hotel bed, staring at Felicity's number on my phone. I haven't contacted her yet, but that doesn't mean I haven't been desperate to. It seems crazy to miss someone I've only spent a handful of hours with, but that doesn't stop the feeling, and I want to talk with her.

So, without thinking any more about it, I click on her contact and type out a message.

ME

Hope your week is going good.

Keeping it simple, I set my phone down on the nightstand and reach for the TV remote, hoping she doesn't keep me hanging. A few minutes later, my phone lights up, and I imagine it's a bit like the look on my face—because it's her.

ANGEL

Hey, yeah, all good here in Seattle. Work's busy, but I'm heading to the gym to blow off some steam. Saw your game last night, played well :)

She watched my game, even when it wasn't at home; does that mean she's been thinking about me? At the thought, a shot of excitement thrums through my body.

Gym, eh? Perhaps we should bench press together sometime ;)

I can't help a little flirtation and almost immediately a reply comes through.

> Ha! Yeah, bench pressing isn't my forte, I'm more of a spin class and yoga girl myself.

Interesting. I decide to take it up a notch.

> Spinning? I do that as part of my conditioning. I have a full home gym, the works. Maybe you could come check it out sometime, and we could see who's got the superior stamina?

It takes several minutes to receive a reply, so I'm fucking relieved when I see her contact flash up on my screen.

> Are you asking me to be your gym buddy, Mr. Morgan?

> You bet I am.

> Well, I see no harm in that.

Fucking hell, I'm hard just at the thought of Felicity in her workout gear.

My fingers fly over the keyboard as I hurriedly type out a response.

Is this a date?

> I'm back in Seattle late Thursday. What about Friday?

Or the minute the plane wheels touch the ground.

I realize this is the first time I've invited a girl over to my place; it's rule number one in my need to stay private. But when it comes to Felicity, I've torn out the page and set it alight. I want to show her my life, show her all of me, and goddammit, I need to know more about her too.

FELICITY

This week has been full-on. Mark has wanted me in every client meeting he's taken on top of my everyday responsibilities, and I am a whole new level of exhausted. At least Darcy has settled well in Oxford. My phone is filled with pictures of her and her friends all making up for lost time. I knew it was the right decision for her and honestly, seeing her happy at least takes off some of the mum guilt that racks through me daily.

I'm due over at Jon's in an hour. *For a spin class.* I can't believe I said yes to him. Being alone in a man's home without properly getting to know him, and then there's the fact I'm going to willingly reduce myself to a sweaty mess right in front of him. Why did I agree to this? Oh yes, because I have no self-control and have apparently lost my mind.

My phone buzzes.

KATE

> I want a detailed report when you get home, missy (I assume you will be returning home tonight!) Don't forget to wear your gift!

I might have lost my mind, but Kate turned certifiably insane this afternoon at work when I received a special delivery, right to my desk. Finishing up an email to one of Mark's clients, Margo, our receptionist slid a beautifully wrapped box to me. "This just came for you, Felicity."

I stared down at it, certain there had been a mix-up, since my birthday isn't for months.

"It's definitely for you—look at the tag."

I THOUGHT WE COULD SYNC OUR SESSIONS.

THERE WILL BE A CAR AT YOUR PLACE AT SIX.

SEE YOU TONIGHT,

J x

Jon sent me the latest Apple watch complete with a gorgeous emerald strap. I wondered how he knew where I worked but then I remembered mentioning Preston & Preston to him at the cocktail bar. He really doesn't miss a detail.

Kate immediately lost her shit and now wants to know when the wedding is. I can't deny it's such a sweet gesture, but the cautious side of me questions his motives. Is this his way of getting into my knickers? Is this all just a challenge for him? He never dates women, so why would I be any different? I try to bury my niggling doubts, but beyond Jon's motives, I'm really not sure what mine are either. I'm not looking for another relationship. Since Elliott and I separated, I've been enjoying time by myself. I want to make the most of being independent. All I've ever known is a controlling marriage, and there's no way I'm allowing another man to dictate my life again.

Five to six, and I'm ready to go. I opted for a pair of black crop leggings and a white sports bra with a sky-blue cami on top, my usual workout attire.

The buzzer goes, indicating the driver has arrived. I grab my water bottle, shove my feet into my trainers, zip up my hoodie, and check I'm wearing my new watch. My stomach feels like an electric mixer, with a healthy dose of anxiety and excitement churning around.

On sight of the car parked outside my building, I realize it's not your usual cab company and the driver looks sort of familiar. "Good evening, Ms. Thompson. Mr. Morgan has asked me to pick you up and take you straight to his apartment. It's not a long drive, about fifteen minutes away."

"You picked me up that night from the cocktail bar?" I ask, suddenly realizing how Jon knows my address.

The driver smiles. "I'm Jon's private driver, Gerard."

Private driver. *Wow.*

En route, I reply to Kate's earlier text and assure her I *will be* returning home tonight, but the jury's out on whether I provide all the details.

Pulling up to Jon's building, I get out of the black SUV and approach the doorman. Apparently, he's expecting me and pushes the door open. "Please take the elevator on the left, Ms. Thompson," he explains.

"Thank you, to what floor?" I ask.

The doorman smiles. "Oh, this elevator only goes to the penthouse, so it will take you directly to the apartment."

He hands me a card with a code and wishes me an enjoyable evening. This really is another world away from my tiny one-bed. I tap the code in and clutch my tote bag to my side as the elevator ascends. Time seems to go by in slow motion as eventually it dings and comes to a stop.

Jesus.

As the doors open, I'm greeted with spectacular gray marble floors and crisp white walls adorned with print after print of what must be Jon's family. There are also some action shots from the NHL, although I don't think any of them are of Jon himself.

Looking up, there are two black chandeliers, sleek and modern in appearance but exuding expense. I think this is his foyer, but it would easily swallow my entire apartment. Up ahead, I spot his kitchen, so I go to kick off my shoes and head in that direction.

"No need to take them off, Angel. But by all means, make yourself at home."

I turn to the right and find Jon standing in an archway to a large room with an enormous stone fireplace roaring behind him. He's dressed in low-slung gray sweatpants and a black wet-look gym tank that hugs every single groove of his torso. I look down at his feet to find them bare, ankles crossed and hands in his pockets. He looks magnificent, his wavy dark hair is tousled and effortlessly perfect, and when he smiles, his dimples pop.

Lord, have mercy.

Taking in his splendor, I feel like I've already completed a three-hour workout.

"Like what you see, Ms. Thompson?"

I don't ask how he found out my last name. I certainly didn't tell him on Friday, but I assume it wasn't hard for him to work out since a quick search on my workplace's website would reveal all.

"Just admiring your sweatpants," I reply with a surprisingly steady tone.

Wait, admiring his sweatpants? Just tell him you were staring at his crotch next time.

Jon pushes off the wall and moves in my direction. I take a step back and bump into a side table I only just realized was behind me.

Holding my gaze as he towers over me, he whispers, "I've missed you."

He's missed me? I'm taken aback by his candidness, but I'd be lying if I said I hadn't missed him too.

Before I can muster up my usual sassy response, he juts his head down the hall. "My gym is this way. Do you need a drink?"

Yes, about three bottles of wine and half a dozen shots.

"No, I'm fine thanks. I've got everything I need." I lift the strap on my bag, indicating I came prepared.

Jon slips on his socks and white Nike trainers, and I follow him through his apartment in silence, the tension between us palpable. I can almost hear the crackles of electricity bouncing off us. We walk through his kitchen first, and it's beautiful with a butcher's-block countertop teamed with stylish light-gray cabinets. Leaving the kitchen, he leads me down another hallway decorated in a similar style to his foyer. There are several doors leading off it, and I wonder if his bedroom lies behind one of them.

"My bedroom is the first on the left," Jon smirks over his shoulder as if reading my mind.

Am I that transparent?

We come to a stop before a thick, wooden door. The room must be soundproofed because as soon as he pushes it open, I'm met with blaring music. "Is that the Spice Girls?"

"I thought it would make you feel more at home."

Joker.

"Well, it's a kind thought, but I'm more of a Marilyn Manson girl myself."

His eyes widen in surprise. "Really?"

Dumping my bag down, I root through the front pocket for my air pods. Popping the lid on the case, I begin putting them in my ears. "Yep, he's my go-to for workouts. "Personal Jesus" is probably my favorite."

Jon props his hands on his hips, shaking his head as he looks down. "I don't think we can be friends anymore."

I mirror his stance. "Why? Don't you like a bit of heavy rock, petal?"

With that, he picks up his phone and swipes the screen a couple of times before Miley Cyrus's "Party in the USA" begins playing through the surround sound.

I can't help but laugh. "Now *you're* joking, Mr. Morgan."

Jon's already on his way to the exercise bikes and shaking his head. "One thing to note about me, Angel. I never joke about Miley."

CHAPTER NINE

JON

W eightlifting is dangerous.
It's especially dangerous when you pay absolutely no attention to what you're doing. I'm benching one hundred and seventy pounds while staring at the finest ass I've ever seen.

We finished our spinning session, and Felicity was seriously impressive, her stamina noted. Afterward, she moved to the treadmill where she's remained ever since, breaking into a light jog. I don't know whether to hate or thank myself right now because the mirrors I installed along the length of the wall give me a perfect view of her bouncing tits while I sit behind, eyes laser-focused on her tight ass, fighting an ever-developing hard-on. If I don't stop gawking soon, there's a high probability that one of these weights is going to end up on my face.

Placing the bar back on the rack, I sit up and wipe my hands on my thighs. "Want to come show me what you can lift?" I thumb over my shoulder to the bar.

She's clearly nervous or maybe a little shy in my presence, and I guess watching me bench over twice her weight won't be helping. She's thrown me a sweet smile now and then, but for the most part, we've been working out and listening to music.

Felicity brings the treadmill to a stop. "I can try, but I tend to stick to stretching and cardio."

Yes, I can see that.

"I can help you, show you what to do, even spot you." I stand from the bench as she bends to collect her water bottle and makes her way over. "Straddle the bench then lean back, keeping your back flat to the surface." I adjust the weight, leaving a very light load before raising the bar and showing her how to lift correctly. Hovering over her, I'm ready to take the bar when she's done. It's easier said than done though because I have an enticing view of her ample cleavage, her tits pressed together in her sports bra. At a guess, I'd say she's a D cup.

Behave, Jon.

After a few reps, Felicity lets out a low groan. *Christ,* this is torturous. "Had enough?" I ask.

She quickly nods her head, and I take the bar, placing it back. "That's harder than it looks, and I clearly have no muscles." She chuckles, sitting up.

Grabbing my Gatorade, I straddle the bench, too, sitting just a few inches away from her so that we're face to face. Even though we aren't touching, it's an incredibly intimate position, and I can tell she feels the same level of intensity.

Taking a drink, I hold her gaze as her eyes drop to my mouth. "I can see a few muscles building in those biceps of yours," I say, reaching up and squeezing the top of her arm gently. Her skin is so fucking smooth, like velvet.

A bead of sweat appears at her hairline, casually making its way down her forehead. Before I can stop it, my hand shoots up and swipes it from her brow.

On instinct, Felicity pulls back, open-mouthed as she sucks in a breath. She shoots to her feet, almost tumbling over the bench as she hurries over to her bag. Shoving her towel, bottle, and air pods in as quickly as possible, she doesn't look up at me. "I should go. It's late, and I need to get some sleep."

I rise from the bench, disappointed she wants to leave but confident her reaction is in response to my touch. "Busy day tomorrow, eh?"

She puffs out a breath. "Yeah, up early, you know."

Sensing this may all be a ruse to get out of my apartment as quickly as possible, I push her further. I don't want her to leave yet. Maybe *ever*.

"Oh yeah, what you got planned?" Felicity isn't a good liar, that much is clear. She goes to speak then clamps her mouth shut, looking down at the floor. I take a few steps closer. "Look, if you want to go then just say so. I won't be offended. A little disappointed maybe. But I'm not about to make you stay or do anything you aren't a hundred percent comfortable with."

Still not looking up, she scuffs the floor lightly with her sneaker. After a beat she breaks her silence, "It's just...I don't know what I was expecting coming here. I guess I expected to find a boy desperate to get in my knickers, not a man interested in spending time with me, let alone actually wanting to work out." She pauses before speaking again, "I expected you to be a bit of—"

"An asshole?" I finish for her.

Bright emerald eyes meet mine and she chuckles. "Yeah, I guess I was. But you aren't, are you? Or maybe this is all part of your plan, your way to get what you want."

It's hard not to let her words show how deeply they cut, but they do. It's clear what she thinks of me, and I can feel my hands begin to tremble slightly at the thought of her walking out of here and never wanting to see me again. I don't want to be the lonely, retired hockey player with no one to come home to. I want someone to share my bed— my life— and meeting Felicity has intensified those feelings tenfold.

I bite my bottom lip, trying to steady myself, and lean down to meet her eyes, Miley's "Slide Away" is soothing my gym speakers. "Felicity, believe me, I want in your pants. I can't lie to you and say I don't because I'm insanely attracted to you. But I have zero interest in getting you naked today if it means tomorrow, you won't answer my calls. Because I will be calling you. I don't know exactly what this is because I've never been in this position before. I just know I want to be in you *and* around you."

"Preoccupied about Saturday?"

I look up from my plate piled high with meatloaf and mashed potatoes and shrug. "Just tired, big practice sessions plus extra time in the gym."

Dad sits across from me, glasses resting on his nose, completing a crossword. He finishes another word and drops his puzzle and pen down beside him. "Fair enough, son, but take it easy and look after yourself. These are key years in your career. How you approach them will likely dictate how long you have left."

Reverting my gaze to my meal, I feel my jaw tighten and nod. "Don't I know it."

Before Dad can reply, Mom is by my side, spooning yet more mashed potatoes onto my plate. "Colorado this week, right?" she inquires, a breezy tone in her voice. She always loves having one or both of her boys home, catering to our every need.

The Colorado Kings are my former team, having played for them straight out of the draft. "Yeah, fly out tomorrow, four-night stay in total. I'll be back late on Sunday."

Mom heads around the table and sits opposite me before Dad comes to join us. We sit in silence for a couple of minutes, but it's a comforting atmosphere. I've never been a fan of silence —it's usually a gateway allowing my mind to wander, typically to troubling places like my future, spent alone as a washed-up pro athlete. Here though, sitting in my family home, my mind stays firmly planted and calm. I love this house. I bought it for Mom and Dad five years ago and paid off their mortgage, allowing my dad to retire early and support Mom and Adam at home. The house also accommodates Adam's needs far better than their old place ever did. It's got an incredible backyard surrounded by tall evergreen trees and shrubs. It's a haven for wildlife, something Adam loves. We also converted the double garage into a self-contained living space for him, complete with a state-of-the-art sensory room. There's everything he could need here when he visits on the weekends.

Which is why it's so difficult when he chooses to stay away and in his apartment rather than come home for scheduled evenings. That's been happening more often, and the frequency of his calls and texts has fallen off a cliff. When we try to call, he rarely answers. I'm worried Adam is becoming more withdrawn. He used to want to attend more of my games, or he would time his visits home to watch them on TV with Dad, but that's also died. The optimistic side of me hopes he's becoming more independent, but the experienced brother says something's wrong. I'd go to him, but he wouldn't appreciate unexpected callers. Lately, I've felt like my brother is drifting away from us, and I know Mom and Dad see it too because it's etched across their faces, and I'm powerless to do anything. The feeling eats away at me because other than our parents, all we have is each other, and that's a frightening prospect.

"Will you be heading out with the Kings after the match on Saturday?" Dad asks between mouthfuls of delicious home-cooked food.

I feel my shoulders tense at the simple question. "Yeah, Trent messaged me last week, asking if I wanted to meet up afterward, so I'll head to one of their usual bars for a few." Trent is the captain for the Kings, and we've kept in touch over the years, he's a good guy, but I've not been out with them in a while.

I should be looking forward to Saturday, but I'm not. The Colorado boys know the old Jon, the crazy rookie with a different woman each night, and that's not who I am anymore. I'm tired of plastering on a façade to meet the expectations of who people think I am based on a version of me that died long ago.

"G OOD GAME, MAN." Jessie claps my shoulder as he walks back to his bench.

"Yeah, bro, you too," I reply.

Jensen, on the other hand, is less levelheaded toward the loss, ripping his pads off before ramming them into his bag, not bothering to have them wiped down. "Fucking good game? Yeah right, we played like shit."

He's not wrong, we did play like shit. My head has been up my ass for days now, and that feeling of dread has only amassed to the point where I got next to no sleep last night. I tossed and turned, eventually giving up in the early hours, then spent an hour searching for Felicity's social media. It's probably a bit creepy, but I followed and added her on every platform I could think of and even threw in a few likes for good measure. She's private on most accounts which isn't surprising, but the few pictures that are public are *stunning*. She hasn't added me back yet, but I'm trying not to read too much into it. Although she hurried out of my place on Friday night, I don't think her body language screamed *I never want to see you again*.

At least that's what I'm telling myself.

Insomnia isn't unusual for me, but it has gotten better over the years since I attended therapy. I started seeing my therapist, Ben, around three years ago when my anxiety and depression began pulling me under. I was barely functioning day to day, and I started to find less-than-healthy ways to cope with my troubles. Hitting the drink too hard or working out in my gym to the point where I could barely walk, desperate to numb my spiraling thoughts of loneliness and self-deprecation. I slept with more and more women, searching for affection and a feeling of being wanted.

I think we all look for validation in our lives, whether it be our successes or simply to be wanted and feel valued, and from the outside looking in, I have all of that, including an awesome but small family. So, when I started to take a downward spiral in my mental health for "no apparent reason" and it seeped into my game, the media started to question what could possibly be wrong. This "has-it-all, women falling at his feet, playboy hockey god." The external lack of validation left me reeling like I had no right to feel the way I did. So, with every bad day, my coping strategies became more extreme, and the compassion I held for myself dissipated altogether.

That was when Zach, the only person I confided in fully, suggested I speak with Ben, a therapist known for working with pro athletes. I've come a long way with his help and still see him each week to keep on the straight and narrow. I've been in more fights than I can recall, had painful insults fired at me from all four corners of the world, and I've had countless coaches tell me my best isn't good enough. Yet it's always the silent games we play with ourselves that hit the hardest.

"You coming out tonight, Jon?" Zach shouts from his shower stall.

"I am, but I'll be wherever Trent and the guys are, so probably the Indigo Lounge. You can join if you want?"

"Indigo, where the fuck is that? Never heard of that one before. But if it sells booze, I'm down. I need to drink tonight's game out of my system," Jensen chimes in.

Form an orderly line.

"Okay, meet me in the lobby at nine, and we'll grab a ride," I shout over the pelting water streams.

"Can't we just walk? I could use the extra cool down tonight," Jensen protests.

"Ha! Yeah, I'd rather not. My legs have had enough exercise

for tonight, plus you remember how it was last season. Colorado away games with their boy, Jon, in tow. The press is always hot on that one, and I don't want cameras in my face if I can help it," Zach answers on my behalf.

"Yeah, fair point, man. Okay, we'll see you at nine and catch a ride from there," Jensen responds.

I turn the shower off and step out into the main locker room. My senses tighten as the cold air hits my wet skin, but I welcome the sensation—anything to take my mind off tonight. Shaking it off, I throw my post-match suit on, forgoing the tie, and head out to grab the team bus back to the hotel.

CHAPTER TEN

JON

I t's ten when we finally make it to the bar.

The press was ready and waiting to take pictures as we arrived which really pissed me off and raised my anxiety levels through the roof. The Scorpions always try to keep their whereabouts private, especially when we head on away tours. But lately, the media has been one step ahead, particularly these last six months, and I've never seen it as bad as tonight. Once again, the cynical side of me can't help but align the timeline with the moment Amie walked into Zach's life. With her job as an influencer, she travels a lot and, sometimes, she'll meet Zach on away games, and she's never alone, often bringing an entourage of bunnies with her. Some of the guys, like Jensen, are welcoming, but I don't like it. Thankfully, Amie isn't here tonight, but that doesn't mean Zach hasn't told her where we're staying. Bringing it up with him though would be like a red rag to a bull, and I've got no firm proof of her antics, only my suspicions.

"Nice to see you, Jon, and even nicer to turn you over like we did tonight." Trent nudges my shoulder and winks.

"Yeah, the quicker tonight evaporates from my memory the

better. Speaking of which, you want another?" I knock my glass against his empty one.

"Why not, man, cheers."

I turn back to the barman, who heads straight my way.

"You bought the whole team with you?" Trent asks, casting his eye across the room and chuckling.

"Yeah, funny enough, they all share my need to drink."

His chuckle morphs into full laughter as we walk toward a booth filled with his teammates. Setting my glass down, I perch on the end of the bench and nod at the guys, some whose faces I know, while others are newer trades.

"Why don't you head back to Colorado, Jon, play out your final years with the Kings? Get back to playing for a *real* team."

I don't recognize the guy who speaks up other than I know he's a defenseman who boarded me hard on more than one occasion tonight. His comment is in jest, but I don't like his disconcerting reference to the end of my career.

I take a deep swig of beer to gather my thoughts and work on a light tone for my reply. "Plenty of time in me yet, and ample to kick your rookie ass."

He snorts along with a couple of head shakes from the other guys, but it's lighthearted in nature.

We sit for a while longer, and I laugh when I catch Jessie and Jensen grinding up against two girls on the dance floor. From the angle I have, they may as well be fucking, one girl is bent fully forward, ass pressed up against Jensen's groin while he firmly grips her hips. *Christ.* A smile breaks across my face, and, for the first time in days, I feel my shoulders drop and some tension start to ease.

I wish I could say the feeling lasted more than a minute though because, without warning, I'm overwhelmed with strong perfume when a half-naked brunette perches herself on my lap. She came out of nowhere—one minute I'm smiling and catching up with Trent, the next I'm playing host to a girl who can't be older than twenty-one. She takes a sip of her Cosmo, which I instantly clock.

I only want one Cosmo-drinking girl on my lap, and this isn't her.

I panic. I don't like how this looks, but what do I do, stand up and let the tipsy girl fall to the floor? Push her off and look like an even bigger asshole? I'd say she shouldn't be touching me without consent, but pretty much every person in this bar knows I've never complained about a smoking hot girl touching me before. And even though she is an absolute smoke show, the thought of touching her or any other girl aside from one rolls my stomach.

"Hey, baby, it's been a while since we've seen you around these parts. Well played tonight."

Huh, she clearly knows nothing about hockey since tonight was anything but well played. I decide the only way to get her off me is to be polite. Without wasting another second, I lean down to speak into her ear to *kindly* ask her to get the fuck off my lap. But she clearly misses the deep frown burrowed between my brows, and as I lean toward her, she fucking kisses me. Full-on, right on the lips. She grabs my head in a vice grip and twists her body around on my lap before moaning into my mouth, trying to part my lips with her tongue. I put my hands up to protest but end up brushing her goddamn breasts as I try to get her off me. I need out of this fucked-up situation ASAP.

Rising to my feet, she *still* clings to me like a fucking koala. This isn't working. So, with a little more force, I manage to untangle her arms and release myself from her grasp, stepping back as quickly as I can. But the panic only rises further, and my brain goes into overdrive.

Shit.

Shit.

Shit.

Technically I've done nothing wrong, but I've been in this game long enough to know pictures of this will be on the internet within minutes and only the most damning images find their way onto social media.

My panic turns to anger as I whip around to face the girl who just sent my life up in smoke. "*What the fuck?* Who said you could kiss me? Sit on my lap? *Touch me?*"

She looks genuinely shell-shocked but still steps toward me once again.

I take another stride back in response, hands up and out in front of me. "That wasn't cool. I have a fucking girlfriend." The words leave my mouth before I can filter them. Her actions weren't cool, but the rest is an outright lie. Felicity isn't even close to being my girlfriend. We've barely spoken since she practically ran out my door on Friday. Not that I haven't wanted to speak to her. *Everyday. Every goddamn minute.* I've just been afraid to go too hard too soon with her and scare her off.

"Well, you sure kept it quiet. The internet says you're single, and anyway, who cares, she knows you're a player."

I shake my head, a futile feeling crushing my chest. The boys in the booth including Trent are all gawking, but as I look around at the rest of the bar, thankfully everyone else is too distracted to notice, including Jensen and Jessie, who are still on the dance floor getting it on.

A wave of relief washes over me but instantly crashes down when I see Koala Girl's friend standing about twenty feet away. *Fucking filming.* Her phone is outstretched on her arm, her mouth gaping open as she shakes her head, but I don't miss the excitable look on her face like she's about to cash in on her viral prize.

In an instant, I'm striding over to her, and out of the corner of my eye, I see Trent shoot up from the booth, tearing after me. "Jon, cool it, bro. It's okay."

Swiveling around, a misty red haze clouds my vision. "No, it's *not fucking okay,"* I drawl back at him, throwing my arms in the air. "I'm supposed to be seeing someone. Well, dating someone." My hands fly to the back of my neck, and I grip hard, my frustration unbearable as I desperately try to describe what I have with Felicity, which right now is nothing, but at the same time feels like everything. "Honestly, I don't know what it is, but it's probably fucked now because these girls—"

I spin back around pointing to...no one. Nothing. Because they've gone. High-tailed their way out of the bar in the split second I turned my back. They must have grabbed their shit and ran out taking their footage, and *my fucking sanity,* with them.

FELICITY

There's nothing better than a sunny Sunday morning, especially one where you can lie in bed, basking in the sunlight as it streams through your blinds.

This is not one of those Sunday mornings.

I'm hungover, and let's just say hangovers are not as forgiving now I'm in my late thirties—this one in particular is sent from the devil himself. It's Kate and my co-worker Taylor's fault, as they came over last night for wine and movies, with the ratio quickly tipping in wine's favor. Taylor works in the admin department keeping us all in check. She's only twenty-six, making her the baby of our trio, but she can drink me under the table, as I discovered last night. My mouth feels like the bottom of a parrot's cage. I need to get up, brush my teeth, and formulate an anti-hangover strategy.

Fighting through the fuzziness of my brain, I hear a *ping* and creak open an eyelid to see my phone screen lit up. I fling an arm to the side and grab it from the nightstand, ripping it from the charging cable.

KATE

Gah! Did I go ten rounds with Mike Tyson last night?

ME

If this message barely makes sense, it's because I only have the use of three fingers and one eye. Never again.

Ha! I guess no booze at lunch.

No booze again. Period.

Fine by me. See you later, XOXO

Battling my body to the bathroom, I brush my teeth and throw my straggly hair into a messy bun and pad into the kitchen. The display of empty wine bottles on the counter acts as an unwelcome reminder of last night's handiwork and another wave of nausea rolls through my stomach. Breakfast is what I need, starting with coffee.

Ten minutes later I'm perched on a barstool armed with bacon, waffles, syrup, and my second mug of black coffee. My stomach instantly wants to reject everything, but I fight through. I only have myself to blame, and that's the worst part of a hangover—knowing it's self-inflicted.

Despite my pain this morning, last night did provide a welcome distraction from my repetitive, bordering on obsessive, thoughts of Jon. I've replayed that moment on the gym bench over and over, the way he casually straddled it and shifted his body toward mine, leaning in to wipe my forehead. His gentle touch felt like a branding iron, and the way his eyes searched mine...my thighs pinch together as I recall it all. I've never been touched so tenderly and to be honest, it freaked me out. My body raged with my head, wanting to lean forward and let him kiss me, take me, have his way with me. But I panicked and practically ran out of his apartment. Since then, I've pretty much had radio silence aside from him adding me on social media and liking a few of my posts. We've exchanged a few texts, but I feel like he's backing off.

But that's what I want, *right?*

It might be the remnants of the wine or maybe my heart outmaneuvering my head but fuck it. I pick up my phone and decide no harm in dropping him a quick message. I know they got beaten down last night so maybe I can make him smile.

ME

> Hey. Hope Colorado is treating you okay. Sorry about last night's result.

I hit send and stare down at the screen, the anticipation of a reply not sitting well with my breakfast and hangover.

A minute or so later three dots appear indicating he's typing a response. *Christ,* I'm giddy at three dots; get a grip, Felicity. But just as soon as they appear, they disappear again. They come back once more, but no reply surfaces. I busy myself clearing away, but after another five minutes, there's still no message. I won't lie, it's kind of disappointing, but perhaps he's busy. Intrigue gets the better of me though, and before I know it, I'm bringing up his socials.

It's hard to describe what I feel when my IG news feed opens. The nausea I felt this morning is dwarfed by the wretched feeling taking hold in the pit of my stomach. Post upon post, image after image, video after video of Jon making out with a gorgeous brunette, probably young enough to be my daughter. Some are of her on his lap, Jon leaning down to talk in her ear, others of her straddling him as they kiss, intensely. But it's the footage of her slender legs wrapped around his waist as he's standing and gripping her thighs tightly that breaks me. Only minutes ago, I messaged him, opening the door to my heart ever so slightly. Well, now I know why I haven't received a response. He's probably shacked up in some hotel with her. I guess I was right when I presumed he was too busy to reply.

My upset is happily replaced with pure rage. I can't believe I nearly fell for his antics and better yet, was actually tempted to fall into bed with this guy. To become another notch on his bedpost.

Stupid girl.

I snatch my phone back up, never wanting to see those images again, and hastily deactivate every social media account I can think of. I need those pictures out of my life, just like I do Jon Morgan.

CHAPTER ELEVEN

JON

The thud as the plane wheels touch down in nighttime Seattle lurches my head forward, breaking me from my semi-conscious state.

I didn't sleep at all last night. Jessie, Jensen, and I left the bar shortly after all hell broke loose and Koala Girl and her accomplice made their escape. The guys only needed to take one look at me to know something was very wrong. I appreciate them, and while I've always known deep down that they're great guys, they really came through for me last night.

We walked back to the hotel and made straight for Zach's room, crashing his and Amie's Facetime which I kind of felt bad about, *kind of didn't.* Zach's solution was simple. Call her and get ahead of her seeing the posts and call my agent and try to block the images from spreading. I'd already been in touch with my agent the moment those girls left the bar with the footage. Like I said, this isn't my first rodeo, but I knew I needed to get in touch with Felicity just in case any slipped through the net.

But by the time I got back to my room, I started replaying everything in my mind, from what she would say to how she would react. While she has social media, she's mentioned to me before that she isn't a big user, and she still hasn't followed me back so, perhaps, she won't see anything until I can get to her and explain everything face-to-face. I want her to look me in the eyes and see my truth about what really happened; it's my best chance to get her to understand.

So here I am, a mess, running on zero sleep, and a desperate man. It's not lost on me how gone I am for this woman I barely know. But I am, and I can't stop thinking about her. I haven't been able to stop since that moment at the stadium, that little squeal, her intoxicating coconut scent, her soft skin against mine. The way she flinched as she felt my touch that day in the gym. The fact that I know she felt it too, the connection, the sexual energy searing between us. And I've fucked it all up before I even got started.

"Just call her," Zach repeats for the tenth time in as many hours. He hands me my carry-on bag from the overhead locker, and we head for the exit ramp. "She already texted you this morning, so even if she hasn't seen the images, she's going to think something's wrong if you don't reply."

"Okay, and say what? Sorry I had my hands all over another woman last night, but I hated it. I wanted nothing more than to be with you, even though all the pictures say completely the opposite. It's not what it looked like? Because that line works every time."

Whichever way I look at this I feel totally fucked. I want to beat the shit out of something, but instead, I run an agitated hand through my hair, pulling hard at the roots, hoping the pain will relieve some of my desperation.

Zach stops halfway down the ramp, turning to me, his finger lifted in the air. "Look, the way I see it is you have two options. One, forget her. Forget you even laid eyes on the girl and move on. Chalk the whole experience up to bad luck and timing." He lifts another finger. "Two. Go after her, call her, message her, tell her what happened, and set the record straight."

I bite my bottom lip and drop my head.

"Or three," Jensen's head pops over Zach's shoulder. "Go with your original plan and *show* her how much she means. Chicks love that shit, flowers, chocolates, all that. Show her that last night meant nothing and was blown way out of proportion."

Zach lifts a shoulder but nods his head. "He's put it terribly, but yeah, get her some 'chocolates and shit,'" he says, mocking Jensen, whose case suddenly finds the back of Zach's heel. "Ow! Fuck, man!"

They might be a pain in the ass, but they're my guys, and they're right. I need to follow through on my plan and go to her and pray for a fucking miracle that she'll understand. Because forgetting Felicity isn't an option.

FELICITY

If it's possible, I feel worse than I did yesterday morning. Only this time, I'm not hungover.

A heavy sense of disappointment has settled over me. The fact that my friendship or whatever the hell it was with Jon is over before it even got started is gutting, and I can't lie and say it's not. That night at the cocktail bar, the glances we stole at each other during games when he was on the bench, when he scored, when he stared me down through the jumbotron. It all felt so much more than to come to this, with me practically blocking his existence from my life. For him to steal moments with me in his gym to then basically fuck another girl in public the next week.

Yet it's not that he hooked up with another woman that gets me so enraged, since he was never mine to claim. It's the fact I'm agonizing that he never was mine. Why do I care what he does? Who he sees? Who he takes back to his bed each night? I never wanted a relationship with him. And was I really that stupid to think he ever wanted something more than casual sex with me?

I burn my mouth on my chai latte, too engrossed in my pointless thoughts to notice the steam billowing from my takeout flask. It's not even nine in the morning and I can already tell how this day is going to play out. It's likely to end with me slouched on my sofa with Ben and Jerry for company while shouting expletives at romantic movies.

"Morning, Margo," I say, lifting my cup slightly as I step out of the elevator doors and into the reception area. "Any messages for Mark over the weekend?"

She shakes her head but keeps eyeing me in a way that makes me feel a bit uneasy. "No, none for Mark, but there is for you."

Huh? Okay, well, to be kept busy today is probably no bad thing. "Okay, just send it to my email, and I'll sort it out ASAP."

Margo's brow creases slightly. "Oh, this can't be emailed." She shifts a little in her chair. "It's on your desk waiting."

Right. Now I'm confused.

Dancing between desks on my way over to my corner of the office, I can feel all eyes on me. What. Is. Going. On?

I round the corner and almost drop my coffee when I spot my "message."

There, sitting on my desk in all his masculine glory, is none other than Jon Morgan. I inwardly curse myself for not making more of an effort this morning. In my dejection, I threw on a gray pencil skirt and a simple white blouse which could've done with an iron. I didn't bother to wash my hair, so I shoved it up in a high ponytail and finished off my gorgeous get-up with a pair of two-year-old, black kitten heels, which have seen better days.

Conversely, Jon is perched on the end of my desk dressed in black trousers and a gray shirt, a couple of the buttons are undone, revealing part of his sculpted chest. Over the top, he has a black and white team-colored Scorpions jacket with the number twenty-two embroidered over his left pec. His floppy brown hair just clears his steely-gray eyes, and he tops his drool-worthy look off with a backward Scorpions cap and white sneakers.

My throat is thick with anticipation as I approach him. What does he want? Why is he here? Placing my bag and jacket down on the other side of the desk, I look around the room to catch thirty heads quickly glance back to their screens, pretending to mind their own business.

It's clear we have an audience, and we need some privacy to talk. "Shall we head over there?" My voice barely comes out as a whisper as I point to a side meeting room I know is free for at least a few minutes.

Jon pauses for a second, his eyes tracing down my body in a way that ignites my soul, and then he stands from the desk. He's smiling softly but it doesn't reach his eyes, and I can tell he's troubled, which troubles me too. "Sure, lead the way."

It's only a few paces to the side room but with every step, my legs get weaker. I can feel his presence and smell his spicy yet sweet cologne. The back of my head burns, and I sense his eyes boring into me from behind. The tension is so thick. I just wish he'd picked a better time to show up rather than Monday morning, at my office, for everyone to witness.

I open the meeting room door and step inside, holding it for Jon, and it shuts with a soft click behind us.

"Take a seat if you like." I point toward the four available chairs surrounding a round table.

He doesn't take a seat, but instead steps closer to me, so we are mere inches apart. Thank God the windows are covered with blinds because this meeting looks *anything* but professional.

"I needed to see you, Felicity." His words are raspy and now that I'm closer to him, I can see the tiredness in his eyes, like he hasn't slept for days. His shoulders are heavy and sunken, and I know he's sorry for what happened on Saturday night. "You saw the pictures, didn't you." It's not a question. Jon goes to speak again but clamps his mouth shut, his jaw straining as his Adam's apple bobs on a heavy swallow. "They aren't what they look like,

Felicity. I know..." He pauses again as his hands fly to the back of his neck and grip hard. "I know *how they look,* but that's not what happened."

I puff out a breath. I'm so freaking tense every muscle in my body is crying. "Well, they looked pretty damning to me, Jon." My tone is incredulous and harsher than I intended. He goes to speak again, but I hold up a hand between us. "Look. It doesn't really matter what I, the press, or the rest of the world think for that matter. You're single and clearly had a good night. The images are no different than the hundreds of others taken over your career and come next weekend, they will be lining everyone's junk folders and wastepaper bins."

The words feel just as ridiculous as they sound. It *does matter* what I think. I've got a pounding head and two empty tubs of Ben & Jerry's at home as a testament to how much it matters.

Jon's brow furrows deep, his eyes almost glazed with pain. He breaks eye contact, staring down at the floor before darting his head back up to me. His gaze turns smoldering, and *Jesus,* this is intense. He steps another couple of inches closer to me until I can feel his breath wash over my face, shooting straight to my heat. "So, you don't care what I do or don't do with other women?" He's so close all I can think about is his mouth on mine.

As if on reflex I wet my lips, my body at war with my mind over this man. "It's not that easy," I explain.

"It's a simple question," he counters, never breaking eye contact.

"Okay. I can't lie and say seeing you with the brunette in that bar didn't hurt me. Because it did, more than I wanted it to, and more than it should have." I can barely breathe my lungs are so tight, but I'm determined to get this all out there. "Because you and I," I motion between us, "we aren't anything. We have no claim over one another." I pause, trying to gather myself. "I'm annoyed at my response. I *shouldn't* have felt that way."

Jon's mouth tips up slightly at the corner and some relief

enters his eyes. His hand lifts to the side of my head as his huge palm caresses my face, his rough, calloused thumb gently stroking my cheek and the motion sends waves of electricity through me. "Would it make you feel any better to know that I've been going out of my mind since Saturday night?" His thumb is still tracing my cheekbone. "Would it make you feel better to know that the girl touched me, sat on my lap, and kissed me, all without my permission?" He leans even closer, our noses almost touching. "Would it make you feel better to know that right after that video ended, I unraveled her clinging legs from my waist and lost my shit, explaining that I had a girlfriend?"

Girlfriend?

"And would it make you feel better to know that since I first laid eyes on you in that hallway, I haven't purposely touched or thought about another woman since?"

There's silence for a few beats, and when he pulls back slightly, his hand is still caressing my cheek as his eyes search mine before falling to my mouth. His tongue darts out, wetting his bottom lip. But he doesn't move to kiss me, although I can tell he wants to. I want him to, even though I can think of a thousand reasons why kissing Jon Morgan is a bad idea.

"Does it make you feel better, Angel?" he asks me once again.

My breath catches in my throat, but I push out the words. "You think I'm just going to fall at your feet like every other woman before me?"

He shakes his head gently, a tender smile tracing his lips. "No, Angel. That's my job."

Jon's lips crash to mine.

They're soft, full, and addictive, just as I expected. It's our first kiss, but he takes my mouth as if it's the last time he'll feel me. Desperate and searching. Hungry and wanting. And when his tongue brushes over my lower lip, seeking permission to go further, my core ignites, bursting into flames, and I could melt into this floor right here.

Our tongues glide together, hot, wet, and in perfect synchronization as our kiss transcends from desperate to a type I can't describe, a kiss I've never felt before. Jon's other hand comes up to my waist, pulling me forward, pinning me to his body, and that's when I feel it. His length. He's hard, and despite several layers between us, I know he's big. And he wants me. Jon freaking Morgan wants *me*. I don't know how long we kiss for because time and everything else ceases to exist.

A brisk knock breaks us apart as my hand flies to my swollen lips. I already miss his touch.

Before I can say anything, Jon answers the door, keeping it half open. "Can I help you?" I hear him say, a hint of exasperation to his tone.

"Sorry. Jon Morgan?" Shit, shit, *shit,* it's Mark. I can tell his voice without needing to see him.

"Yes, that's me," Jon replies. There's a beat of silence before Mark speaks again.

"I'm looking for Felicity. One of her colleagues said they saw you disappear into this room together." Mark is no fan of ice hockey, or any sports for that matter, but in this city, everyone knows Jon Morgan, and I can tell there's a level of trepidation to his tone.

Jon straightens. "Yep. I turned up first thing this morning and spoke to your receptionist, Mandy, is it?"

"Margo," Mark corrects.

"Margo. I was making an inquiry, looking for some legal advice actually. Margo said Felicity would be the right person to speak to. So here we are."

I have to hand it to him; he sure thinks quickly on his feet.

Sensing it's my cue, I move around into Mark's line of vision. "Hi, can I help you? We were just finishing up." I know my lips are obviously red and swollen, and I inwardly cringe at what I must look like—like I'm post make-out, I would imagine.

"Actually, I have a couple more questions for Ms. Thompson before I leave," Jon chimes in with utter conviction.

Mark's attention darts between us before taking a couple of steps back and straightening his tie. "No problem, Mr. Morgan. Thank you for your inquiry." He then turns to me but doesn't look angry, more bewildered. "I just needed the files for my ten-o clock, Felicity, are they ready?"

I nod, very pleased and relieved for knuckling down on Friday and getting everything ready in advance. "Yes, they're waiting on your desk."

"Excellent. Well, nice to meet you, Mr. Morgan," he finishes before turning and striding away, revealing a sea of inquisitive faces as they all dart back to their screens in unison.

Jon shuts the door hastily before turning and striding over to me, hands flying to either side of my face, ready to kiss me again. I take a step back, shaking my head.

"We can't do this here. This is my work, and we almost got caught; I need this job! Why did you come to my office?" My tone is once again harsher than I intended, especially after the tender moment we just shared.

He closes the space between us again. "I know, and I'm sorry. But I knew if I turned up at your place you might not answer the door to me, and you wouldn't hear me out. I had no way of contacting you since you blocked me. I needed to see you." He raises his hands to my waist but at the last minute changes his mind, redirecting them to his pockets.

He's probably right. I'd have done all I could to wipe him from my life. "I didn't block you. I deactivated my social media accounts." I can feel my face flushing at the confession. "I needed away from reporters and Saturday night, and yes, I needed away from you."

Jon's head tips up, his eyes reaching the ceiling as he nods in understanding. "We need to talk, Felicity, not here, but soon." He pulls out his phone and scrolls through a couple of screens, taking another step toward me. "Come to my place tonight. I'll send a car for you, and I'll make you dinner. I want to talk with you. We've got so much to straighten out."

I can see the pulse thrumming in his neck as he waits for my answer.

"Haven't you got practice tonight?" I reply.

"Nope, night off."

"Meetings?" I have no idea why I'm making this so difficult.

He quirks a brow. "Meetings? No. I haven't got any meetings, Felicity, and even if I had, I would cancel them. Stop searching for obstacles."

I check my watch and shift from one foot to another. I've lost so much time this morning, and I'll have to work late to get everything done I need to today. "I'll need to work late to make up time," I explain. "I won't have time to go home and get changed and then come to yours."

"You drive a hard bargain, Felicity Thompson," he chuckles. "In that case, I'll come pick you up tonight and take you out to dinner. I'll be here at six, out front."

"Dinner? Like out? In public?" I parrot back at him.

"Yes, Angel, dinner, at six."

"Seven."

"Okay, seven."

I nod in agreement, all common sense and caution firmly out the window. It's only dinner.

We walk through the office, and I try not to let my paranoid brain run away with thoughts of what the observant faces are thinking as we pass. It's unusual for prospective clients to simply waltz in and have an appointment with anyone, but I suppose there's nothing normal when it comes to Jon Morgan.

As we approach the elevator back down to the lobby, he turns to me, stepping slightly closer. I can feel Margo's weighted stare on the back of my head and, clearly, so can Jon, who casts a quick glance at her over my shoulder. Returning his eyes to mine, he gently smiles, and I feel his knuckles lightly trace the back of my hand which I'm sure isn't accidental. "Tonight, at seven," he confirms again.

I pull my bottom lip between my teeth, glancing down to my shoes, which really *are not* date-worthy.

Wait. Is this a date?

But I decide not to ask; I'll find out later tonight. I think Margo and Co. have had plentiful entertainment for a Monday morning. "Okay, but nowhere posh." I flick my hands up and down my body then feel a tinge of embarrassment at my apparent assumption that he would take me anywhere fancy.

"Chick-fil-A it is then," he teases.

"Fine by me," I retort. "Drive-through would be preferable."

Jon pushes the button to call the elevator and then turns back to me, edging only slightly closer, reserving a professional distance between us, but the heated look in his eyes says differently. "Felicity, there's only one reason we'd use a drive-through, and it's got nothing to do with your outfit and everything to do with me keeping you all to myself. See you later."

With that, he steps inside, leaning against the back rail as the doors close between us.

CHAPTER TWELVE

FELICITY

I can't take my mind off tonight.

Apprehension and excitement eat away at me as the hours tick by to seven p.m. I'm nervous to go out in public with Jon. I'm a private person, and the thought of having my face plastered across the web and labeled as his latest conquest gnaws away at me.

Not just that, but what about my family? Jack would likely be delighted but Darcy. Seeing her mum being cast across media outlets with a world-famous athlete known for his playboy ways? Shit, this is a bad idea, and I need to squash it, fast.

I need to cancel.

I quickly grab my phone to text Jon and explain but see the time is now six-thirty. *Double shit.* He'll be on his way by now.

So instead, I scroll past his number and land on Kate's. Thankfully, at this time the office is mostly empty, and other than a few cleaners and Mark, who's tucked away in his office, the coast is clear.

Kate answers on the second ring. "Missing me already?" she purrs down the phone.

"So, I have an issue."

"Okay, go on."

"How do I put this? Well, it's like this. I got into work this morning and...um."

"Just say it, babe." Kate gets to the point, but her tone is one of gentle concern.

"Jon turned up at my office this morning, you know after the pictures went public from Saturday night. He wanted to explain, which he did. He then asked me to go out with him for dinner tonight so 'we can talk' as he put it. He's picking me up outside the office at seven, and I'm dressed like an old woman who can't be bothered. I don't even have perfume in my bag. I haven't washed my hair and God only knows what he wants to talk with me about or where he's taking me and—"

"And breathe," Kate interjects before pausing for a few seconds.

I can hear voices in the background on the phone, and I worry that I'm disturbing her evening, but then she continues. "Look, my best advice is to go out with him, let him talk with you and see what he has to say. If you don't, I know you, babe, and you'll be ruminating forever if you don't hear him out. That said, honey, just..."

Kate pauses again, blowing out a breath. "Just be clear on what you want from this evening. I get good vibes from him, and I trust him to take you out but don't get carried away and *don't* let feelings come into it. He has a reputation, and you're fresh out of a marriage wanting to 'enjoy your independence again,'" she quotes my previous sentiment back at me. "If you want to have fun with him then be my guest. Christ, I couldn't blame you for wanting to climb that like a tree!" She releases a girly giggle before her tone snaps back to serious once more. "But for all that is holy, *don't* get emotionally involved with him. Seeing you so upset at lunch yesterday reminded me of how vulnerable you are, and I don't want to have to kick his ass when I'm picking you up off the floor if he breaks your heart."

She's right. *Oh my god,* she's right.

I drop my elbows onto my desk and lean forward. "I'm also worried about being seen out with him. What are people going to say about me? I've got my children to think about and you know how the press is."

"This is different. It's not some random Saturday night hookup, heading back to a hotel where you're all over each other. Plus, the press can predict where he'll be after games. A random Monday night, not so much. This isn't his first rodeo, babe, and he knows you won't want attention. Just go with it."

I exhale a deep calm breath. "Why are you so wise?"

"Not just a pretty face."

I feel the tension in my shoulders begins to ease. "I needed this. I needed you to talk me down from the ledge and knock some sense into me."

"So, what are you going to do about tonight?" Kate asks.

"Exactly as you say," I confirm without hesitation. Sitting up straighter in my chair and with more conviction to my voice. "I'll let him take me out, hear what he's got to say, and if he does suggest more, I'll tell him no. I don't do hookups, Kate, you know I never have, and I don't think I can see sex as casual without catching feelings for someone. So, we remain friends, and I definitely can't kiss him again, because...wow."

"I'm sorry, come again?" Kate blurts down the phone.

"I sort of kissed him when he came to the office. Mark pretty much caught us in the act too."

Kate bursts out laughing, like proper cackles. "Yeah, good luck keeping this one strictly friends, babe. Something tells me there's going to be benefits along the way and, hot damn, I'm jealous."

Recalling the kiss we shared earlier today sends my mind into a dreamy state. I can feel his touch on my cheek, the way he wrapped his rough palm around my nape, his hard length against my body, and how he took my mouth with his. I've never felt so possessed by a man, so wanted. But the hard truth is we aren't on the same wavelength.

"I can't romanticize Jon Morgan." I release a heavy sigh and feel my shoulders sag with the weight of my reality.

"I think that's for the best, honey. I just want you to be happy," Kate replies before adding, "I gotta go, but call me, and let me know how it all went, and you know where I am if you need me tonight. I'll have my phone on me."

I grab my jacket and bag and make my way downstairs to meet Jon. "Love you, babe, mwah!"

We end the call just as I reach the elevator. Hitting the button for the lobby, I inhale a few calming breaths and repeat my mantra not to fall for this guy.

MY MANTRA WENT STRAIGHT out the window the moment I stepped outside the doors.

He's going to be the death of me. Leaning against a gleaming pearly white Dodge Charger in dark gray trousers, a long-sleeved, white shirt, and smart, black dress shoes, Jon Morgan exudes sex. When I say sex, I don't mean the *thank you very much that was a lovely night* kind of sex. Oh no. I mean passionate, all-night-long, *rail you into the mattress until you see stars and then rail you some more* sex. Fucking you in each room of his apartment, taking you on every surface, and worshipping your body until your voice fails you.

As I walk toward him, his corded muscles strain against the white fabric of his shirt and his trousers cling to his incredible thighs, showcasing the delights that no doubt lie beneath. His dark-brown hair is styled back and away from his face tonight, and I can tell he's had the sides freshly clipped. His steely-gray eyes sparkle from the city lights, and his perfectly full lips curl up into a smile, popping his dimples as I near him. He's shaved since this morning too, but I can still see a small amount of stubble cast across his strong jawline.

He is truly a work of art, worthy of taking center stage in any gallery. Without a doubt, he is the most beautiful man I have ever seen, and as he steps forward to take my tote bag from my shoulder and open the passenger door for me, I'm also certain he is the most beautiful man I will ever lay eyes on.

"Good evening, Your Highness," Jon greets me in his deep smooth voice and there's a cocky glint in his eyes.

"Why, thank you." I play along taking the passenger door from him before getting into the car. A very nice car. All black inside with fancy, green interior lighting. It smells of Jon; his spicy cologne wraps around me which I admit does tingly things to my lady parts. I wonder how many other women have sat in this seat and felt the same? He leans across and buckles me in, and that simple act alone sends a need straight to my core. This man does things to my body and heart I'm scared to admit.

Turning to me with one arm draped over the steering wheel he lightly drums his fingertips on the dash, and I can't help but notice his gaze move from my eyes to my mouth. I automatically sweep my tongue across my bottom lip, remembering what happened the last time he looked at me like that. I half expect him to lean in and kiss me again. I know I want him to, even if we shouldn't.

He doesn't though, instead, moving his eyes back up to mine. "How was your day, Angel?"

"Busy. I had so much to get through, made worse by this random man turning up at the office first thing this morning, demanding to talk and take me out tonight." I can't help but tease and yes, flirt. Because I have zero self-control. Nada.

Jon's eyes sparkle. "Oh, is that right? Well, I need the details on this guy for making moves on my girl. Can't say as I blame him for trying though."

My girl. My. Girl.

Oh, Jesus.

"So, where are we off to then? I could go for fried chicken." I'm not joking. I'm absolutely starving, having worked through my lunch break.

"Sorry to disappoint, but no fried chicken tonight; we're hitting up the finest restaurant in town." Jon cranks the engine as it roars to life. It's an absolute beast. I love cars and have a decent knowledge of them. My dad was a fan of racing, having spent many years marshaling at events, and I guess to some extent, his passion has rubbed off on me, especially when I went along with him as a young girl to places like Silverstone, Mallory Park, and Donnington.

In stark contrast to the utter masculinity around me, Miley Cyrus's "Midnight Sky" starts up, and I can't help but burst into fits of giggles. After a few seconds of trying to settle my hysterics, I look over to find Jon side-eyeing me with a full pout spread across his face.

"Oh, I'm sorry, I didn't mean to hurt your feelings, petal."

He shrugs before putting the car in gear. I hadn't noticed it was a manual car and there's something about the way he shifts between gears and presses the pedals that has me fluttering all over again. "That's okay, baby. We can't all have great taste in music."

We both laugh at the same time, and any tension my body was harboring in anticipation of this evening instantly eases. There's clearly far more to this man than the bravado the press portrays—or perhaps what he lets the world see.

Clearing my throat and trying to stay on task for tonight, I gaze out the passenger window, the street looking somewhat familiar. "Where are we going?"

"I told you, the best restaurant in town."

I look down at my old gray skirt which is now sporting a coffee stain from earlier. "I told you; I'm not dressed for anywhere nice."

Jon turns to look at me, eyes ablaze with heat that instantly radiates to my cheeks. "You look fucking stunning."

I scoff at his comment. I'm by no means vain, but even I can see I'm hardly dressed for fine dining. "Oh, come on. I look like I haven't washed my hair and just finished a long day in the office. You, on the other hand, you look like..." I stop, my eyes taking him in, my body heating to boiling point at the sight. "Well, you look lovely."

Jon chuckles quietly. "You think I look lovely do you, Angel? Why, thank you."

I flush, hard, and turn back toward the window to hide my reaction. *Fucking lovely?*

On a Monday evening, the streets are relatively quiet, so we reach our destination quickly. Jon indicates, pulling into an underground garage and the electric doors open automatically.

I'm now more than curious. "So other than it being the finest restaurant in town, where exactly are we?"

He pulls down a ramp into a small car park lined with at least half a dozen beautiful vehicles. Amongst them, I note a black Audi A7 with all-black wheels, a silver Porsche Cayman, a midnight-blue Mercedes G-Wagon, and a BMW M 1000 motorbike. Whoa, we really are somewhere nice, and exclusive, clearly.

Thankfully, there's one space remaining, so Jon swings the car around before shifting into reverse. He throws his arm round the back of my seat and fires a wink at me before backing into the space. "You'll see. You're not good with surprises are you, Angel?"

Well, wherever we are, I'm heading straight to the bathroom to change my underwear.

He kills the engine. "Hang on."

He jogs around to my side, tapping his knuckles lightly on the hood, and then opens my door and reaches across to release my belt; he smells insanely good. Taking my hand, he helps me out of the car and places my tote back on my shoulder. At this point, I'm wondering whether to issue a missing persons ad because every ounce of feminism has abandoned me, and even more worrying—I'm not that mad about it either.

There's at least a foot in height difference between us, and it shows as I glance up at him. "Thank you."

He smiles sweetly then laces his fingers through mine and leads me to a pair of black double doors. Pushing through, we're met with an elevator, and once inside, Jon leans across and presses a button behind my back. His eyes find mine again, and as the elevator begins to climb, he doesn't say anything, just simply studies my face. I've noticed him looking intensely at my eyes a few times, almost like he's enraptured by them. I could say the same about his.

The elevator pings as it comes to a stop, and the doors slowly open to reveal...his apartment. I throw my head back in laughter as he steps out, taking my hand once again.

"Told you, Angel, the best restaurant in town."

"Oh, is it now?" I jest.

"Better believe it," he shoots back.

"What did you do? Hire a private chef or something?" I pull up onto my tiptoes to get a better view of the kitchen over his shoulder.

Jon's hands fly to his chest, clutching at his heart in mock hurt. "Private chef?" he exclaims. "No need for a chef when you possess these cooking skills." He wiggles his fingers in front of him with a cheeky grin on his lips.

Yes, and I can imagine those hands aren't just good for cooking either.

"Well, something certainly smells gorgeous." The aroma making its way down the hallway toward me is delicious.

"Oh, it definitely does," Jon smirks. "Come on, let's go eat." He waves at me over his shoulder as he walks into the kitchen. "I need to check on the beef."

CHAPTER THIRTEEN

JON

I'm so nervous.

My hands tremble as I open the oven door to check on the Beef Wellington I've spent the best part of the afternoon preparing.

When Felicity agreed to meet me tonight, I knew she'd be nervous to go out anywhere in public together, and the last thing I want to do is embarrass her or give her another reason not to see me again. I wasn't sure I'd get her back in my apartment after she practically ran out of my home gym the last time she was here, and tonight, I want to get to know her. I want to try to make her feel at ease around me. But I can't deny I'm nervous as hell. I know she doesn't see this as a date. I know enough about Felicity to work out she doesn't date someone unless she sees a possible future with him, and if I'm brutal in my assessment, I'm not sure she sees beyond the next hour in my company.

I don't let that deter me though, because there's something about this woman that keeps me on my toes. She couldn't give a fuck who I am or how fat my bank balance is. Status and cash don't impress her; she runs deeper than that. Trouble is, I don't think she thinks that of me. I have a reputation as a good time, a one-night-only guy ready to rock your world and then send you on your way, and as I stand in my kitchen, watching her look at framed photos of my mom, Dad, Adam, and friends, I know my playboy days are actively working against me right now, and that's everything I've always feared.

"How old were you in this?" Felicity asks as she holds up a photo of Adam and me at Disney World. I'm in a Mickey Mouse hat complete with ears, and Adam's in a flowery Floridian shirt, both of us beaming at the camera on Main Street with the castle set behind us.

I was in my sophomore year of high school. "About fifteen. So, twenty years ago, jeez that's a long time." I chuckle. "We went on a family vacation and stayed on International Drive. Adam loved it."

"Is Adam your brother?" Felicity asks, her eyes visibly warm.

I stand at the counter and begin chopping up potatoes. "He is; he's three years younger than me."

"Oh wow, he's super handsome. His smile is so bright." The apples of her cheeks turn a cute rosy pink. She's so sweet and genuinely kind.

"Is that so? You netted the wrong brother then." I'm joking around, but I can't hide the slight twinge in my chest at the thought of her with someone, anyone else.

"Maybe. But Adam's brother isn't too bad, I suppose. Do you have any other siblings?"

"No, it's just me and Adam. Mom and Dad decided the pair of us were enough to keep their hands full for a lifetime." I smile at her as she replaces the picture and checks out one of the Scorpions prints from last season when we lifted the Stanley Cup for a second time. I don't keep many hockey photos on display, especially with me in them, just a few in the hallway, but the look on Zach's face in that shot is pure joy. "What about you?"

"Hmmm?" She seems engrossed in the photos but then shakes her head slowly, still staring at the frame. "Oh, no. It's just me." I don't miss the slightly flat tone to her response, almost like there's a story behind it, but I decide not to push.

"Can I get you a drink? Wine or a cocktail?" Did I go out and buy ingredients to make a Cosmo and then spend the afternoon studying how to make them? You best believe it.

"Oh, you mix cocktails, too? Is there any end to your talents?"

Heading toward the fridge I pull out the mixer and then fetch a martini glass from the cupboard above. Yes, I bought glasses too. I've had a busy day. I grab the vodka and triple sec and set everything on the side along with a lime for the glass. "I'd reserve judgment on my skills until you've tasted it."

Felicity approaches the counter and sits on one of the high stools, which for her height and in a pencil skirt is impressive. From where I'm standing, I have a perfect shot of her cleavage, the top two buttons of her white blouse undone, and my dick twitches at the sight. Jesus, she's something else. I swear I can see the edge of her white lacy bra, sitting against her flawless creamy skin. If she's older than me, she sure as hell doesn't look it. Her body and face are youthful, but her sunny personality also radiates from her. She's totally out of my league in every way.

She scrunches her nose in confusion as I start filling the single martini glass from the shaker. "Aren't you having one?"

"No, I don't drink much during the season, just the odd beer."

"So, you don't drink cocktails?" she presses.

"No, it's not really my thing, Angel."

More confusion fills her face along with another gorgeous flush right down her sweet neckline. "So where did all this come from?" She casts her hand across the counter pointing at the glass, fresh cocktail ingredients, and shaker.

I casually lift a shoulder. "I got everything earlier while I was shopping for dinner."

"W-what?" Her brows knit together slightly. "You bought all

this in, for me?" She shakes her head. "Jon, that's...that's so sweet. Thank you."

I hand her the glass, complete with a slice of lime attached to the rim, and smile. "I wanted you to have something you like."

She takes a sip and moans in pleasure. *Fuuuuck,* that sound does things to me. Not now, Jon, not now.

"I've never had anyone think of me or remember the little details like that."

I balk at her comment, finding that very hard to believe. How any man could be in the same room as Felicity for longer than five minutes and not want to know everything about her is beyond comprehension. She's the type of woman who once you meet, she hijacks your every waking thought. "I find it hard to believe that you're not etched into the memory of everyone you meet since you've invaded every part of mine."

FELICITY

"Okay, that was gorgeous. You might just be the finest restaurant around," I say, placing my knife and fork back down on my plate. *And it was* gorgeous. It's clear this man can cook, that's for sure. I wonder how many other women have been bowled over by not only his legendary bedroom skills but also his abilities in the kitchen.

"Probably not one of my best. The beef could've done with more seasoning, but I'll take the compliment, thank you," Jon replies, leaning back in his chair across the counter from me, his corded forearms folded and flexing, providing a very welcome view.

"If that's average for you then your best must rival Gordon Ramsey because that was perfect to me," I reply, draining the last of my Cosmo.

"Tell me something I don't know about you?" Jon asks a couple of beats later.

"Oooh, I like this game. Okay, well I've always wanted to go to Norway."

Jon shuffles forward on his stool, folding his hands together and resting his chin on them. "Anyone ever told you you're random?"

"A few. It was something my dad and I always wanted to do, to see the northern lights. The aurora is a bucket list item for me." I clear my throat from emotion, wanting to move on. "What about you, tell me something no one else knows."

Considering my question, Jon swipes a hand over his mouth. "I've never been to McDonalds."

"No, freakin' way," I laugh, I can't believe he's never tried the legendary Big Mac.

"It's true; in fact, I can probably count on one hand the number of fast-food deliveries I've had."

"Because you're a fighting-fit athlete?" I reply, flexing my biceps.

Jon smirks at me, his shoulders vibrating with laughter. "Something like that, Angel." He grips his half-empty water glass. "I guess my life has always revolved around hockey. It's always been pretty one-dimensional..." his eyes meet mine, "until now."

He rises to his feet and rounds the counter, swiveling my stool to face him. He steps closer, and I look up at him where he towers over me. "You're so fucking beautiful, Felicity. I wanted to see you again tonight because I can't bear the thought of you thinking for one single fucking second that I have eyes for anyone else. You're all I see."

He nudges my chin up with his index finger and slowly lowers his lips to mine. Hovering just over me, my core tightens and pulses with need. "Can I kiss you again?"

I know I shouldn't. I had a plan tonight, to remain platonic.

But the need to kiss him overwhelms me, leaving me powerless. "Okay."

He closes the space and smiles against me. Jon groans at the contact, and as his tongue swipes across my lips and explores my mouth, I know this won't be the last time I kiss him.

"HOW'S JACK doing in college? He make it on the team?" Jon's still standing over me, his left hand drawing pattens on my thigh.

"Yeah, he's made a couple of appearances, but the forward positions are hard fought over. He called me last night and was a bit at sea. A lot of the guys have more game experience, and I think he's struggling to make his mark on the team and get involved in the social aspect. That's unusual for him—he normally makes friends easily."

Totally engrossed in what I'm saying, Jon nods his head in thought. "How long has he been playing?"

I tap my chin, thinking over the timeline. "Uh, well I guess he started playing at eight." I let out a sigh. "Trouble is, there aren't nearly as many opportunities in the UK compared with the US and Canada, so he's been playing catch up." I pause, not sure how much to reveal about my past life, but there's something about Jon that makes me trust him like I can talk freely around him. "When my ex-husband, Elliott, got offered a job out in Seattle on an eighteen-month contract, Jack jumped at the chance to move out here. I kind of knew he'd want to stay and apply for college in America, but he's not had an easy start to his freshman year." I wave a hand in front of me. "And it's not like I have any clue how to help him. I can't even lace up my skates, let alone advise him."

Jon's tone is very matter-of-fact. "Has he got what it takes? Most guys step onto the ice as soon as they can walk, so eight is late to begin playing." He continues drawing circles on my thigh, his touch is soothing.

I shrug a shoulder. "He's still made it into a strong college team. I know he's fast on the ice and that's his main threat, but his coach says his technical skills are behind the others. I worry he's putting too much pressure on himself and should be enjoying his college days, but instead, he's running himself into the ground." I feel my voice shake. "Not to mention his parents have just divorced and his dad and sister are now halfway across the world."

Wow, the evening has gone from light-hearted to me basically unloading my parental neurosis and worries over my son onto this man. Yet, I can't stop talking; it pours out of me like a river breaking its banks. "So yeah, other than that, I'd say he's doing okay."

I lift my gaze to find Jon's unreadable stare, and if I didn't know better, I swear I see a glossy glint in his eyes. Still, he doesn't say anything, doesn't try to fill the void with meaningless chatter. Instead, he slowly takes my hand in his, lifting it to his lips as he lightly brushes a kiss over my knuckles. A jolt of electricity shoots straight down my spine to my toes. This man's touch is dangerous, enticing me to take leave of my senses. Before, I could counter my feelings with the belief that he was a shallow playboy, a star on the ice, and a good time between the sheets. But with every hour spent in his presence, layers are peeling away, revealing a man who both excites and terrifies my delicate and battered heart.

JON

Felicity Thompson is well and truly under my skin, her presence as permanent as a tattoo.

As she bares her concerns over her son, I hear the emotion in her voice, and it does something to my chest. I want to soothe her anxiety, ease her upset, and take it all away. I open my mouth to comfort her, but words are cheap. I need to *show* her I care. I want to know more about her, about her past and her family, but I don't want to push her too far. It's clear my girl doesn't trust easily, and the reasons behind why she doesn't send an uncomfortable bristling sensation through me. Who hurt her? And where are they now? "When did Elliott head back to the UK with Darcy?" I ask cautiously.

"Just before the hockey season started. Unlike Jack, she couldn't wait to get back home. She missed her boyfriend, Liam. But I miss her terribly. It's hard, you know. Building a new life, trying to plant roots without those you love near you."

I want to tell her that she can plant roots with me, that she doesn't need to feel lonely, but I hold back. When it comes to us, she's on a completely different trajectory. I'm way out in front, ready to jump in with two feet, and if she gave me the green light, I'd gather her up in my arms, march her toward my bedroom, and lay her down on my bed, not resurfacing for days. But she's eons behind, and I know I need to gain her trust before I can even consider her heart. But I can't help wondering why she's so guarded when it comes to men. Is this exclusive to me and my reputation as a womanizer or due to another man hurting her? My fists ball at the thought of the latter.

"Why did you and Elliott split?" The words are out of my mouth before I can stop them.

She lets out a low chuckle. "How long have you got?"

For you? A lifetime.

I don't say anything, just continue to draw patterns on her thighs as I've been doing the last half hour, like a lovesick puppy.

"We met when we were young but grew apart. I had Jack at twenty-one, and I guess getting married was the obvious choice." Her brows furrow, pain etched across her face. "I suppose he loved me in his own way."

Suppose he loved her. Yeah, that's not sitting well with me. I can't help my growing frustration; she isn't the type of woman you take for granted and something tells me this asshole, Elliott, did exactly that.

"It just didn't work out, and I guess I lost myself along the way." Her shoulders straighten along the back of the stool as she lifts her chin. "But I want to find myself again. My children are growing up and finding their own way, so now I want something for myself. I want to work on my career, make friends, and spread my wings. Even at thirty-nine, it can't be too late."

With so much packed into her words, my head spins, trying to process the meaning. I hear she wants to find independence, but how would a new man fit into her future? How would I fit into her future?

"You're thirty-nine?" It's hardly an old age; she's still young. But I had her pinned at only one or two years older than me.

She sighs. "Yep, I turn forty next July."

I take a seat on the stool next to her and rest my chin on my palm, fixing her with a playful grin. "So does this make you my sugar mommy?"

She balks. "Sugar mommy? No, Jon, it makes you cheeky."

"Cheeky, hmmm. I can work with that." I wiggle my eyebrows.

"Don't push it, Morgan. You've done so well feeding me amazing food and thoughtful drinks. Our friendship has gotten off to a strong start."

After today and the kisses we shared, I'd say we're way past friends.

CHAPTER FOURTEEN

JON

I'm in a bad mood, and I have been for days.

I could lie to myself and pretend our back-to-back home losses are to blame, but this isn't my first rodeo. Form on the ice comes and goes, and despite Coach ringing us out in practice earlier, my mood reflects an issue closer to home.

It's clear Felicity is determined to position me firmly in the friend zone. She said it herself on Monday night—she wants to "spread her wings." I spent all six periods over the last two home games unable to keep my eyes from her and Jack. She threw me the occasional smile, but after I dropped her back at her place, I know she's pulling away. The kisses we shared in her office and then at my place were indescribable. I've kissed many women in my lifetime, but none have ever made me feel the way I do with her. It feels so easy and natural with Felicity, yet she seems determined to deny what I know she feels, too, and it's frustrating the shit out of me.

"Morgan, my office, now." Coach Burrows's harsh tone ricochets across the locker room, interrupting my thoughts. I stand from the bench and throw on some sweats and a hoodie, ready to face his wrath.

"What did you do now, Jon?" Jensen drawls in a teasing tone, but I'm in no mood for joking around.

"Just worry about your own game," I bite, grabbing my bag and storming out of the locker room toward Coach's office.

I stop outside his door when my watch buzzes violently. I glance quickly at the screen telling me my resting heart rate is one-twenty beats per minute. I'm not surprised; it feels like it's about to crash through my chest and my body temperature is ablaze.

Dismissing the notification, I take a few centering breaths just as I've practiced with Ben over the years and try to recall my go-to calming visual: Me lying on a beach in Mexico, the sound of the ocean waves lapping at my feet. But lately, every time I close my eyes, all I can see is Felicity, smiling at me in my kitchen, and with each second I recall her perfect smile, my heart rate slows. The palpitations noticeably subside, and the anxiety attack I know was brewing eases far more quickly than I've ever known it to in the past.

How can the woman who sees me as no more than an unreliable playboy be the source of my turmoil yet my antidote all at the same time? She wields the kind of power over me that has the capacity to make or break me at the snap of her fingers, and the truly scary part is, I don't think she has any idea.

"Sit down, Jon." Coach points to the black leather chairs opposite his desk. I drop my bag and take a seat, resting my leg over the opposite knee. I might as well get comfortable because when Coach uses first names, you know shit's got serious.

"How can I help you, Coach?" I try to keep my tone relaxed as I grind my molars.

"I'll get straight to the point. You and I have worked together for long enough to know your mood stinks right now. Your performance has been off, and that's putting it fucking mildly. And your teammates? Well, they see it, and it's bringing the entire locker room down."

I think he's finished when he takes another deep breath, leaning back in his chair, his eyes glued to mine.

But then he goes on.

"However, it's not necessarily your volatile form on the ice that worries me, it's your mindset. I'm seeing a pattern emerge, and I don't like how it looks. When was the last time you went out with the team post-game?"

He raises a hand to shut me down before I can even begin to answer. "And I don't mean turning up for an hour and then clearing off back home or to your hotel. I mean as the Jon of old, out for the duration, bringing the rookies into the team and making them feel welcome. Sure, you still sink the puck and have the odd strong game every now and then, but honestly? You've lost your way. So, tell me, what the fuck is going on."

My stomach twists at the truth in his words. He's right, and being honest, I thought I'd done a better job at hiding it. How the fuck am I supposed to tell the man who's invested so much into my career, made me captain, and stood by me when I mentally broke, that I'm struggling with my love for the game? That despite this sport making me the highest-paid player in its history, showing me the world, and opening every door to my dreams, that I've started to resent it. I lean forward, resting my elbows on my knees, and drop my head between my shoulders, shaking it slowly as the tremors start in my hands.

I know I'm not captain material any longer; in fact, I'm probably the last choice for the coach and GM right now, but they've stuck with me purely out of loyalty. I know that based on my current state of mind, they should hand the C to someone else. They should also bench my ass and give someone more deserving a chance. But the cold truth is if they do that mid-way through a season, my career is toast, and after years of pouring my soul into this game, I'll finish up exactly as my nightmares predicted: a washed-up, lonely-as-fuck, former playboy with nothing but a garage full of cars and a stack of cash to show for it. At thirty-four, I should be heading back to my girl and curling up on the couch with her, watching movies and talking about our days.

I finally find the energy to speak but keep my eyes on the ground; no way am I letting him see the wetness that's blurring my vision. I clench my jaw and pinch the inside of my thigh, hard, trying to get a hold of my emotions. "I don't know what to say, Mike." I blow out a shaky breath. I don't think I've ever used his first name before, but this conversation is far more personal than just hockey. "I can't argue with anything you've said. You're dead on with your assessment of my game and head space right now." Resigned to my fate and depleted of fight, I continue. "So, I guess all I can tell you is I'll respect whatever decisions you and the GM make. I'm committed to my contract and giving this team the best I have, and that won't change."

There's a stretch of silence between us.

"Look at me, Jon." Coach's tone is softer as he addresses me as Jon the person rather than the player. "Look at me."

"I can't," I say. "Just let me keep this to myself, please." I don't want him to see me like this. "I'll talk with you again when I can."

"Jon, you are a true professional, and everything you have done for this sport is unmatched. I don't know how much longer your career is set to last, but no one knows your game like I do, and believe me when I tell you that when you do decide to hang up your skates for the final time, your name will be spoken along with the likes of Gretzky. But you need to take time to care for your body and mind. I've watched you fight mental health battles before, and I'll stand by you again, but I really hope it doesn't come to that."

A few beats pass, and I finally have the courage to look up at him, my eyes slightly drier and my emotions back under some sort of control.

"I don't want to see you at practice tomorrow. Take the day, go see Ben, talk with your family, do whatever you need to get your head on straight for Saturday because I need you against Dallas, and we need to get our home record back on track."

I nod and don't even fight him on the practice. Other than through injury, I can count on one hand the number of practices I've missed, but even my hazy, spinning-out brain can see that I need this reprieve. "You got it, Coach. I'll see you at early morning skate on Saturday," I reply.

He nods and stands from his chair, shrugging on his jacket. As I grab my bag and turn to leave, he catches me once more. "And Morgan?"

"Yes, Coach?"

"I'm not going to take this conversation to the GM. But know that he's noticed your shift in mentality, and I don't just mean on the ice. You and I both know he's not afraid of pulling the trigger, so I'm giving you this time and Saturday to show me that I was right to keep this conversation in this room. But I can't hold him off indefinitely. If he thinks the captaincy and starting center belong elsewhere, then he'll do just that."

His words hit me like a thousand knives, but I steel my resolve, tip my chin up, and say, "Understood, Coach. I appreciate your loyalty."

As I step out into the hallway and head straight to the parking lot, I don't once look up at staff, players, or anyone else who crosses my path. I just need out of here as quickly as possible. It's not lost on me, and I know it definitely won't be on Coach, that I didn't assure him I wouldn't let him down because, frankly, I never make promises I can't keep.

Yanking my phone from my pocket I unlock the screen and scroll right to the bottom of my contacts. There's only one person I can think to call right now.

CHAPTER FIFTEEN

JON

"Good evening, Mr. Morgan." Sergio, head of security, opens the door to the apartment block.

"Hi, Sergio," I reply. Normally, I spend a couple of minutes talking with him, but today I need to get upstairs and away from people.

Heading across to the elevator, I punch in the code I've known by memory for years and ride the eleven floors to the penthouse.

"In here," I hear Zach's voice call through the dark as I walk through his hallway, kicking my sneakers off. I find Zach sprawled across his couch with the only light coming from the enormous TV mounted on the wall.

"What game are you watching?" I ask, dumping myself down on the opposite couch.

"Dallas footage. Want a beer?" He tips his bottle toward me. "There's some in the fridge if you want."

I'm surprised. Zach rarely drinks, especially during the season, but what the hell, after today, why not? "You read my mind." I stride across the open-plan living space and grab a beer from the fridge before heading back.

We spend at least an hour saying very little, simply studying game tape and exchanging the occasional thought or opinion ahead of Saturday. When I called Zach earlier, I asked him if he was home and if he had company, aka Amie. He knew I needed to talk but didn't push it any further, just told me his door is always open. In many ways, I see him as a brother. He's always been there for me, offering advice, even when it's not something I want to hear. Over the last six seasons, we've formed an unbreakable bond, and I trust him with my life.

"Coach told me to stay away from practice tomorrow and to take a rest day." I broach the subject first, draining the final dregs of my beer.

"How do you feel about that?" Zach sits up from his lying position on the couch, placing his empty bottle on the table in front of him.

"Honestly? Relieved. Kinda feels bad to say, but I don't want to be around people right now."

Zach bobs his head; he's already worked that one out based on my mood these past few days. "What's going on, Jon?"

I let out a low chuckle, gripping the back of my neck. "My game's going to shit, and I can't seem to get a handle on it."

"Yeah, I can see that, but why?" he pushes.

"Nothing's working out, and I'm frustrated."

"By nothing, you mean a certain girl?"

He called me out, no holding back, "Ugh, yes, no, I mean maybe."

"She still giving you the cold shoulder after the away game in Colorado?"

I shake my head. "No, worse. I turned up at her office, kissed her, then invited her back to my place for dinner. All was going great until she basically friend-zoned me and told me she wanted to 'spread her wings' and be independent since her bastard ex-husband made her feel undesirable and trapped in a loveless marriage." I huff out a breath, running a frustrated hand through my hair. "So yeah, I know she feels something for me, and I know there's a part of her that wants me, but her worry over relationships and losing her newfound independence means she won't trust or date. It's obvious and there's fuck all I can do about it."

Zach stands from the couch and moves toward the kitchen, returning thirty seconds later with another beer for each of us. Flicking the cap off, he hands me the bottle and I take another swig.

"This might seem obvious, but have you told her how you feel? Because from what I'm hearing and seeing, bro, you are fully gone for this girl, and it's fucking with your head."

"Yeah, I think I made it pretty clear when I made out with her in the middle of her office and then invited her back for dinner and kissed her again," I bite out.

"All good and well, but how does she know *what you want?* Look at it from her point of view. This world-famous hockey player starts pursuing her, texting, and inviting her to his place for dinner. But he's got a reputation as a playboy with a different woman in his bed every night." He takes another swig of his beer, tipping the bottle toward me. "I know what I'd be thinking. I haven't jumped into bed with him at the first opportunity, and now he sees me as a challenge. Think about it, Jon, if you were a chick, would you want to be another notch on your bedpost?"

I swipe my hand across my face, giving it some serious thought. "Yeah, it's a possibility I guess, and no, I wouldn't want to sleep with me either. Not unless I knew there was more to it than just meaningless sex."

"Exactly." Zach sits back on the couch. "I've never met the girl, but Jensen tells me she's the type of woman you marry, not someone you have a one-night stand with. So why would she open the door to you if she thinks you only want one thing? And frankly, I know you have only great intentions with her; I can see the seismic shift in you. But based on your past, why would she see that?"

Christ, that stings. Yeah, I knew all this deep down but hearing it validated out loud, it's hard to take. I shrug. "Yeah, but that still doesn't help with her need to be independent."

Zach nods his head in understanding. "Look, man, I'm no expert, but has it ever occurred to you that her only experience in relationships has been controlling and unhealthy? That's what she's used to. She hasn't seen anything different, so she doesn't know what it's like to be with a man who shares her interests and wants to help her achieve her dreams and goals."

He waves a hand in front of him. "So really, it's simple: *show* her what she could have and that you want her for more than a cheap fuck. Women like her don't fall easily."

"And what if she still doesn't want me after all that? I genuinely don't think I could handle the rejection."

"Well then, she doesn't want you, but what are your alternatives? Walk away and don't try? I don't think I've ever known you to back off from something you want. Spell it out to her, take the risk. That's the best advice I have for you, buddy." Zach kicks back and lies down on the couch again.

"I thought I had," I reply, peeling the label off my bottle.

He low chuckles. "Nothing worthwhile ever comes easy, man."

I don't say anything, instead letting his advice sink in. He's right; I know he is. Still, it doesn't make putting myself out there for her any easier. I've never dated a woman in my adult life, let alone gone after someone for a full-blown relationship, and to be brutally honest, anything less than that with Felicity won't be enough for me. All my instincts tell me she's everything I want, everything I need.

Placing my half-finished beer back on the table, I decide to enter potentially dangerous waters. "So how are things with Amie?"

Zach scoffs, tipping his head up to the ceiling, "So Jensen told you then?"

I've no idea what he's talking about. "No, told me what?"

He looks genuinely surprised I don't know but answers me anyway. "Rumor has it she's been seen out in New York with Alex Schneider."

My jaw hangs open. *What the actual fuck.* "Fucking Schneider. Where did you hear this?"

He drains the last of his beer, and I can tell he's starting to feel its effects. "Well, I say rumor. Apparently, he posted a photo of her and him getting cozy in some club downtown last night. The photo was up for all of five minutes before it was taken down, but the damage was done, screenshots taken, and I've seen the evidence. She was blowing my phone up all night, denying there's anything going on before I switched the fucking thing off, so you're lucky you got hold of me. I was ready to throw it out the window."

I shake my head. I mean, I've always had bad vibes from Amie but cheating? On a guy like Zach, with a scumbag like Schneider? That's lower than I thought she'd ever go. "Shit, man, I'm sorry. You're sure she's been playing away?"

Nodding, he replies "She sat on his knee, arms wrapped around his neck, so yeah, it seemed pretty damning." Zach continues to stare absent-mindedly at the TV, the game footage having stopped several minutes ago.

I feel like the shittiest friend. Here I am coming to unload my issues onto him when the guy's girl has just been caught cheating on him with the worst possible person. It's clear Schneider is using Amie to get to Zach off the ice. He's that sort of person.

"I'm sorry I haven't been there for you, man; I've had my head so far up my ass."

"It's okay, not like you could do anything or change the fact that she's a cheating bitch."

"You really cared about her, huh?" I can see how much this is tearing him up. Now the beers, drawn blinds, and pitch-black apartment make sense.

"Yeah, I thought she was the one, but like I say, I'm no expert in relationships." He blows out a humorless laugh. "Just goes to show what I know."

"Never blame yourself for trusting the person you love. She's the one at fault here. Other than that prick."

Zach's jaw pops. "Yeah, and you've probably done me a favor tonight. I was googling flights to JFK when you called. Ready to track him down and beat the living shit out of him for touching my girl but..." he pauses, "that's probably what he wants."

"Yeah, you got that right, and she's not worth it. Hurts like hell now, but in a few weeks, you'll wonder why you ever bothered with her."

My best friend stands, swiping his bottle from the table. "Yeah, and on Saturday night when we crush Dallas, I'm heading out to celebrate with a puck bunny or two."

I want to tell him that searching for affection in empty hookups isn't the answer, but who am I to talk?

"Anyway, fuck it, whatever. You down for some Warzone?" Zach thrusts a PS5 controller in my hand.

"Yeah sure, but I'm not taking it easy on you." I clap a hand on his shoulder and come to sit next to him.

"Likewise. Just stop pussy footing around Felicity, yeah? It doesn't take a genius to work out that women like her don't stay unclamied for long, and if you're as serious about her as I think you are, then you need to lock it down."

I smile, recalling how her skin pebbled under my touch. "She's all I want."

CHAPTER SIXTEEN

FELICITY

KATE

I'm wearing my favorite jersey for tonight's game ;-)

ME

Oh yeah, whose day are you making?

That's for me to know and him to find out.

Okay. You can't say things like that and then not spill. Tea, please.

Hmm...JJ

Huh? JJ?... As in the goalie, Jensen Jones?

Maybe.

Oh, so you do have the hots for him!

Girl, I have eyes, who doesn't?

He is pretty, no doubt. I need to know more.

And I have to go. See you tonight xoxo

See you later but just know—this conversation isn't over xoxo

She's such a tease but I can't say I'm surprised. The eyes she gave him that night at the cocktail bar when Jensen and Jon approached our table gave it away. He's definitely her type, but from what I hear, he's also a player, almost as prolific as Jon. But he'll be no match for Kate. She'll chew him up and spit him out. I gotta hand it to her, she knows what she wants and how to get it, and something tells me Jensen is next on the menu.

It's a little after ten on Saturday morning, and I've barely moved from my sofa despite the caffeine overload from my fourth coffee. I feel overwhelmed by thoughts of Jon and the time I spent at his on Monday night. The way he showed a sensitive side, especially toward Jack, was totally unexpected, and I wasn't prepared for it.

So, what did I do? I ran back to my apartment before he could show me any more of himself. For the last five days, my brain and heart have been at war with each other. My brain repeating Kate's warning to not catch feelings, and my heart telling me to trust him and do just that. And argh, it's exhausting.

I'm contemplating paying a visit to the supermarket as I have nothing in for breakfast when there's a knock on my door. It's probably another parcel for my neighbor, Audrey. Since she discovered Amazon, her online orders have been relentless. I wouldn't mind taking the odd one in, but she spends half her time at her boyfriend's, so I've inadvertently become her personal postal service. But it's not like I have anything better to do.

Making sure I'm at least half decent, I swing my door open, ready to sign for another parcel. But it's not a delivery for Audrey.

Instead, it's Jon Morgan, propped against my door frame, hands tucked in the pockets of his gray sweats. White Nike trainers complete with a Scorpions hoodie. The gods are clearly conspiring against me because there's catnip, and then there are black backward caps.

Jon's eyes rake over me from head to toe, a small smile pulling at his lips when he clocks my fluffy bunny slippers. "Nice outfit," he teases, pushing off the door frame.

"Thanks, I made a special effort this morning." I hold the door open, moving aside to invite him in.

Stepping through the door, Jon stops beside me, sliding a gentle hand across my hip before stepping past, and the way my body responds to his is undeniable. "It's definitely up there for me."

Closing the door behind me, I quickly turn and watch him stride down my hallway, his athletic ass hugged perfectly by his sweats.

"I smell coffee, baby." Jon chimes from the kitchen while I hurriedly check my hair in the mirror above the console table, casually trying to ignore the *baby* reference. I look like I just got up and then decided to pull myself backward through a few hedgerows before opening the door. Oh, and there's a smear of last night's mascara under my left eye. Excellent. I've no idea why he's here, but he looks incredible and smells good enough to eat, sending tingles throughout my body.

Stepping into the kitchen, I find him sitting at my counter, both elbows propped up typing something on his phone.

"How can I help you, Mr. Morgan?" I ask, heading to the refrigerator with no particular purpose but to busy my wandering eyes and distract my racing brain. *Why is he here?* "Can I get you anything?"

Jon sets his phone down and looks up, fixing me with his trademark steely gaze. "I'm here to take you for breakfast."

"Oh, I uh, I'm not dressed," is all I can manage, glancing down at my bare legs and sleep shorts.

"Yeah, I can see that." Jon swipes a hand over his mouth. "I can wait. I had an early morning skate and thought I'd stop by to see what my girl was up to."

My girl. There it is again. I can't work out if my body's trembling from caffeine overload or his presence, but either way, I don't want him to leave.

"Give me fifteen."

JON

I fight to tear my eyes away from Felicity's ass as it sways down the hallway toward her bedroom.

I need to play this cool, but my dick clearly didn't get the memo as it twitches in my pants. I can't say I blame him; I wasn't lying when I said this outfit was up there for me. She's spectacular in tiny pink sleep shorts and a white short-sleeved T-shirt. Her chocolate hair is thrown up in a messy bun and strands delicately frame her petite heart-shaped face. She's an absolute dream, even in her crazy bunny slippers. I can't help but imagine her wearing something similar as she climbs into bed beside me each night.

"This is a little upmarket for an impromptu breakfast, don't you think?" Felicity turns to me, tucking a wave behind her ear, a tinge of uncertainty in her voice which I can't help but find endearing.

"I need a breakfast fit for a king after this morning's session and ahead of tonight's game. It's a must-win." Coach's words from Thursday replay in my mind, and for me, tonight feels like a Stanley Cup final.

"I can't imagine *the* Jon Morgan is nervous about any game."

She lightly prods me in the ribs with her elbow, flashing me a warm smile. *Damn, she's cute.*

"Yeah? You'd be surprised. Anxiety's my middle name." I don't know why I say it. We weren't even talking about anxiety; she was referring to pre-game nerves. But the word tumbles from my lips so easily. For a minute I think about taking it back, but the seriousness of my tone gave me away.

Felicity stops in her tracks, twirling a few strands on the fringe of her trademark emerald scarf around her pointer finger. "Want to talk about it?" she asks, a tender tone laced through her voice. I love that she doesn't assume I want to dive headfirst into my issues with her and doesn't start probing for information. She just leaves the door ajar in case I want to step through.

We're standing right by the Seattle waterfront, the chilling winter freeze slicing through the air as it blows her silky waves around her flawless fair complexion, her rosy lips shine with a gloss she applied before she left her apartment.

I tip my head down toward her, bringing my height closer to her level, our foreheads only a couple of inches apart. "Not much to tell," I say in a whispering voice. I close my eyes, inhaling her addictive coconut scent, made even more intense by the swirling wind, and it's at this moment I want to kiss her again. But I'm still unsure of her boundaries. Zach's words from Thursday night ring in my ears: *"Lock that down."* And I want to, so badly, but when it comes to whatever this is with Felicity, I'm navigating it without a map or GPS. Every time I think I've found my way with her, I come up against a roadblock and the last thing I can afford is for the wheels to come off completely. I see her tongue dart out wetting her bottom lip, and I know she feels it too, that she wants this, or at least to feel my mouth on hers again.

Despite every cell in my body screaming to kiss this woman in front of me and make her mine, I lift my head and glance at my watch. The reservation I made when I arrived at her apartment was set for five minutes ago, and given I emailed the owner asking to seat us in a private area so last minute, I feel like a dick for not being on time. "We need to head inside," I thumb over my shoulder, still lost in her emerald eyes as she searches mine for answers to my earlier admission. The way she's looking at me, Jon Morgan, not the NHL star but the *person,* the man beneath the pads and bravado, simultaneously eases and spikes my anxiety all at once. Having her here with me and knowing she cares soothes my worries, but not knowing if that look is from a friend or a woman who wants more but is too scared to let it show, leaves my heart dangling over a precipice. But I'm too far gone to pull back now. Regardless of whether or not she'll catch me at the bottom, the truth is I'm falling, or maybe even fallen for her, but I'm going over the edge no matter what.

I turn to walk toward the restaurant, and as I do, she catches my hand. Her tiny warm fingers wrap around mine as they dwarf her soft touch. "Wait." Her voice comes out shaky, and her breathing is fast-paced and shallow as she pulls me back around to face her. Her hand darts up toward my face as she gently pulls on my cap, bringing my head down closer to hers.

At first, I wonder what she's doing, but I'm not kept guessing for long as she rises on her tiptoes to close the final space between us, gently tracing her sweet plush lips against mine. Her breath is minty and when she lets out a tiny, sweet sigh, any self-control I was nursing a moment earlier rapidly disintegrates as I gather her in my arms, pulling her closer to my body.

I desperately want to feel her pressed against me once more, but I'm also aware of the biting chill and I don't want her to get cold. Releasing one hand from her waist, I bring my finger up and under her chin, tipping her head slightly to deepen the kiss. This kiss has so far been tender and a little unsure, both of us dancing around, enjoying each other's touch. But now I want to taste her again. Her tongue peaks out to gently caress mine in perfect harmony, and I smile against her lips, our foreheads resting against each other.

"Christ, what are you doing to me, Angel?"

I ask the question, but I don't need to hear the answer. It's becoming clearer and clearer. Friends don't kiss like this; friends don't feel all I know she's feeling right now. And as I break our connection and take her hand in mine, walking her toward the restaurant, I can't help but think she might break my fall after all.

CHAPTER SEVENTEEN

FELICITY

"Here we go!" Kate screams in my ear, practically deafening me. "Oh my god these seats are awesome! You lucky bitch, getting to enjoy this view every home game."

I hand her the loaded nachos she ordered and wave at a couple of people sitting close by. Over the weeks, I've started talking to the other regular fans, and it's hard to miss that more people have started to take an interest in the growing dynamic between Jon and me. I won't lie—it sort of makes me a bit uncomfortable, but I think people are largely being respectful.

"Yeah, well this *lucky bitch* is considerably less well-off thanks to these seats," I retort. I've saved for years for Jack and Darcy's eighteenth birthday presents and thankfully had some money left over from the inheritance I received from my parents. The season tickets are a dream for Jack, and I'm so pleased my mum and dad's legacy could go some way to making it a reality for him.

I'm also pleased I can bring Kate; she occasionally attends games but largely watches on TV. Jack's game clashes with this one, so he can't make it, and when I can, I plan to go to watch his games more now that he's breaking into the team and getting ice time. He needs his family and support in the stands, and over the past couple of weeks, he tells me his form has improved and his coach is pleased with the advancements he's making to his technical game. I'm proud of him but still worried he's going to burn out.

My jacket starts vibrating and I pull out my phone, and ugh, Elliott's name flashes across the screen as I hit reject. This is the third call I've had from him today followed by a couple of texts asking me to call. I replied asking if Darcy was okay to which he'd said yes, but he needed to discuss something with me. I've learned over the years that when Elliott wants something, it has to be a priority for everyone else, and he expects all those around him to drop everything for his needs. But now, unless it involves our children, he can wait. Besides, I'm in the middle of a deafening hockey stadium.

"Oh, hold these again for a quick sec." Kate thrusts the nachos back into my hands, and I roll my eyes. I knew the popcorn, big gulp, and nachos would be a handful, but she was determined to get *all the snacks.*

Kate winks at me before removing her black jacket revealing Jensen's jersey with his number eight-eight stamped on the back, sleeves, and chest. She leans forward and pulls her long blonde hair to the side, revealing *Jones* and giggles to herself.

Taking the nachos back once again she shoots me a smug smile. "Do you think he'll notice?"

Oh, he'll notice. Jon always stops by my spot on his routine lap around the ice, and if Jensen doesn't clock it right away, Jon definitely will. "I think that's a dead cert, babe."

"Excellent!" she replies, sounding pleased with herself. I've got to hand it to her—confidence oozes from every pore. She's one of those women who truly doesn't give a shit what others think, save for a few she's close to. She's unapologetically Kate, with a bright smile and a feisty temperament in just the right measure.

A few minutes later, the players are being introduced onto the ice, ready for warmups. Music beats around the stadium and strobe lights chase across the walls. Butterflies erupt in my stomach, and a chill races down my spine. I love this part of attending games, the display and drama they put on for the fans, but I'm not going to deny the truth of why my body reacts as it does.

Every time I see him, he sends my heart rate racing, but when his tall masculine body is clad in hockey gear and gliding effortlessly around the rink, my pulse hits overdrive. It's useless denying the effect Jon Morgan has on me, and when he enters the rink and slows, dragging his gloved hand across the plexiglass with a dimpled smile reserved only for me, Kate sees it all in live color. His smile, the deep pink flush on my cheeks, and the way my breathing picks up. She grins, popping another piece of popcorn into her mouth, happy to be here for more than just one show.

The game between Dallas and the Scorpions is tight, with both teams all square at zero-zero as we get close to the end of the first period. Jensen is playing incredibly, making crazy saves even my uneducated eye recognizes to be out of this world, and Jon has been picking up defense more than usual. I've never seen him so locked into a game before. He's running the show out there, but both he and number ninety-eight, who I don't really recognize but Kate tells me is Jessie Callaghan, giving me all the gossip on his trade last season, have been denied in front of goal.

The end of the first period and the players begin skating off the ice. I catch sight of Jon, who's skating backward, removing his mouthguard. He flashes me a cheeky grin before disappearing down the tunnel.

Jensen, on the other hand, is still skating across the ice, his gaze firmly planted in Kate's direction. "I think he's spotted the jersey," she comments, a giddy tone to her voice.

"Uh, yeah, it's safe to say he's clocked it," I reply, chuckling and shaking my head. The way Jensen's looking at her though, there's a possessive darkness in his eyes. Even from halfway across the ice, it's plain to see something is being shared between them, and I'm not entirely convinced it's just playful innocence.

IT'S three-two to the Scorpions deep in the final period.

The whole team has been playing incredibly, but Jon's game has hit another level, and every time he gets the puck, there's a hum of anticipation in the crowd, like he could do anything. And he could. He's a magician on the ice, his brain a step ahead of all those around him.

"Your boyfriend is so freakin' amazing," Kate shouts.

"He's fantastic, but he's not my boyfriend," I shout back, clapping at the latest move.

Kate scoffs. "Ugh yeah, he is."

"Have you just forgotten the conversation we had a couple of weeks back? We can't be any more than friends. We're too different." But at this point, even I'm struggling to buy my bullshit.

"Yeah, well I don't think you need to worry about catching feelings anymore."

I turn to look at her. "Why not?"

She exhales a laugh. "Because he's definitely beaten you to it."

I'm about to argue that she's wrong, but the noise level in the rink rises higher, and I look back to see Jon going one-on-one with the Dallas keeper. He sells him the wrong way and sinks the puck in the top right-hand corner, making it four-two and a definite win for the Scorpions.

I lose it and throw my arms up against the plexiglass in celebration and the whole team is piled on top of Jon, clearly knowing how much that meant to him.

When he finally gets back to his feet, he makes a beeline in my direction, stopping dead in front of me, and sending up a spray of ice. Removing his mouth guard he shouts, "Angel!" and all heads turn my way as I feel my cheeks warm. "That was for you." Jon smiles down at me through the glass then skates back to center ice, leaving the crowd reeling. It's the most public display he's shown to date, confirming all the recent rumors that the captain of the Scorpions has eyes for a fan.

"Like I was saying," Kate sings at me when I retake my seat. "He beat you to it."

JON

Life has never been so good.

Sure, it's not perfect, but it's damn close. I've just played the best game since I can remember, acknowledged by a clap on the back and a knowing smile from Coach Burrows. I know my position as captain and starting center is still far from secure, but tonight was a start. Dallas is top of the league, and tonight was always going to be a hard-fought battle, especially since we desperately needed the W before we hit the road for a two-week away series.

"The fuck was that pass, Jon!" Jessie fist-bumps me as we head toward the showers.

I haven't pulled off a pass like that in years, even surprising myself. "Moment of inspiration, I guess," I shout over to him and turn on the faucet, the steaming water hitting my body and easing my aching muscles. I'm going to be sore in the morning, since I pushed myself to the limits tonight.

"Screw the pass! I want to know what the hell's going on with you and that hot-as-fuck brunette we saw all that time ago in the cocktail bar. You've been eye-fucking each other for weeks, and don't think we didn't notice you skating over to her and declaring your love at the final buzzer," Kyle Johnson shouts from across the locker room.

Jesus, for a rookie he really does have some balls, much of it misplaced when he's addressing me as his captain and even more so when referring to Felicity as *hot-as-fuck*. My spine steels at the thought of another man's appreciative eyes on her. "Shut the fuck up and wipe down my pads, will ya? They smell particularly bad after my performance tonight." The rest of the guys laugh.

Thoughts of that moment I shared with Felicity at the end of the game replay in my mind. I've never seen her so animated, and the way she cheered me on, it was like she was there to support me as my girl, like she was totally invested in me and my game. My chest fills with warmth, and I realize I need to see her again tonight. I want to capitalize on what we shared over breakfast, the kiss by the waterfront, and the easy conversation.

Grabbing my towel, I throw it around my waist and head for the locker. I pull out my phone, hoping she and Kate haven't left the stadium yet. The game finished at least twenty minutes ago, and I was going to head to the baths and gym for a light cool down given the state of my body. But something tells me being in my girl's presence will do more to soothe me than any cool down ever could.

ME

You still at the rink, Angel?

It feels like we're hovering in this space between friends, *who kiss,* and something more, but today she let me in slightly, and I have to keep trying. With Zach's advice forever on replay, it feels like it's now or never.

I throw on a pair of black pants and a button-down white dress shirt—rolling the sleeves to my elbows because I'm still overheating—and slip on some back dress shoes. My hair's still wet, so I grab a clean black Scorpions cap and throw it on.

"In a hurry?" Zach sidles up to me. He's already dressed and ready to leave.

"Yeah, hoping to catch Felicity before she heads out."

A smile tugs at his lips.

I check my phone. Still no reply, and she hasn't even read it. Shit.

"You coming to Riley's tonight?" Zach asks with a hopeful look in his eye.

It's then I take in his outfit. Zach is a good-looking guy, and tonight he's dressed with purpose in a tailored suit and his hair is styled. He's out to drown himself in beer and, at my best guess, pussy too. My best friend has never done hookups, and at the look in his eyes, he needs someone to accompany him and make sure he doesn't do anything, *or anyone,* too stupid tonight.

"Yeah, why not. Gimme five, and I'll meet you out in the parking lot." I grab my bag and pull out my phone again, scrolling for Felicity's number.

"I'll drive," I tell Zach.

He throws me an appreciative smile before exiting the locker room.

I'm walking down the private hallway on my way out toward my car when I dial Felicity. She's still not seen my text, and an uneasy feeling comes over me. I don't know whether she's ignoring me or genuinely hasn't seen my message, but either way, I don't like it.

Finally, she answers on the last ring. "Hello?" I can barely hear her, the sound of voices and blaring music overpowering her soft voice.

"It's Jon. Are you okay? Where are you? Are you alone?" The questions spill out of me in a panicked tone I can't hide. I'm powerless when it comes to this girl. It's clear she's in a bar somewhere, without me. She looked stunning at the game today; tight blue jeans, a white sweater, and a black leather jacket with her signature emerald scarf popping the color in her eyes. Guys are going to be all over her.

I throw the double doors open to the players' parking lot and spot Zach leaning against my car waiting for me.

"Where are you?" I repeat, almost shouting now, my voice sounding way harsher than I intend.

"Hang on," she yells. I hear a few more voices and Felicity replying before the noise dies down, replaced with traffic and horns.

"Ugh, that's better. I can actually hear you now," she huffs out.

"Where are you? I messaged you, but you didn't reply." I pop the trunk on my car, and Zach throws his bag in before we both get in and my phone connects to the Bluetooth system.

"Oh sorry, didn't see that. I'm in some bar with Kate. We came here for a few drinks and food. Sorry we didn't wait, but Kate saw Jensen after the game, and he mentioned you would be coming here and—"

"So where are you?" I cut her off and feel like an absolute asshole. Jesus, what's gotten into me, and why am I so tightly wound up?

"Alright, cool your jets, Grandma. We're in um..." She pauses, clearly checking where she is, and I inwardly chuckle. She's so fucking cute. "Riley's," she finally confirms.

"Yeah, Jensen would be right then." I crank the engine on my Porsche, pleased with my choice of car so I can get to her and the lecherous men as quickly as possible.

"We'll be there in ten, baby," I confirm, tagging on the *baby* because fuck it. I'm done messing around.

CHAPTER EIGHTEEN

JON

We get there in nine minutes.

Throwing my car into park directly in front of the bar, Zach and I hop out, immediately attracting attention from those smoking and loitering outside. Ideally, I shouldn't park my car in public sight, but I'm done caring. I just want to get inside.

"Step it down a gear, buddy." Zach plants his palm on my shoulder, halting my advance toward the entrance. "You can't head in there all guns blazing. You and I both know she's understated and won't appreciate the captain of the Scorpions flying in to stake his claim."

I deflate because he's right. I need to relax and while I still have no claim over her, the thought of her talking or even flirting with another man ignites a fire, singeing me from the inside.

The bar is absolutely heaving, bodies everywhere, but thankfully, security recognizes us immediately and escorts us to a reserved booth at the back. I fully expect to see Felicity with the rest of the team, but she's nowhere to be seen. Kate is, though, sitting next to Jensen, the pair of them getting close.

"Where is she?" I ask Kate. I know I sound like a dick, but that seems to be my default these days when it comes to my girl and making sure she's okay.

"Well, hello to you, too." Kate waves a sarcastic hand in front of me, and Jensen snickers next to her. This girl has sass in spades, and it might just be that our goalie's met his match.

I pull at the back of my neck, trying to steady myself. "Yeah, sorry, I just want to make sure she's okay. It's packed with God knows who in here."

"She's fine," Kate drawls, tipping her glass in the direction of the bar. "She's ordering a—"

My feet are carrying me over there before Kate can finish her sentence.

FELICITY

"No, I'm fine, thank you," I tell the tall blond guy next to me. He's offered me a drink at least three times since I've been standing here waiting.

"Did you go to the game today?" Blond Guy persists.

"Yeah, I did. Intense game," I reply, trying to sound friendly but uninterested. In my thirty-nine years, it's a skill I've yet to master.

All I want is to get my Cosmo and head back to the booth to wait for Jon. It's been at least ten minutes since he called, so he can't be far away now.

"You here on your own?" Another question from my new friend.

I peer up at him, braving potential eye contact. He's a good-looking guy, maybe a couple of years older than me. He catches my gaze and moves closer behind me, his front pressed up against my back. At a similar height to Jon, this guy towers over me, and I'd be lying if I said I wasn't a little intimidated. "No, I have my friends here with me."

The girl in front of me finishes getting served, and I thankfully have space to move forward, but that means nothing to this guy, as he simply steps forward maintaining the distance between us, which is nothing, nada.

He leans over my shoulder, his nose almost nuzzled in my hair, as he sets his empty beer glass down on the bar.

"I don't see them." His tone is almost suggestive, and I can smell the alcohol on his breath. My stomach turns at his presence; I need to get out of here.

"They're right here." A deep, familiar voice cuts through my discomfort, enveloping me in a sense of safety.

It's Jon.

When I turn to face him, he's right behind me, the blond guy having taken several steps back. His eyes are soft but wear a sense of concern behind them like he's silently asking if I'm okay. I nod, reassuring him I'm fine.

Blond Guy's eyes have bugged out at the sight of Jon, clearly having a hard time processing that the captain of the Scorpions is standing right in front of him.

Jon places a firm arm around my waist, pulling me into his side. His eyes are dark and possessive, leaving no doubt who I am to him.

"She's here with her boyfriend. Me." Jon's voice is hard and unwavering. *Boyfriend.* That singular word ignites my core, sending shock waves throughout my body.

Calm down, Felicity; he's just playing it up to make a point to this creep.

"You okay, baby?" Jon asks me in a gentle voice.

"Yeah, I'm good. Just been waiting to get a drink for an age." I gesture to the crowd all pushing to get to the bar.

My bag starts buzzing, and I reach in to fetch out my phone. It's Elliott, again. I send him a template message saying I'll call him later. He's really stepping his contact up today, and I know I can't keep holding him off forever.

Jon's brow furrows when I disconnect the call. I don't know if he saw who it was, but he doesn't say anything. Instead, his hand travels to my lower back, and he dips his chin, hovering it above my head. "Leave the drink with me. I got it." And with that, he lifts his hand in the air toward one of the bar staff, who immediately looks up, almost like they knew he was there all along. "Cosmo for my girl please, buddy. Over there." Jon points to the booth I vacated what feels like hours ago.

"You got it," the barman shouts.

I turn to look at Jon, an incredulous expression on my face. He smiles at me before leading me back to the booth, his fingers interlaced with mine. "Don't wander off on your own in bars, Angel. There are pervy guys around," he whispers softly in my ear as we take a seat opposite Zach, Kate, and Jensen.

"Pervy guys like you?" I playfully respond. Okay, I'm full-on flirting, but no judgment, please. I've got Jon freaking Morgan's hand round my waist and his lips tickling my ear.

"These eyes are only for you, and for the record, I'm the only guy who should be checking you out." He pauses and then continues, "I don't know if I mentioned it, but you look beautiful tonight."

I'm unraveling right before him. Every last shred of willpower to resist this smooth-talking man is deserting me.

"Zach, all okay, man?" Jensen breaks me from my Jon-induced trance.

Zach is staring ahead past mine and Jon's shoulder, his eyes flaming with an emotion I can't quite make out. He doesn't look happy though, not at all.

"Zach?" Jon tries to get through to him, to no avail.

I peek over my shoulder and spot a group of girls on the dancefloor, the vast majority being tall, blonde, with legs for days. Stunning.

"Ah, shit."

"W-what is it?" I ask Jon, slightly concerned.

"Amie," he drawls but doesn't add anything else.

"Who's Amie?" Kate interjects, looking as confused as I feel.

"My ex." Zach's tone is harsh, bordering on angry. His eyes

are still boring into the group of girls dancing and gyrating against each other.

"I'm gonna head to the bathroom," I say to Jon. I need a reprieve from the tension that's building around the table.

"Want me to come?" Kate asks.

"No, it's fine, babe, but thanks." I grab my bag, feeling a little squeeze from Jon's hand around my waist as he lets me go, and I make my way to the bathroom.

Pushing through the door, the cooler air from the partially open window hits me. It feels nice and refreshing, a stark contrast to the sweltering heat radiating from the main bar area. I don't need to use the bathroom; instead, I use it as an excuse to take a breather from the intensity. I decide to use the time productively though and reapply my lip gloss and blush.

I'm halfway through my refresh when the bathroom door flies open. A tall scantily clad blonde I half recognize from the dancefloor stands before me, a snide smirk pulling at her red pouty mouth.

"So, you're flavor of the month then."

I place the cap back on my lip gloss and turn to look at her properly, checking she's definitely talking to me. I've never seen this woman before tonight, and she finds it necessary to speak to me like this.

"Excuse me?"

"Oh my god, you're British too." The last part she attempts to say in her best posh British accent, sounding more ridiculous than anything else.

"Yes, I'm British, and?" Seriously, who does this woman think she is?

"Well," she scoffs, "you must be some sort of princess to nail down Jon Morgan."

"I'll take that as a compliment, thanks," I respond, my tone sounding unimpressed. "But I'm not *nailing down* anyone. I'm here with my friends."

The girl's eyes grow wider with frustration. "Oh, come on.

We've all seen footage from tonight's game. What did you do, get knocked up so he had to take you on? You're hardly his type." Her eyes trace over my body, a look of disdain on her face. "Jon goes for more..." she waves her hand in front of her, "glamorous women."

I draw in a sharp breath, shaking my head in a pitiful manner at her pathetic display. "Look, whoever you—"

"Amie," she interjects curtly.

"Amie," ah Amie, Zach's ex—it's all making sense now. "Look, Amie, I'm way past my days of catty exchanges in dingy bar bathrooms, and I'm certainly way past caring what you or any of your *friends* might think of me. I'm here to enjoy a nice evening celebrating a Scorpions win. So please, if you wouldn't mind." I point to the door, indicating my wish to leave. She doesn't move though, instead remaining in front of the bathroom door.

"Don't say I didn't warn you," Amie throws out as she finally steps aside, letting me make my leave.

I turn back to her, halfway out the door. "Warn me of what?" I'm exasperated now, fed up with her games, and ready to get back to Jon and the group.

"Of Jon. He has a different woman in his bed every night, always has and always will." She struts over to the mirrors, pulling out her scarlet lipstick and applying another coat. "No one ever keeps him for long." She huffs out a laugh. "Just ask half the girls in this bar or Sarah and Bryony. They're out with me tonight; I'm sure they can vouch for his ways." She pauses, catching my eye in the reflection. "Sure, he's a good time, but you don't actually think he wants you for more than that, do you?" she mocks in a patronizing tone. "Aww, you did. Cute."

I shake my head at her before turning to leave, letting the door slam behind me. *Fucking bitch.* Yeah, Zach is better off for being shot of her.

But as I make my way back to the private booth area, I can't help but feel the weight of her words sink into my skin, taking residence in my consciousness. *They can vouch for his ways.*

Amie's friends are still dancing when I take a seat, some guys having joined their gyrating session. I wonder who Sarah and Bryony are and whether they've slept with Jon or if it's just mind games from Amie. Either way, my thirty-nine years tell me she screams trouble.

Today has been a long and trying day. I just want to go home and get away from the hordes of people. I need peace and quiet and the safety of my apartment.

"All okay?" Jon asks as the back of his hand brushes the top of my arm, setting off another wave of goosebumps across my skin.

"Can you take me home, please?" I ask, turning to him. My voice is laced with more emotion than I intended, but it's all too much today. Kissing Jon this morning, the game, the attention from the crowd, the calls from Elliott, the guy at the bar, and now Amie.

His brows knit together with concern etched across his face. "Yeah, sure. Anything you need." He downs the rest of his drink, and I stand, pulling on my jacket.

"What's happened, babe?" Kate asks. My face must be giving away more than I hoped.

"Honestly, I'm fine, just tired," I lie.

"I'll text you," she offers, and I nod, smiling weakly at her.

And then Jon's leading me out of the bar, tucked under his protective arm.

CHAPTER NINETEEN

JON

I open the passenger door of my Porsche, and Felicity gets in as I do up her belt.

Jogging around the back, I climb in the driver's side and fire up the engine, flicking her heated seat on full blast. It's early December and cold out, but Felicity's shaking, badly, especially since we just stepped out of a sweltering bar.

Something happened in there. I don't know if it was the blond dude who I wanted to lay out as soon as I saw him zeroing in on her. Or was it something else, maybe in the bathroom? She's clamming up on me though, I can tell.

"Sorry to drag you away from your celebrations." She offers me a tiny smile, but her face is washed out and her eyes are heavy.

"If you need to go home, then I'm always going to be the one to look after you." I could've stayed for another hour or so, and I was supposed to be keeping watch on a volatile Zach, especially with Amie around, but I've no doubt Jensen has that covered.

I place my hand gently on her thigh, desperate to bring her comfort. "Want to tell me what's wrong?"

"Not really. I'm just tired. Long day."

I know that's not all, far from it. But she didn't push me earlier when I alluded to my anxiety issues, so I repay her the favor and focus on the road and getting her home.

I pull into her apartment complex parking lot alongside a green Mini Cooper. I don't need to ask to know whose it is, but I do anyway. All I want to do is make her smile again.

Tipping my head in the direction of the car. "Did you ship it from England?"

"Yes, I did actually, but you do know they sell them here. In case you're interested and fancy trading your Porsche in for an upgrade."

I burst out laughing, sassy Felicity is back and I'm here for it. "I doubt I'll get one leg in that thing."

"That thing? By *that* I assume you're referring to Martha."

"Martha," I repeat, laughing even harder.

She looks hurt at my mocking. "Yes, Martha Mini, and that's a little presumptuous since I haven't invited you for a spin."

"Shame, I was looking forward to a ride." At this point, we both know I'm no longer referring to Martha.

Felicity looks away, her shy demeanor returning at the flirtatious turn our conversation has taken. I wonder if she's always been this reserved with men or if it's the effect her bullshit ex has had on her. That thought alone makes me want to pummel him into the ground.

"I haven't got much in food-wise." She changes the subject as we head to the stairwell.

"That's okay, Angel, we can order something in. I'm on cheat day tomorrow, I can just bring it forward a few hours." I pull out my phone to place an order. "Pizza?"

She lets out a hearty sigh. "Ah, yeah that sounds perfect."

"Any preference?" I ask as we climb the stairs to her place on the third floor.

She taps her finger on her bottom lip, considering her options, but all I can think about is how that perfect mouth feels on mine, and I almost lose my footing on the next step. "I'm fairly easygoing, but black olives are an absolute must."

I screw my face up. "No danger of that. The devil's food."

"What?" She stops in front of me. "Your lack of pizza topping sophistication is disappointing, and since you can count on one hand the number of takeaways you've had, I say my knowledge is superior."

"Well, pizza rookie or not, you're stuck with me now, woman."

I haul her over my shoulder using one arm to carry her the rest of the way to her apartment, and I fight back the urge to bite her perfect, round ass resting just next to my face. She squeals and tries to break free, but she's so light, she's not going anywhere. I even manage to complete the order with my other hand. "I've put black olives on the pizza, but you should know I wouldn't do that for anyone else."

Her tiny fists beat on my back in mock protest. "Oh, I'm such a lucky girl."

"Hell, *yes* you are." But not half as lucky as me.

FELICITY

"Felicity?"

Jon comes to a complete stop as we reach the third floor, my ass in the air and back to my apartment door. I recognize that voice, one that racks a cold shiver through me.

"And you are?" Jon asks, his tone suspicious.

"I could ask you the exact same thing."

It's Elliot. I wouldn't miss that self-assured, superior tone anywhere.

Jon pulls me off his shoulder and sets me down so I'm standing beside him, though I'm still pressed firmly to his side. "What are you doing here, Elliott?" I sound exasperated, and I am. Seeing Elliott outside my door is the last thing I need.

"I've been calling and texting you for the past three days," he snipes.

"Can we just go inside?" I step away from Jon, opening my front door. "I don't want to make a scene here."

"I'm not making a scene."

Once inside, I kick off my boots and stride down the hallway toward the kitchen before turning to Elliott. "What can I do for you? I thought you were in Oxford, and where's Darcy?"

"I've been back here for the last couple of days, checking in with the fund manager's performance and making sure all is going smoothly since I left. Darcy is with Liam like she always is," Elliott replies, all the while keeping an eye on Jon, who's standing in the kitchen entryway, fists balled at his sides. "You haven't answered my calls, and I need to talk to you. I fly back home tomorrow, so you left me no choice but to come to your apartment and wait."

I look to Jon, who's barely moved from his position, continuing to stare Elliott down. I drop my bag on the counter, still not meeting Elliott's eyes. "You told me whatever you had to say has nothing to do with Darcy or Jack, and our divorce has been finalized. I don't see what more there is to talk about."

He deflects my statement, angling his head toward Jon instead. "Who's this guy?"

"I'm her boyfriend." He comes to stand beside me, wrapping a strong protective arm around my waist.

That's the second time he's referred to himself as my boyfriend tonight, and I kind of like it. Even if we both know it's not true and he's saying it only for my benefit.

Elliott looks to Jon and then back to me, his jaw agape. "You're joking, right?" His voice is laced with pitying amusement.

I don't deny it and decide to follow Jon's lead. I want Elliott out of my apartment as quickly as possible and this seems like the best plan. "What do you want?" I ask again.

"Seriously. You're with him?" Elliott looks to the ground, his hands coming to his hips as he shakes his head in disbelief. "What, are you having some sort of mid-life crisis now, Felicity? Messing around with dumb jocks? Jesus, you've really let yourself go—"

It happens faster than I can register.

Jon is across the kitchen and in his face, pinning him against the wall with one arm under his chin, his other fist bunched at his side, ready to unleash. "What did you just say to her, asshole?"

Elliott's eyes go wide, a terrified look strewn across his face. "Let go of me you thug."

"It's okay, Jon," I reassure him, although I'm shaking with anger myself. Drawing in a steadying breath, I decide to ask Elliott one final time. "Why are you here?"

Now released from Jon's hold, although very much still under his towering gaze, he brushes himself off, straightening out his collar. "I want to talk to you in private."

"You can say to her whatever you need in front of me."

For the first time, Elliott looks uncomfortable, his shoulders slightly slumped. "I wanted to talk about us." He takes a step toward me, a look of vulnerability in his eyes, one I don't think I've ever seen before. "I think. I think we made a mistake. I miss you, Felicity."

I'm fixed to the spot. I don't know how much time passes, Elliott staring at me, Jon staring at Elliott with a murderous look in his eyes, and me? I'm just zoned out, looking right through Elliott. I hear his words, but they mean absolutely nothing. I feel nothing at all for this man. My ex-husband and father of my children.

Finally, I break the silence, shaking my head as I do. "I'm sorry, but I think we made exactly the *right* decision. Separating was the best thing that could ever happen to me. I was miserable in a loveless marriage, and if you're being honest, I know you felt that too." My voice begins to crack but I press on, desperate to get the words out. "I felt unloved and unappreciated. Our entire relationship revolved around *you* and what *you* wanted, where *you* wanted to be. Your job came first above us all, and lately, I've been able to find myself again. Make friends, go out, have fun."

"So that's it, huh? Almost two decades of marriage down the drain all because you want to go out and *have fun?*" he retorts in a mocking tone, his fists propped on his hips.

I shake my head and take a step toward him, trying to steady my breathing. "No. Our marriage has been over for many years, way before we came to live out here. I'm moving on with my life, and you should, too."

"Moving on with him?" he bites out, pointing a finger in Jon's direction. "Some NHL playboy? Surely you don't think it's possible to have a serious relationship with someone like him. He'll take what he wants from you and dump you the first chance he gets." A disgusted sneer crosses his face as he casts his eyes down my body. "Jesus, he probably already has. You should get yourself checked out."

"You fucking *what?*" Jon grits out, his jaw ticking. I can tell he's about to lose all control, but something holds him back, and I know it's out of respect for me. But if I gave the word, I suspect my ex-husband would be flat on his back, nursing a broken jaw at best.

Steeling my shoulders I reply, "Who I do or don't date has nothing to do with you anymore. You lost that right the moment you started treating me like a second-class citizen." I've never stood up to Elliott, always choosing to back down and yield to his demands. But not tonight, not anymore. I'm worth more than the way he treated me. "I think you should leave." I point to the front door.

He scoffs, "You're kicking me out?"

"She asked you to leave. Now go before I put you through the fucking wall." Jon strides across the room once again, Elliott's palms flying up in front of him in surrender. He's clearly intimidated.

"Okay, fine. I'm gone. But this isn't over, Felicity. You're making a mistake. Darcy wants us to give it another go, and I think she's right. If she finds out you're shacked up with some hotshot hockey player, she'll be devastated. Is that the example you want to set for your children? That their mum has lowered herself to some sort of puck bunny? I'm giving you a second chance, an opportunity to come home to your family. Just, think about it." Then he turns, strides down the hallway, and yanks the door open, leaving it to slam behind him.

I fall to my knees, every emotion that's been simmering under the surface finally erupting out of me. And I sob. All the while, I'm being held in Jon's comforting arms, his hand gently smoothing my hair as he rocks us slowly, reassuring me it's all going to be okay.

CHAPTER TWENTY

JON

"Stay with me?"

Elliott left around twenty minutes ago, and I've finally managed to calm her enough to get her to eat at least a slice of pizza, complete with gross black olives.

We're sitting on her black corner couch, my back against one of the side arms as she sits between my legs, her back pressed against my chest. The position is intimate, but she's been way too upset because of that asshole for me to even think about anything other than comforting her.

"I'm right here," I softly reply into the shell of her ear, smoothing her shoulder with my palm. In this position, I can inhale her gorgeous coconut scent that I've figured out is her shampoo.

She turns her head around to face me, her eyes slightly puffy from crying, and her cheeks still stained from tears. "No. I mean stay with me. Tonight. Here."

I can't lie, I'm taken aback by her request, but being totally honest, I hadn't planned to leave her. Not until I knew that fucker was back on a plane to London and out of this country. I want him nowhere near her. I rub my thumb lightly across her cheek, drowning in her slightly red but still beautiful, emerald eyes. "I wasn't planning on leaving you tonight, Angel. I can take the couch."

She shakes her head, her lids fluttering shut at my touch. "No, I mean stay with me. In my bed."

I freeze. I was not expecting her to say that. "I can sleep on here; it's no problem."

She sets her half-eaten slice back on the plate and turns her body toward me fully so that she's on her knees and between my legs. Despite my best efforts to keep this PG, my dick twitches, and I run my hands down her sides, feeling her firm body beneath my palms.

"No, I want you with me. I need you, Jon. I feel safe when I'm with you. In your arms."

Fuck me. My heart squeezes at her admission. The trust she places in me, the way she's looking at me with longing and expectation. It's everything I've hoped for.

I've shared a bed with many women over the years, but never like this. And never with a woman like Felicity. In my past, being in bed with someone has only resulted in one thing for us both. But tonight, Felicity wants me for an entirely different reason, to hold and comfort her. I'm in uncharted territory, and I'd be lying if I said I wasn't scared shitless.

IT'S ELEVEN P.M., and I find myself in Felicity's tiny bathroom feeling like a sixteen-year-old about to lose his virginity. The thought of sharing a bed with the woman I've lusted after for months has got me all twisted up. Not to mention my dick which clearly hasn't gotten the memo that tonight will likely get no further than first base.

"There's a spare toothbrush under the sink," she shouts from the other side of the door.

At least that's one dilemma sorted. I've fantasized about sharing a bed with her hundreds of times—okay, probably thousands, most ending with me getting myself off in the shower to the thought. But I was not prepared for the way tonight has unfolded.

Don't get carried away, Jon. She wants you to stay and comfort her. I mentally will my dick to stand down and my brain to get a grip.

But fuck me is she beautiful. And cute, so cute. Her coconut shampoo, the scent that's been driving me crazy since late September, sits at the side of the tub along with a matching conditioner. I make a mental note of the brand. Would it be weird if I bought a bottle just to keep at my place, for times when I don't get to see her? *Christ, who are you and what have you done with Jon Morgan?*

With one final pep talk, I pull the door open and step out into her bedroom. The room is glowing in soft light courtesy of a single lamp on her nightstand. The sage-green comforter on the queen-size bed is pulled back, but it's missing a particular someone. I wiped down the kitchen and plates after our pizza, so I doubt there's much to do in there.

So where is she?

Just then, the door to her closet opens, and out steps Felicity, sporting tiny pink silk sleep shorts and a matching cami top that scoops low at the front. She's no longer wearing a bra, and I catch my first glimpse at the shape of her perfectly perky tits and nipples, which are slightly peaked. Shit, is she turned on or just cold? I can't tell because the heating in this place is crap at best. No wonder she has a thick comforter piled with blankets. The thought of my girl living and sleeping in a cold apartment pisses me off, and I make a mental note that it's something I need to address and fast.

"Hey." She pauses as she closes the tiny closet door which

stays ajar due to the number of bags and scarves hanging over the edge.

"Hi," I squeak out. Shit, I'm so nervous. Looking at my dream girl dressed in barely anything and standing before me in her bedroom. I'm still in my dress pants and button-down shirt, having only removed my jacket and shoes much earlier in the night.

"You look, um, nice." *I'm so smooth.*

She smiles sweetly, with an edge of uncertainty to her still slightly puffy eyes.

"Do you have a favorite side?" she asks, looking over at the bed.

As long as it's next to you, then no.

"No. I." I pause. I can't believe I'm saying this, but I want her to know me, the good, the bad, and everything in between. "I've only ever slept alone, so I've always just taken the middle."

"You've never shared a bed with another woman?"

My skin itches, flushing hot. "No, well, yes. Not all night."

She looks confused, her lips twisting to the side as she considers my response. "So, just one-night stands?" She asks the question but there's no judgment in her eyes, just a hint of intrigue.

"Yeah." I start unbuttoning my shirt, desperate for something to do with my hands. "I sort of had rules when it came to women."

She starts climbing into bed before moving over to the far side closest to the window. Once settled, she leans her back against the wooden headboard pulling the comforter up and over her chest, clearly aware of her peaked nipples as her face flushes with a touch of embarrassment. I don't like it. I never want her to be embarrassed around me.

Tipping her head slightly to the side, her eyes cast down over my chest to my abs. My shirt is undone but not removed, hanging open at the front. I start undoing my belt, unlooping it slowly. Returning her eyes to mine, I swear there's a heat in them that wasn't there before. I can't deny I'm a good-looking guy with a thick muscular body, and taking my clothes off in front of a woman has never been anything other than routine in the buildup to sex. But this, tonight, here with the girl of my dreams as she watches me strip to my dark-gray boxer briefs, every cell in my body is ignited with hyper-arousal and awareness. If the apartment is still cold, I can't feel it. I've never experienced anything this hot, yet sex isn't even in the cards.

I climb into bed, my weight shifting her ever so slightly closer as I feel our thighs brush together, a fleeting touch that jolts through me going straight to my dick.

Shit, not now.

Keep it together.

Think of anything. *Anything else.*

"I don't know if I want to ask about your rules." She breaks the short silence.

I too shift back against the headboard, close enough so our shoulders touch, sending a similar physical reaction through me. The way Felicity responds, I know she feels it too. "I don't want to keep secrets from you, Angel. You can ask me anything and I'll always be honest. Even if it isn't what you want to hear." I can't say I'm proud of some of my past, but I'm serious about this woman, and I'll show her all of me.

She doesn't say anything more. So, I offer up the information I think she wants. "I never stayed overnight with any hookup. Once we were done, I'd either get dressed and leave her place or call her a taxi from the hotel to make sure she got home safe." I turn to look at her, analyzing for any trace of judgment in her eyes. Still none.

"So, it was a one-and-done type of arrangement?"

"Not quite, my rules meant I couldn't hook up with the same woman more than twice. That was designed to stop them from catching feelings, in case they got the wrong idea of what it was. Which to me was always sex. Meaningless, but with a purpose of release and a connection with someone on the shallowest of levels."

"Oh." Felicity brings her knees up and under her chin. "And they were okay with that."

"Yeah, for the most part, I never had any issues. They knew what they were getting with me. It suited both parties. I got what I wanted and needed, and they got what they wanted too. Some wanted to brag about being with me, and others were more tight-lipped, just in it for the great sex."

She smirks at that, and there's a twinkle returning to her eyes. "Great, huh? Don't mind Mr. Modest Morgan over here."

I chuckle, feeling my shoulders relax just a little. Instead of running for the hills, she appreciates my openness with her. Fucking incredible. "I told you, I'll always be honest with you, so yes, the feedback I've received over the years leads me to believe I'm decent in bed."

"H-How much feedback have you had?" I don't need to be a genius to work out that's a loaded question. She's asking me for my number and suddenly, the eased tension returns tenfold.

I grip the back of my neck, trying to soothe away some of the discomfort. "A lot... More than I can count." Which is the truth. I have no idea how many women I've been with. If I averaged hookups twice a week, which is conservative given my rookie years, then we'd be looking at a big number, but that doesn't account for the fact that on occasion I'd find myself with more than one woman at a time. Especially during my darker moments before I started seeing Ben and was drinking more than I should.

I desperately want to change the topic of conversation but work through the pained silence, giving her an opportunity to ask anything more.

But she doesn't push me any further, and for that I'm grateful.

"I've only ever slept with one man."

My jaw nearly hits the floor. Christ, our pasts couldn't be any more different, but it means so much that she's offered up a part of herself in return for my candidness and it fills my chest with warmth. Once again, my mind is taken back to that poor excuse of a man she calls her ex-husband. "Elliott," I grit out, jaw clenched.

"Yeah." She blanches slightly, and I wonder if it's at the mention of his name. "We met at university. I fell pregnant with Jack and by twenty-two, I was married with two children. Darcy followed not long after Jack."

It's my turn to blanch. "So, you had two children while still in college?" I try to keep my tone as even as possible, desperate for her not to think I'm judging, which I in no way am.

"Yeah. Elliott said I should just quit school and focus on bringing up the children. In fact, he was determined for me to, but my mum and dad stepped in and helped care for them both, so I could continue studying and finish my degree."

They sound like amazing parents. The opposite of her douchebag ex. "What about his parents? What about *him?*"

She scoffs at the mere suggestion. "Oh, no. His parents were high-flying professionals, no time for me. They didn't like the fact I'd had Jack, never mind Darcy. They thought I'd gotten pregnant to ensnare their perfect son who was bound for great things in finance. They never stopped to think that Elliott was responsible for his actions. In fact, he was—" she hurries out and then stops.

"He was what, Felicity?" My tone is way sharper than I wanted, but the way this is going, I know I'm not going to like it.

She frustratedly gathers her beautiful chocolate wavy hair into a messy bun, securing it with the black elastic band around her wrist. "He told me he wanted more children. He said he wanted to have them young so we could concentrate on our careers. He told me I was it for him, and at such a young age I fell for it. I mean, I guess I was it for him, but not in the way I hoped. Not in a romantic way. As the years passed by, it became clear that I was responsible for bringing up the children, and he was the sole breadwinner." Her voice is shaky and laced with emotion, and I can tell she's trying to keep herself together. A lone tear pools in the corner of her eye.

My heart cracks open. I can't bear to hear or see her upset. On instinct, I pull her into my side so her head is resting on my chest, and it's then I feel more dampness.

I think she's finished talking, but then she continues.

"Don't get me wrong. He isn't a bad dad; in fact, he's got a great relationship with Darcy. They're close. Jack not so much, but he's always been good to them, providing everything they need. But our marriage? Well, we were on very different paths. I wanted to be a human rights lawyer, and he wanted me to drop my career and be the *perfect wife*." She says the last bit in a mocking tone. "There's nothing wrong with raising children and staying at home if that's what you want to do. But I wanted something for me. I love Jack and Darcy with all my heart, but women can have it all. The career and the kids if that's what they want. When it became clear that I was going to continue working, he started setting up interviews for me with his connections. I got shoe-horned into being a PA for Mark Preston. It's a decent job and the salary is okay, but it isn't my dream."

So, he's a controlling mother fucker, keeping her right where he wants her, and over time, it looks like he wore her down. From time to time, I've witnessed that spunk in Felicity, the spark I know she has when she gives me shit. I saw it the moment I laid eyes on her at the stadium, but it's offset by a woman who lacks confidence in herself and her amazing capabilities. It's clear she's incredibly smart. If I had my best guess, I'd say she threatened his superiority. His position as the main breadwinner and head of the house. So instead of helping her with her dreams, he controlled her and clipped her wings.

Dick.

Zach was spot on that night at his place.

"What does he do for a living?" I know he works in finance,

but if one cent of my money is invested and benefiting this fucker, then I want out. I want him out of our lives, out of hers. My gut tells me what she's shared tonight is only the tip of the iceberg.

"An equity fund manager." Her voice is a little steadier as I trace my fingers up and down her arm. In the last couple of minutes, she's gone from being tucked into my side to my arm around her back, pinned between her and the headboard as my fingertips dance across her goose-pimpled skin. "One of the best in the UK, but more recently, he's moved to head of the US equity team, and that's what brought us to Seattle. He's been working on a new fund launch. Well, more like overseeing its progress."

"And then you divorced him, and he moved back home?" I ask cautiously.

"Yes. We divorced eight months ago and that's when I moved out and into this apartment."

I look around. Seattle is expensive, but if the financial settlement has been completed, I'd expect her to have a nicer place given the money he earns.

As if reading my mind she clarifies. "This is rented, and I could afford better based on the settlement I got from Elliott, but I want to keep hold of that money, not eat into it too much. My life is so upside down, and with two children still in education, Darcy about to start university next summer, I want to pull my weight. I don't know what's going to happen with my job or if my living in Seattle will work out. I could find myself unemployed at some point, so I need to hang onto the savings I have. Besides, the settlement from Elliott was okay, but it wasn't great."

I pull back and peek down at her. Anger swelling in my gut once again. "Wasn't great how?"

She puffs out a breath, staring straight ahead at the cream-colored wall in front of us. "He didn't want to divorce; I drove the breakup. I hadn't any real grounds to divorce him other than on no-fault terms, so finally, after years of me growing more distant from him, he agreed on the basis that I settle on a smaller proportion. I wasn't prepared to go through a battle over money. As long as I had enough to get by and support the kids, I was happy. Money never has and never will mean much to me. Unlike Elliott who is obsessed with it. My freedom and happiness meant more than a higher share of his estate."

There's so much for me to unpack and process in what she's told me. Felicity has given me a window into her life over the last fifteen minutes and since I got into her bed, she's shared with me details that make so much sense. Why she is like she is, nervous about another relationship. Constantly keeping me at a safe distance. Here's this playboy NHL hockey star pursuing her, asking for her number, asking her on dates, flirting like hell on nights out. Another successful man with deep pockets.

It all makes so much sense.

Yet despite her past and damaged heart, she's still found the strength to let me in and try on some level. She's incredible.

CHAPTER TWENTY-ONE

FELICITY

J on Morgan is in my bed.

And boy is he glorious.

After the shittiest evening on record, involving a bitchy Amie and an unwelcome visit from my ex-husband, I lost all self-control and invited the beautiful hockey superstar into my bed. And I don't regret a thing.

"Thank you for sharing with me." Jon's arm is wrapped around my waist where his fingers have been tracing slow, languid patterns up and down my left arm for what feels like hours. All while he's listened to me pour my heart out over my failed marriage.

I guess I decided to unload in response to his openness about his past sexual encounters. He laid down a lot of truths about his playboy ways and the rules he abides by. Could it be that he's breaking one of his rules for me tonight by staying in my bed?

"Likewise. I mean, I knew you hooked up with women, but no judgment on my part. You do what makes you happy." I yawn and shimmy out of his hold but lie down, settling on my side, my hands clasped beneath my cheek as I face him.

He mirrors my actions until our faces are only centimeters apart. I can feel and smell his still slightly minty breath as it envelops me. "It doesn't make me happy. I mean, at one time it did, but not anymore."

I wonder why hooking up with a multitude of gorgeous women wouldn't make any hot-blooded man happy. "Women must throw themselves at you, so it's no wonder you have rules."

Jon's brows crease together. "*Had* rules." His hand darts out, his rough thumb gently brushing over my cheek. "I had rules, Felicity. I don't anymore."

"Why not?"

"Because you're breaking them, Angel. One by one."

My breath catches in my throat, and I fight to keep the butterflies from fluttering out of control.

On instinct, I reach out to retrieve a loose eyelash, save it from falling into his eye. "I've never seen an eight-pack before. Only on posters and billboards," I muse, thinking back to the way Jon undressed right in front of me, giving me the best show of my life.

"Hm, are you sure it wasn't my photo you were gawking at?"

"You've been a model before?" I sound surprised but really, I'm not. I mean, come on, Jon's body doesn't need an ounce of airbrushing.

"Not so much now, but in my rookie years, yes."

"What did you model?"

"Underwear."

"Now *there's* a surprise. Why don't you anymore?"

Jon shifts, and I notice it's closer to me. My core tightens at our reality, in my bed, talking about his chiseled body, lying so close it heats my own.

"Putting myself out in public kind of lost its appeal years ago."

"I get that. I mean, I can't begin to know how it feels to be in the public eye, but I understand why you want your privacy.

You're so much more than just an athlete. You're a person too, Jon, and a very good one."

He swallows thickly, and I see the way the columns of his throat works. We stare at each other for a few beats. His eyes are slightly glassy, and I wonder if it's in response to my words. I hope so; I hope they resonate with him in some way because I get the feeling he needs to hear it more often.

"Your apartment is cold." Okay that's not where I thought this conversation was going but he's right, it's freezing. My nipples tell the story—well that and the super-hot man currently lying beside me.

"Yeah, my landlord is kind of a dick and hasn't had the heating system serviced in forever. Plus, it's an old building." I wince. "I'm sorry; if you want to head back to your place to get warm, I understand."

A mischievous look crosses his face, one I've grown familiar with over the last couple of months. "Bring it in here, I run hot and can keep you warm." He flips his hands toward him, inviting me to snuggle.

Chest to chest, our body heat mingles, his chin resting on top of my head and his big strong arms wrapping around my body, offering me the comfort and safety only Jon has ever been able to bring. A simple tip of my chin would mean our lips meet, and the pooling heat gathering at my center reminds me of how turned on I am right now. He wraps his leg over mine, so we're completely tangled in each other.

"That better, Angel?" His voice is gruff and heady, drawing me further under his spell. Despite my shitty evening, I can't help but remember the kiss we shared on the waterfront this morning. The intoxicating way his tongue massaged mine. I want to kiss him again.

"Jon," I say, hoping he can decipher my need from his name alone.

"Yeah?" He leans his head down further as I tip my chin up

to his. And then our eyes connect, his steely-gray gaze searing straight through me.

In an instant, our lips are clamped together with a gentle closed-mouth kiss as we enjoy the feel of each other's touch. Jon makes me feel a kind of sexy I never thought possible. His tongue caresses my bottom lip and I part, allowing him to brush slow, gentle strokes against mine. My natural reaction is to let out a needy whimper which is met with a guttural growl from deep within his chest.

Turning me onto my back, all the while keeping our mouths fused together, Jon's upper body hovers over me, his thick fore-arms caging me in on either side. I'm overwhelmed with his presence, and I want more. I want him. I want him to take me, to own my body. To give me what I need. This playboy superstar is slowly winning me over and showing me parts of the man he really is beneath it all, and I want every piece he has to offer.

I know he feels my aching desire as he lifts his head and looks into my eyes, his pupils blown wide from raw hunger. "What do you want, Felicity?" It's a simple question; still, the answer is incredibly complicated.

But the only word my heart and head are screaming is, "You."

He sits back on his heels, his thighs spread slightly apart. "Come here then."

I lean up on my elbows, curious as to what he's doing. Holding out his hands, I place my right palm in his as he pulls me up until I'm straddling him. I can feel his enormous hard length against my heat as he gathers me in his arms.

"Hang on, baby." He reaches down and grabs a stray blanket from the bed, wrapping it around my shoulders. "Better."

His eyes rest atop my head, and I feel a gentle tug as my hair cascades around my shoulders and he smiles as strands of wavy chocolate locks frame my face. "I see you, Felicity, all of you. Inside and out, and you're so unbelievably stunning." He kisses me again, his hand lightly gripping my chin as he works his tongue into my mouth, sending me into sensory overload. I've never been kissed like this. Not even the kisses we've shared before match the urgent nature with which he devours me. "You drive me fucking crazy, Angel. Tell me, is this what you want? Is it too much? I can slow down."

"No, don't stop. More."

He breaks our kiss, his slightly calloused thumb tracing over my bottom lip. "Tell me if it's too much, okay?"

Jon moves with such confidence everywhere in his life, including the bedroom, but I can't ignore the slight tremor racking through his hands as he lays me back down on the bed. "Are you nervous?"

He smiles, the kind that reaches the creases at the corners of his eyes. "A little, yes. You do things to me I can't explain. I just want everything I do for you to be perfect."

"This is perfect." Bringing my hand to the side of his cheek, I hold eye contact to silently tell him I trust he won't take it too far, not tonight.

Our mouths meet once more, but this time his hand runs up my outer thigh as he holds his weight over me on his other arm. His roaming hand pokes beneath the hem of my silk cami as he scrunches the material, tugging it upward before I feel his palm brush the underside of my left breast, and *oh, holy shit.*

It's electric. My nipples harden, and my core pulsates. "Ohmygod, yes!"

He smiles against my mouth, bringing his lips to my neck, where he sucks and lightly bites at my sensitive flesh, navigating his tongue to soothe the slight sting.

"What are you doing?"

"Marking you, Angel. Just claiming what's mine." He pulls back then, looking into my eyes with genuine concern. "Is that, okay?"

I should hate it. After all Elliott has taken. I should never want to be possessed or controlled again, but I don't mind it coming from Jon. Quite the opposite. I love the way he makes me feel. Like I'm his, but rather than as a trophy or belonging, he's honored to hold me, kiss me, and maybe one day even love me. "Keep going."

He wastes no time exploring my body. His hand moves to my other breast, softly kneading and flicking. "I can't wait to suck on these, baby. I'm gonna make you feel so good."

I moan through parted lips, my chest heaving as he sits up, slightly pulling on the bottom of my cami, asking me for permission to remove it. I arch my lower back off the bed, granting him the access he needs. Then my top is swiped clean over my head in a smooth and skillful motion.

He doesn't lower himself back onto me though. Instead, he stays sitting up, his eyes journeying the length of my top half, from my navel to my breasts, leaving a trail of fire along my skin with every inch he consumes. "I-I. Fuck, Felicity. You are...you're something else. Where the fuck have you been?"

"Just here and there, I guess."

"In my fucking dreams more like." He ducks his head, dipping straight for my breasts before he stops once more. "You take my fucking breath away."

Then he sucks me, feasting on my nipples as he releases each one with a pop. Straddling the line perfectly between pleasure and pain. He shifts his whole body, settling between my thighs, where I feel his hard shaft graze my clit.

Even though there are two layers of material separating us, I feel the intensity as if he were inside me, giving me the friction I'm yearning for. "Oh my god, that's incredible. More. Give me more."

He rubs my nipple between his thumb and forefinger while he licks and increases the pace with which he grinds against me. My body is completely at his mercy, primed and ready for him to do what he wants.

Dark wavy hair falls over his slick forehead, resting across his intense, feral eyes. "You're such a greedy girl for me aren't you,

Angel? I love it. Now come, scream my name, and make my wildest fantasies come true."

His filthy mouth sends me over the edge, and I go off like a firework, sparks dancing at the corners of my vision as he delivers the greatest orgasm I've ever experienced. All without ever touching me below the waist.

I'm in so deep with this man, and I'm running out of excuses to deny it.

CHAPTER TWENTY-TWO

JON

What the fuck is that noise?

Prying an eyelid open, I'm immediately met with bright sunshine illuminating the entire room. Jesus, Felicity's blinds are as effective as the heating in this place.

But I can hardly complain given who I'm tangled up with. My girl, the only woman I've ever wanted like this, and here I am, in her bed, having spent the night with her. My face is buried in her silky hair as it cascades across the pillow, infusing my senses with her signature scent. Her body is pressed flush against mine, with my right arm tucked beneath, holding her to me firmly. I woke up this way, and I wonder if subconsciously, I've held her like this all night.

Unsurprisingly I have a raging boner and a serious case of blue balls. My cock is resting against her ass, nestled between her silk-clad cheeks. It's perfection and torture all at the same time. Have I been hard all night? Probably. After I made Felicity come just from sucking her nipples and shamelessly grinding against her like a horny teenager, I pulled her into my arms and held her until she fell asleep. It took me a while to drift off, my mind caught between the realization that I'm finally making progress with the only woman who's ever captured my heart, and murderous thoughts about Elliott, whose face I'd love to connect with my fist right about now. Men, and I use that term loosely, like him give guys a bad name. They don't deserve to breathe the same oxygen as women like Felicity, let alone marry them and get to call them theirs. He treated her like some sort of possession above his fireplace, a pawn in his life, and it pisses me off.

Buzz buzz.

My phone on the nightstand lights up with a text notification.

Carefully, I scoot my arm out from under Felicity and turn to grab it.

> ZACH
>
> I'm in your apartment lobby but apparently you aren't home…?

He sent the text fifteen minutes ago. Shit. I quickly write him back.

> ME
>
> No, I'm out. What's up?

> Was going to take you out for breakfast. Woo you with some pancakes. It's cheat day.

> I'll have to take a raincheck, buddy. I won't be home for a while.

> Where are you?

As my best friend, I hate keeping things from him, but I don't know how much Felicity would be comfortable with me sharing.

> Out. Anyway, why are you on my side of town?

I look at the time. Jesus, it's only just turned eight on a Sunday morning, and he's outside my place?

> It's just hit eight in the fucking morning.

> More to the point, where have you been?

Nice deflection. As you're my bro, and bros tell each other everything, right? I didn't go home last night.

> Who did you go home with?

> ...

I stayed at Amie's.

Ah fuck.

> FFS man.

We didn't fuck.

> Well, that's something.

We just talked, and I took the couch.

> And?

And I don't know. It's all fucked up. Just wanted to clear my head. Hence why I came over to see you.

I look over at Felicity. She's still sound asleep.

> You still around now?

Nah. In an Uber on the way back home.

> I'm headed home for lunch today at Mom and Dad's but could swing by your place for six?

It's a date.

I expect candles and a gourmet meal.

Fuck off. I can't cook for shit. Unlike some.

I'll compromise on tacos.

Done.

See you later and keep your head on until I get there.

Tell Felicity I said hi.

P.S. if you've been texting me while still inside her just know, that sort of shit doesn't get me off.

Fuck off and fuck off.

I close my message thread with Zach and open the other text I received this morning.

MOM

Hey honey. Great game last night, but oh my god, who was that woman you were pictured with? It's all over ESPN! She's beautiful. I'm so proud of you. Please tell me you're still coming over for lunch. I need all the details!

I shake my head. Mom never changes.

ME

Hey Mom, firstly, yes, I'm still coming over for lunch. Secondly, her name's Felicity and it's nothing official.

Yet.

Three dots appear in record-breaking time. Okay, Mom's excited.

> Oh, what a beautiful name! But will it be
> official? Do you like her? She's not another one
> of your women, is she?

The last line of her text twists my stomach into knots. The thought of Felicity being lumped in with my previous women nauseates me.

> No. Definitely not another one of my women.
> We're kind of seeing each other but it's
> complicated.

> Well hold onto this one. I can tell, she's
> different. The media is saying you're in love
> with her, and by the look on your face, I think
> they're right.

Are they right? Maybe. I'm in over my head, I know that much.

> I'll do my best. See you later.

> I'm so happy. My boy's FINALLY been knocked
> on his ass by a woman.

I close out the message thread and smile at the unintentional truth in Mom's words. The way we collided in the hallway, her tiny frame practically sending mine to the ground.

"Morning."

I turn over to find a pair of emerald eyes staring straight back at me. She's wide awake.

How long has she been awake and, shit, did she see any of my text exchange with Mom?

Pushing my paranoia to the back of my mind, I scoot closer so both our heads are on her pillow, lips merely inches apart. "Morning, Angel."

Felicity slaps a palm over her mouth, her eyes going wide. "Oh my god! I must have the worst morning breath."

Like I give a shit when I've got the most beautiful woman lying right beside me.

"Hmmm, I can't smell anything other than coconut but, here, let me check for you." I close the distance between us, bringing one hand to the nape of her neck. Placing a soft kiss across her lips, I brush my nose gently over hers and then scrunch it up in mock disgust. "Yeah, it's terrible. Unbearable in fact."

She swats at my chest, a playful giggle bubbling up. And if it isn't the most beautiful sound I've ever heard.

It's taking every shred of self-control to keep my hands to myself. I might've stolen a quick kiss but the things I want to do to her right now are borderline criminal. Seeing her fresh morning face, hair sprawled across the pillow, and big green eyes staring up at me evokes a response I'm barely able to contain.

I'm not ready to get dressed and leave. I want to spend more time with her. Ride this high I find myself on. But I've gone from having most of the day free to barely any time at all, and today is the last day before I head out with the team for two weeks of away games. Plus, Elliott is still in Seattle, his plane leaving later today.

Taking leave of my senses and without considering the potential complications this could bring I ask, "What do you have planned for lunch?"

FELICITY

"What do you have planned for lunch?"

Well, I was sort of hoping to stay in bed all day with you but...

"Um, nothing I don't think?"

Honestly, I can't recall if I have plans. If you asked me my own name right now, I probably wouldn't be able to tell you. That's the effect this man has on me when I'm in his presence, let alone lying next to him and having spent the night together where he gave me the best orgasm of my life. So yeah, I think it's Felicity Thompson, but who knows at this point? "Why?"

"I've got a stacked day today, but I have a two-week away series starting tomorrow, and I thought maybe we could spend some more time together before I leave. If you want that?"

My heart drops. I completely forgot about his away series. Two weeks seems like an eternity. But I don't let it show and play it as cool as possible. "What do you have in mind?"

Jon shifts slightly, a small v appearing between his brows. "Ah, well this is where it gets interesting."

I arch a brow. "Interesting how?"

"The kind of *interesting* that involves my mom, dad, and possibly my brother."

I fly up to a sitting position, the bedding pooling in my lap. Thankfully Jon handed me my top before we went to sleep last night, so I'm not free and exposed to the morning air. "As in lunch with your family?"

"At my parent's house." Jon sits up alongside me, his rippling bare chest on display.

"You want me to meet your family? Jon we barely—"

"You can come as my friend. We don't have to say any more at this point."

I can feel the panic rising in me. *I can't* meet his family. It's way too soon. We don't even know what we are. This is a bad idea. But then I'm reminded that after today, I won't see him for another two weeks, and a wave of disappointment washes over me. *Just friends.* It could work if we keep it simple. I've been around to Kate's parents' for dinner before. So, this is no different, right?

I drop my head and cover my face with my palms, thinking through my options.

"If you don't want to, it's fine, I get it. I can see you when I get back."

"Okay," I respond.

"Okay?" Jon repeats.

"Yeah, okay. I'll come with you but as friends. *Only* as friends."

His full lips tip up as he pushes my hair back off my shoulders, exposing my neckline, a place I know he discovered last night is hypersensitive for me. Goosebumps erupt where his fingers graze my skin, and as he notices, his eyes drop to my mouth. "You might want to wear something that covers your neck." He part winces, part smiles.

I trace the side of my neck and feel the sensitive skin as delicious memories remind me of how the marks got there.

Jon chuckles deeply and kisses them, a sarcastic lilt to his voice. "Oh, absolutely, only as friends. I'll need to swing by my place on the way to get changed."

I nod and begin climbing out of bed. "Sure. Coffee?"

"The woman of my dreams," Jon replies, leaning back against the headboard, his arms folded behind his head. I can feel his penetrating gaze course through my body as I make my way to the closet, grab my robe, and then head for the kitchen.

JON

ME

Will lunch stretch to another person?

MOM

Oh my god!!

Cool your jets. She's coming as a friend.

A friend? Really, Jon?

Yes, really. Can you contain yourself for a couple of hours or should I revert to the original plan?

No, I mean yes. Yes, I can definitely behave myself.

Good. She's skittish and it's complicated, so just play it cool, okay?

As a cucumber.

Good.

What the fuck am I doing?

CHAPTER TWENTY-THREE

FELICITY

"Must be nice to have your family live so close."

We're in Jon's Mercedes G-Wagon making our way across to his parents' house in Bellevue for lunch, and honestly, I don't know how I'm going to eat a thing. My stomach could go for Olympic gold in gymnastics. I'm so nervous. Even though Jon has promised several times this morning that we're going "as friends," I have no doubt his mom, dad, and probably brother watch ESPN, and there's no hiding the intimate moment we shared at yesterday's game.

It's not that I don't want to be associated with Jon romantically; any woman would give her left tit to be in my shoes. It's more that I don't know his—or my—full intentions at this point. When I left Elliott, I didn't want to jump straight into another relationship. But here I am, feeling like that's exactly what I'm doing. Yet I can't seem to say no or stay away from him, and I get that the feeling is mutual. The way he touched me last night, kissed me, whispered dirty things in my ear. Jon Morgan is slowly weaving himself into every part of my life, and I feel like we've barely scratched the surface.

"Yeah, I got traded from Colorado six years ago to be closer to them. I hadn't really been around since the day I left for college, and my parents needed the support, so I put in a request."

It's a bright and sunny December afternoon. Jon looks glorious, his thick, wavy, dark hair peeking out from under his trademark backward cap. He's gone casual today, wearing a long-sleeved white top and blue jeans. Both must be tailored because they hug every single curve and line of his body. I'm even crushing on his white Nike trainers and aviators. The way he casually holds the steering wheel with one hand, glancing over at me from time to time. It's all too much for my mortal body.

"Tell me more about your family. I feel I need some material before I head into the lion's den." My voice is lighthearted, but I can't deny the element of truth in my words.

Jon switches hands on the steering wheel so his nearest is free. He rests his palm on my knee and begins rubbing soothing circles over my black leggings. Each pass of his thumb radiates tingles straight to my core as I recall his mouth on me last night.

"Not too much to tell. My dad, James, had a regular job before he retired. My mom, Jennie, has been a stay-at-home mom since I can remember. They moved to Bellevue when I bought this house for them a few years back. It was largely to help with caring for Adam."

I'm about to ask more about Adam, but he continues anyway. At the mention of his brother, a proud smile breaks across his face, his dimples popping and on full display. "Adam's autistic, and he has some sensory processing needs too. He lives in an apartment across town with a support worker on hand if he needs them, and generally, he comes home on the weekends. The last house my parents had wasn't suitable for him. It was too small with no space for a sensory room. Plus, he's only a few years younger than me, so he needs his privacy. He can largely look after himself but can get overwhelmed with too many people. He needs peace and alone time to regulate. The outdoors is his sanctuary. He loves birds and wildlife, and this house offers him that. We converted the garage into a self-contained apartment for him."

"Oh, wow, Jon, that's amazing. You did all that for your brother and family."

"It's just money, Felicity. At this point in my life, I have more than I know what to do with. My brother is ten times the man I am. He deserves the world. My parents too."

The way he puts himself down doesn't sit well with me. For a man who's achieved so much, his lack of self-confidence off the ice is a little shocking. "Never underestimate how much good you do and have done for your family. You sound very lucky to have each other."

Without thinking any more about it, I grab his hand from my knee and interlace our fingers, resting it on my thigh.

Jon quickly glances down at our joined hands, his features softening. "Can I tell you something? Well, two things actually."

"Sure, you can."

He hesitates for a brief moment, clearly unsure of his next words. "Number one. I'm not the person they make me out to be. The womanizing cocky bad boy. It's all just a front, you know? Engineered to keep people from discovering that underneath the bravado, I'm pretty weak. A trembling mess consumed by anxiety over mine and my brother's future."

I squeeze his hand tighter. "That doesn't sound like the words of a weak person to me."

He puffs out a breath, one devoid of humor. "So, I've been told before. It's funny though, isn't it? The bad things people say are always easier to believe."

I nod, staring out the passenger window. "I can definitely relate to that."

There are a few beats of silence, but it's not uncomfortable. We simply sit with each other's truths.

"What's number two?" I finally ask, turning back toward him.

"Number two is dependent on number one."

"What do you mean?"

"Because if you're okay with number one, then when we get out of this car, I'd really like to kiss you again."

"IN THE KITCHEN, HONEY."

Stepping through the front door of Jon's parents' house, I'm met with the heavenly scent of home cooking. We take off our shoes at the front door, and Jon takes my jacket, offering a reassuring smile. It's not only the nerves twisting my stomach into knots but also the feeling of a family. The safety and comfort of coming home to Mum and Dad. I miss this.

"They're amazing, and they're going to love you," he whispers in my ear as he guides me down the large entryway toward the back of the house. It's a big corner property with a wraparound porch. The house is painted an ivory color with a red door and two bay windows each with seats, the perfect place to curl up with a book I imagine. The house is classically styled with dark hardwood flooring throughout, and as we make our way down the hallway to the kitchen, I cast a quick glance left and then right into the main living room. There's a feature fireplace along the back, with sky-blue walls and a large cream sofa. I can hear the TV, a hockey game is clearly in progress, albeit it's out of sight. The dining room on the left is already set up, the table laid for royalty. My stomach flips once again. It's clear Jon's mum has gone to a lot of effort.

Entering the kitchen, I'm blown away as it spans the entire width of the property with a garden room attached at the back. The back wall is completely glass, offering an incredible view of the backyard, which is *huge*. Fir trees line the end of a beautiful garden, and to the bottom left I can see a raised pond, and the two acres, by my best guess, are decorated with a combination of camellias, cherry blossoms, and rhododendrons. It's too early in the season for many of the shrubs and flowers to bloom, but I can tell this place is a sensory paradise.

"Oh, honey, it's so good to see you. I've missed you so much." Jennie spins around from the stove where she was stirring a pot and makes a beeline for her son, wrapping her arms around him and pulling his large frame to hers.

I'd say Jennie is no taller than me with shoulder-length dark brown hair not dissimilar to Jon's. When she turns to face me, her gray eyes warm instantly; I can totally see where her son got his looks. She's beautiful.

"You only saw me last week, Mom." Jon kisses her on the cheek before turning to me as well. "Mom this is—"

"Ohmygod, Felicity, it's so amazing to meet you! Ah, you're so pretty!" Her hands fly to her cheeks as she takes me in from top to bottom. "Jon, you never said she was this beautiful."

Jon flushes, and it's possibly the first time I've seen him a little embarrassed. It looks cute on him.

"As a cucumber. Yeah, right." He rolls his eyes and stuffs his hands in the back pockets of his jeans.

"Oh!" Jennie waves her hand in front of her. "Never mind that."

"Mom, this is Felicity, my *friend,* and Felicity this is Jennie, my slightly deranged mom." I don't miss the accented way Jon says friend, but he's sticking to the agreement, and I appreciate that. After all, we aren't anything more and we don't have any other label.

"Nice to meet you, Mrs. Morgan." I go with a traditional greeting and hold my hand out to her with a sweet smile.

"Wait? What! Sh-she's, y-you're, British?" Jennie's mouth hangs open and Jon smirks. He clearly didn't tell her that part.

"All the way from sunny blighty," I say, exaggerating my accent a little.

"So cute!" And with that, Jennie pulls me into the biggest, and possibly tightest, hug of my life. "I love her already!"

"For fuck's sake," I'm sure I hear Jon mutter under his breath. I get the feeling Jennie likes to wind her son up and it would appear she's pretty good at it, too.

"Where's Dad?"

"He's out the back with Adam. They're putting up lights to get ready for the holidays," Jennie finally releases me from her vice-like grip.

"He's home?"

"Yes, honey, he made it back this weekend, but he's only staying tonight. He seems to be in good spirits, but his support worker, Angie, tells me he's had another difficult week," Jennie replies, making her way back to the stove.

"Want to come meet them?" Jon eyes me and tips his head to the back door.

"Yes sure, let me just grab our shoes."

We make our way out the back and across the gravel drive-way, which runs the length of the property. "This is an impressive place."

"Yeah, it's perfect for them. Even though we didn't grow up here, it feels more like home than the previous house ever did. As soon as I bought it, my dad was able to quit work, no longer having a mortgage to pay, and spend time with Mom and Adam. It's the best thing hockey has ever done for my family."

He's incredibly generous. This house is a small estate which no doubt cost more than I will ever see in my lifetime. "It's beautiful. Do you think you'll live here when you're older and you know, your mum and dad pass?" I don't know what makes me ask the question, but from losing my parents so unexpectedly, I guess it's always at the back of my mind.

"No. The house is written into Adam's name." We round the side of the garage. Adam is attempting to detangle a string of lights, and James is halfway up a ladder.

Placing his hand on the small of my back, Jon steps forward a couple more paces. "Alright, you two."

James's head whips around and Adam's eyes shoot up. "Son,

great to see you." His dad's eyes then meet mine. They're a deep-brown color and his hair is even darker, almost black, from what I can tell under his gray baseball cap. I'd pin James at around six-foot-one and Adam at a similar height. However, Adam has the most beautiful blue eyes. I first noticed them when scanning photos at Jon's place, but they're even more striking in real life. His hair is slightly lighter, a mousey brown, tousled and thick. He's a gorgeous man with a chiseled face and strong jaw. In fact, the whole Morgan family is beautiful. There's no doubt they have strong aesthetic genes.

Jon lifts his hand to Adam, offering him a fist bump. "Alright, bro, great to see you."

Adam's eyes dart from Jon to me and then back to Jon again. Initially, I think he's a little overwhelmed with my presence, but then he surprises me and smiles, and oh boy, he has dimples too. Adam's smile reaches his eyes as he returns the fist bump and quickly resets his attention to unraveling lights.

"You must be Felicity," James says as he climbs down the ladder, wiping his hands together before offering one out to me.

"I am; nice to meet you, Mr. Morgan."

James stills and looks across at Jon.

"Yes, she's British. Yes, Mom was shocked, too. And no, she doesn't live in a castle."

James throws his head back and laughs. "I'll assume you've been Jennie'd in that case."

"Yes. She's a liability."

James lets out a knowing laugh. "That she is, but she'll never change."

"Need any help?"

"Ah, no, son, you spend time with your girl. Adam and I have got this covered, haven't we?" James looks over his shoulder at Adam, who's crouched by a box, and he hums in agreement. "Food shouldn't be long, and then we'll be in."

"Okay, I'll take Felicity back inside, but let me know if you need anything."

"Felicity?"

"Yes, Mr. Morgan?"

"Please call us James and Jennie, and it's great to meet you. Never did I think I'd see the day when my son brought a woman home."

I hear Adam snicker from behind his dad, and Jon low groans.

"You too M...James."

CHAPTER TWENTY-FOUR

JON

"Are you into hockey?" Dad asks Felicity.

Lunch was incredible and Mom thankfully kept it light. Homemade chicken noodle and French onion soups, grilled cheese, and salads. I had visions of us sitting down to a Thanksgiving meal but being the incredible cook she is, she can pull off anything and make it five-star. Mom taught me everything I know in the kitchen, and when I was younger, if I wasn't playing hockey with Dad, I'd be helping Mom prep food.

So far, I'd say Felicity has handled the occasion well, although as she sits next to me, I can feel the tension rolling off her. I kind of feel bad throwing her into meeting my parents so last minute, but she's been a champ and smiled through the afternoon. My parents, especially Mom, can be overwhelming, to say the least, and as the day's worn on, she's not reined it in at all. If anything, she's becoming giddier at the thought of me having a girlfriend. I can only hope Felicity isn't scared away, which is a real possibility, and that thought cuts through my bones, leaving me cold.

"Yeah, well sort of. I'm getting more into it now that I have a season ticket to the Scorpions. I got it for my son, Jack, when he turned eighteen. He's playing college hockey and is totally obsessed."

"Oh great. How's his season going?" Anything hockey and Dad's all ears.

She sets her water glass down. "A bit mixed. He seems to be finding his stride though. He's fast on the ice, but his technical skills need work. Although recently they've come on, so he tells me. I'm going to one of his games this weekend."

I look over at her. "You are?"

"Yeah, I'm going to drive over and watch. He needs someone in the stands for him."

"That he does." I smile and squeeze her thigh under the table.

She looks incredible this afternoon; black leggings and a fitted cream fluffy sweater showcase her gorgeous hourglass figure and her hair falls in waves across her shoulders, her scent is driving me crazy. But not as crazy as the knee-high black leather boots she wore out.

Jesus.

When she stepped out of her bedroom, I wanted to turn her around and take her straight back in, lay her down on the bed, and unzip them with my fucking teeth.

I want her so badly.

The taste I got last night has only served to drive me to the edge of my sanity. It took everything in me to hold back from going further last night, and I don't know how much longer I can hold out. I want to be inside her; I need to feel her squeeze around my cock. I need to bury myself in this woman and claim her as mine. I just hope she won't make me wait much longer because I'll wait a lifetime for her. Even if she's my undoing.

"Can I help you with the dishes, Jennie?" Felicity breaks through my haze of dirty thoughts I absolutely should not be having at the table.

Waving a dismissive hand, Mom starts collecting empty

plates. "Oh thanks, honey, but no, you're our guest. Jon, why don't you show Felicity the rest of the house? I'm sure she'd be intrigued to see your old room."

Adam chuckles from the side of the table, his head buried in his phone, but he hears everything that's being said.

"Yeah," Dad cuts in, "We've taken down most of the posters in there, but there's still one or two left up. I'm sure she'd enjoy seeing your previous interests."

The "posters" he's referring to are of my boyhood crush, Pamela Anderson. Given the fact they've only lived here six years, I'm confused as to why those posters have made a reappearance. I swear to God my parents collectively set out this morning to embarrass the shit out of me. Too bad at thirty-four I've passed that point, but I guess this is the first chance they've had to make me blush in front of a girl since I've never brought one home before.

Plastering on an unaffected smile I place my hand on Felicity's lower back and guide her out of the room. When she's out the door and safely out of eyeline, I turn back to face my family and flip them the bird. Dad throws his head back in laughter, practically choking on his water.

Instant karma.

I GLANCE at my watch and notice it's now five. Shit. I need to be over at Zach's in an hour. I spent the last thirty minutes showing Felicity my old room. She asked me about every single one of the trophies and medals stacked in my cabinet, carefully reading the engravings. I was going to store them at my place, but Mom wanted to keep them here, a reminder of what I achieved when I was younger. True to form, two posters had been hung back up and it wouldn't surprise me if it was Adam's doing. I've got to hand it to him, he's always had the knack of winding me up; call it sibling intuition.

"Where's Felicity?" I ask Mom as I exit the downstairs bathroom. After the house tour, I took a call from my agent that couldn't wait, and Felicity wandered back downstairs.

"She's out in the backyard with Adam, honey. They've been out there for a good while now."

"With Dad?"

"No. Just them."

I peer over Mom's shoulder to find Felicity and Adam standing at the raised Koi Pond. Adam's bent over, pointing at something, an animated look on his face, and Felicity matches his level of enthusiasm. The pair look like kindred spirits, each as engrossed as the other. I can't recall the last time I've seen my brother so engaged with another person; let alone someone he's only just met. He's always preferred his own space.

"I think you might have a little competition for her attention." Mom's teasing tone penetrates my trance.

A smile pulls at my lips as I continue to watch them. "Yeah. Have they been like this for a while?"

"Yes, well, initially he was showing Felicity the waxy leaves on the camellia. They were both feeling them. Then they moved onto the fir trees. Adam then pulled her across to the pond, and they've been there ever since." Mom pauses, shaking her head in wonderment. "She's really something, isn't she?"

"Amazing." I'm still staring at the woman who seems to capture the attention and hearts of everyone she meets.

This woman. If I wasn't completely gone before, I sure as hell am now.

"Thanks for coming today," I say to Felicity as we make our way back to downtown Seattle.

"I enjoyed myself. Your family is lovely."

I know I'm lucky to have them in my life.

Felicity turns on my playlist but keeps the volume low, and Ed Sheeran's "Lego House" starts playing softly through the speakers. "You like Ed Sheeran?"

"Don't tell me you're going to trash him as well as Miley? I don't think my heart can take it."

She laughs, a sound that makes my heart swell once again. "No, I love him. He often joins me on my end-of-week wine dates."

What the fuck? "Huh? Is that some random British saying?"

She laughs again, pressing her palm to her sternum.

"Alright, Mary Poppins, it's not that funny." Fuck knows where that came from, but her posh British accent, flawlessly pretty face, and dark hair kind of remind me of her, along with the fucking massive tote bag she carries around everywhere she goes.

She whips her head over to find a shit eating grin on my face. "Oh no, you didn't. Joker." She then turns the volume up louder on Ed.

I immediately reach over and turn it down, sensing my opportunity to push a little further.

"What are your plans for the holidays, Mary?"

She casts a glance over her shoulder to the empty back seats. "What're you doing?"

"Just checking for someone called Mary."

I tap my fingers on the steering wheel. "Are you going to stop being a naughty girl?"

Felicity shrugs innocently. "Didn't think I was."

I switch lanes and then throw a quick, heated glance her way. "Oh, you are. And that's punishable behavior in my book."

Her mouth forms a perfect "o" and the apples of her cheeks pinken.

My dick twitches at the sight of her lips parted like that. "Can you not?"

"Not what?"

I shift in my seat, trying to get myself comfortable with an ever-hardening dick. "Hold your mouth like that."

She drops her head down, her shoulders shaking with laughter. "Aw, does it make you uncomfortable?"

"You could say that."

And then she does something I really, *really* wasn't expecting. Placing her left hand on my inner thigh, she slowly runs her palm up from my knee to my groin, her fingers dancing and teasing as she makes her ascent.

"Fuck." I throw my head back into my seat, gripping the steering wheel with white knuckles. "You're gonna make me crash, Angel."

"So, it's Angel now? Is that my bad girl name?"

A low growl escapes my chest. "Don't push me, not unless you're prepared."

That's met with an evil chuckle, but she takes mercy on me, stilling her hand mid-thigh.

Trying to gather myself and regain some control behind the wheel on a freeway. "You haven't answered my question."

It's as if the playful, flirty, steamy Felicity leaves the car. Taking her hand back, she twists her fingers together on her lap, dropping her head so her hair falls in front of her face. "Heading home for a few days and coming back New Year's Day."

I sort of expected her to say that. Why wouldn't she be going home to see Darcy and her family? "Okay," I say, drawing the word out to indicate my confusion at her sudden shift in mood.

"I'm desperate to see Darcy. Jack's coming home with me too. We fly out on Christmas Eve."

Then it hits me. The potential source of her discomfort. "Where will you be staying?"

She pales slightly, turning her face to catch my straining jaw.

"Where are you staying, Felicity?" I bite out, more of a demand than a question at this point but I'm far from anything but concerned for the woman I care so deeply about.

"In Oxford."

"Where in Oxford?"

Her voice is barely audible, "My old house."

My stomach falls through the floor as both anger and, I'm not ashamed to admit, jealousy coarse through me. "With *him?*"

Growing defensive, she replies. "Well, yes. It's what Darcy wants, for us to be together on Christmas morning, and I put my children first."

When I was eighteen, I was more interested in going out, playing hockey, and spending time with friends. "Has Darcy specifically told you that? Won't she be with Liam most of the time?"

"Well, no. Sort of. Elliott's been texting me, telling me I owe it to the kids to give them the Christmas they deserve."

Emotionally manipulative bastard.

I'm desperate for her to see what Elliott's game is. "So, stay somewhere else and go see them in the morning. You can't stay in *that* house. With *him*. I see you, baby. I've seen what he does to your confidence, the way he speaks to you. Can't you see what he's doing even now? He's got you like a puppet on a string. Using your children to manipulate you. Christ, he told you he wants you back. Can't you see?"

Sitting on her hands to prevent the nervous fidgets I've just made her aware of, she shakes her head. "I've nowhere else to stay."

"Friends?"

"Haven't got any back there. They were all affiliated with our marriage."

Jesus, he's a fucking narcissist, cutting her off from all connections. "Then stay with your mom and dad." He can't possibly have turned them against her too.

"Can't," is all I get back in a clipped and defeated tone.

"What do you mean you can't? Even if they're away, stay at their house."

"Because they're dead, okay? They're gone. Both of them.

Eight years ago, they both died of cancer. I sold the house because Elliott said it was a structural liability and the garden was too big to manage."

A sob breaks free as she spins her body around to face the passenger window and my heart plummets. It hits the fucking floor, ricocheting around my ribcage on the way down. She lost her mom and dad, at thirty-one, in the same year. I don't have words and frankly, how can anything I say next do justice to what she's been through? So instead, I act like the dickhead I am and say in a soft tone, "You can't stay there, Felicity."

She ignites. Like a wild animal backed into a corner, she rears up, throwing her arms in the air. "Well, funnily enough, Jon, you don't own me. You don't get to tell me what I can and can't do and who I can and can't stay with. I mean, ugh, what are we even doing here? What is this?" She furiously motions between the two of us. "Do you not see the irony? You question his controlling and borderline abusive actions, and all the while, you're telling me who I can see and where I can go for the holidays. No one owns me like that."

Her words hit me like bullets. She's right. I'm acting like a total asshole, but the inner need buried within me to protect this woman wins out. I draw in a calming breath and finally say, "It isn't borderline abuse, Felicity. You physically shake whenever his name is mentioned. Has he ever touched you?"

Her sobbing shoulders still. "What do you mean? I've had two children with him."

"You know exactly what I mean. Has he ever *hurt* you?"

"No." Somehow, despite Elliott being the lowest version of a man I can think of, I believe her. "Okay."

We drive the rest of the way in silence. Unlike previous times where we've sat comfortably in each other's presence, this time it's unbearable. The air is charged with our joint anger and frustration. But mostly at this point, I feel sad, desperate for the loss of her parents, and destroyed by her tears. The thought that I caused her to cry makes me ache.

I pull up outside her apartment block and cut the engine. I don't want to leave, but I have twenty minutes to make a thirty-minute journey to Zach's, and I can't let my best friend down again.

Unbuckling her seat belt, Felicity wipes at her cheeks. "Thank you for today."

She reaches for the door handle, but I stop her, gently grasping her other arm at the elbow.

"Look, I'm sorry. You're right. I can't and don't have any right to tell you what to do. But know this, if you were mine, then things wouldn't be any different. I'd still let you know that I didn't like you spending time with that asshole because he hurts you, but I would never, *ever* try to control you. I just want you to be safe and happy. What happened to your mom and dad, shit, I'm so sorry, Felicity."

My words are sincere, but I can tell they do nothing to penetrate the walls she's rebuilt back around her once more. Her face is expressionless as she nods her head in acknowledgment and reaches for the door of my car. "Thank you, Jon. Good luck with your away series."

And then she's gone. Shutting my car door and walking to the entrance of her apartment building. Leaving me in a state of shock, sadness, and fury. How the fuck did the best twenty-four hours of my life go so wrong in the space of ten minutes? One thing I am sure of though is that I can't bear to see her hurt or upset in any way, and I'll do everything I can to show her how much she means to me. I pray to God that one day I'll call her mine, but I know right here and now she'll own my heart for a lifetime.

CHAPTER TWENTY-FIVE

FELICITY

M y self-pitying routine goes something like this.

Me, slumped on the sofa, a tub of Ben & Jerry's in hand, generally cookie dough, with Ed Sheeran serenading me.

Ugh. I'm so pissed. But you know what's worse? The fact that every time I recall reasons why I am pissed at him, my resolve weakens, and I begin questioning exactly what it is he did wrong. The fact is, he's concerned about me staying with Elliott. Well, based on the evidence, I'd say he's got good reason to be. He's also concerned that Elliott's using Jack and Darcy against me. He's probably right about that too. And the fact that Elliott wants me back? Well, he did tell me just that less than twenty-four hours ago, in this very room, right in front of Jon. The more I search for reasons to be annoyed at the muscled, gorgeous, and protective hockey player, the more I come up wanting.

So yes, I'm pissed off, but mostly at myself for snapping in the car and practically comparing him to my ex-husband. He's nothing like Elliott. Everything Jon does is without an agenda. His acts are selfless and authentic and what do I go and do?

Push him away.

I wouldn't be surprised if that's the last time I see him outside of the hockey arena.

Ping.

Spoon hanging halfway out of my mouth, I sit up and look for my phone. It's unlikely to be Jon. He looked just as pissed as I did when he drove off, and I imagine Zach has already advised him to keep his distance.

KATE

I haven't heard from you since last night at Riley's. Tell me you are okay.

ME

Yes and no, but it's got nothing to do with last night.

Okay. What's happened?

Honestly, I don't want to talk about it, but suffice to say my Jon Morgan era is likely over.

I highly doubt that.

Oh, trust me, you didn't see me earlier.

I still highly doubt it.

Why?

Girl, does it really need spelling out for you? You're thirty-nine.

Apparently, it does.

The man is infatuated with you. Obsessed. Like, gone for you. It will take more than a hissy fit to drive that man away. (I assume that's what's happened).

Yes.

Thought so.

I decide it's time to turn the spotlight on my best friend.

> So where did you end up last night? Your last known whereabouts was Jensen's knee.

> Your arms around his neck.

> Sucking his face.

> While wearing his jersey.

Can we not?

> Not what?

Talk about him.

> Oh, Kate.

All I'll say is this…

Number one, he's a dickhead.

Number two, he's a dickhead.

Number three, he's a…you get the point.

> What did he do?

More like who did he do? Last thing I saw was him leaving Riley's with a redhead.

> WHAT?! He was with you.

Yeah, well we sort of had a disagreement. It was stupid. I stormed off and the next thing I know, he's moved on.

So, he's a dickhead.

> Clearly! And what were you doing while he was getting into it with Red?

That's beside the point.

Kate.

...

Talking.

To?

An attractive male.

So, you tried to make him jealous?

It just happened. I went to get a drink and the next thing I knew a tall, dark guy called...(okay I can't remember his name), started talking with me.

Convenient.

Yes, very.

Anyway, whatever. He slept with someone else the day I tried to make my move and wear his jersey. I curled my hair and wore my best jeans and everything. I'm over it.

As long as you're okay.

I am. Glad you are too, and trust me—all will be fine with Jon.

Ugh, if you say so. See you tomorrow?

Yeah, but I've got an appointment first thing. Lunch?

You read my mind.

XOXO

XOXO

AN HOUR later I'm at the gym, killing myself on the treadmill. Anything to relieve stress and work off the copious calories I just inhaled courtesy of my ice cream addiction. I wasn't lying when I told Jon I work out to Marilyn Manson. Somehow his angry and explicit vibes make me pound the treadmill harder. Intense, but I've never been able to come to the gym and "take it easy." I guess it's partly my way of coping when life gets a bit manic or tough. When my parents died, I practically lived in the cardio suite.

Returning home, I drop my gym tote to the ground along with my yoga mat. I always finish any gym session with ten minutes of stretching. It helps reduce sore muscles, and let's be honest, I'm not exactly twenty-one anymore, so still being able to touch my toes is a win in my book.

I haven't heard from Jon all evening, and I'm not surprised. The more I analyze my behavior and the way I went off at him, the more I've convinced myself he's run for the hills. I could lie, trick myself into believing it's for the best, but the truth is, if I never heard from him again, I'd be devastated. I never felt for Elliott what I feel for Jon. As clichéd as it may be, I now know precisely what they mean when they talk about butterflies and swooning. Jon Morgan embodies dream-man characteristics, and even if he doesn't see it in himself, he is the ultimate catch. Not because he's super wealthy, famous, or hot. *Okay, maybe it's a little bit to do with his abs.* But rather because of everything I never expected him to be. Kind, caring, protective, and funny. Off the ice, he is so much more than what people see through the plexi-glass, and I suspect he's quickly become someone I could never live without, as scary as that thought is.

Knock knock.

I'm post-gym and pre-shower, which isn't a great combina-tion. I wasn't expecting anyone. Maybe it's Kate and Taylor with another round of wine and movie night? I'm hardly dressed for it in black Nike gym shorts and a matching sports bra. Throwing on a pink hoodie to cover up, I slide across the two deadbolts and swing the door open. It isn't Kate and Taylor waiting for me on the other side, nor is it my friendly pizza delivery guy who I've been known to, once or twice, order from and then forget they're coming.

It's none of them.

"Alright, Mary."

Jon stands at the entrance to my apartment, his arms above his head, braced on either side of my door frame. His biceps bulge and strain against the simple black T-shirt he's since changed into. His tailored black jeans are clearly made to measure, hugging his thighs and calves to perfection. Let's not mention the black backward cap he's wearing, because I swear, he does it only to tease me, and it works. And those butterflies? Well yep, they're here and doing the tango.

"Mary isn't here; you must have the wrong place," I reply, an involuntary smile breaking out over my face as I cross my arms and lean against my wall, giving him the space to enter. I'm excited but mostly relieved to see him, having convinced myself I'd blown whatever we had.

"Oh, she's definitely here," he remarks as he walks past me and into the hallway.

Kicking off his gray Converse, he pulls my body to his as he wraps an arm around my waist. His familiar spicy cologne sends shockwaves through my body, pooling at my heat, and I fall into his embrace.

Kicking the door shut behind him, he places a kiss on my forehead before dropping his to mine until our noses brush. "I've been over this so many times in my head."

"Over what?"

"This. What I want to say." With a steadying breath he continues, "I have no idea what I'm doing here, Felicity. I've got no experience with women other than how to please them in bed. I don't know if I'm what you want, but I also don't think I'm a bad bet. You rock my world, consume my thoughts, and make me feel like I can be a better person. It's like you're the antidote to my demons, and I'm hooked."

I don't know what to say, so I don't say a word. Instead, the silence is replaced by a pounding sensation, and at this point, I'm not sure if it's my heart or Jon's.

"Date me."

"W-what?"

"Date me, Angel. Let me show you how a man should be. Let me hold you, kiss you, take you out, and spoil you. Let me call you mine because, *goddammit,* I need to call you mine."

I shake my head in disbelief. "I, Jon—"

He cuts me off, and his hands fly to cup my face as he holds my gaze intensely, his piercing gray eyes searching mine. "I know you've sworn off relationships and with that guy you call your ex, I'm not surprised. But don't let him ruin what I know could be something amazing between us."

I bring my hand to his cheek.

"I'm going all in here, Felicity. I don't know if it's going to backfire and crush me, but I have to try. I need to try with you." He closes his eyes and rests his forehead back against mine. I can see the anguish written across his face as he waits for my answer, but really, there was only ever going to be one outcome. Yes, it's so soon after my breakup and yes, I swore off relationships wanting to choose my independence first, but honestly, I've never felt so free as when I'm with Jon.

"Okay."

He pulls back, hands grasping my shoulders. "Okay? As in okay, okay?"

I smile up at him. "As in okay, okay."

Before I know it, I'm seeing my hallway from upside down as he marches toward my bedroom.

"Jon, I just got back from the gym." I giggle.

"And it's driving me crazy. I need to taste you."

"T-taste me?"

He throws me on top of my bed, ripping his shirt over his head. There's a sense of urgency to him I've never seen before, almost like a starved wild animal finally unleashed on its prey. And I have a feeling that prey is me.

"Do you trust me, Angel?"

"Yes," I gasp.

"Then let me make you feel all the things I already know about you."

Oh.

God.

"Sit up."

Slowly unzipping my hoodie, he bites down on his bottom lip as he drinks me in. Next, my sports bra is lifted, his fingers caressing my skin as he guides it over my head, leaving me bare from the waist up.

"You ready to let me take control?"

A delicious shiver racks through my body. "You like to be in control?"

"With you, I'll be anything. But yes, I like to dominate."

My heart pounds in my chest at the thought. "Then dominate me."

Pinned to the mattress, my arms above my head, Jon holds me by the wrists as he straddles my body, his jeans and belt undone at the waist and hanging open. He's gentle in his touch but assertive enough to leave no question as to who's in charge.

My bedroom is lit only by moonlight and the streetlamps below. "I haven't closed my blinds."

Pressing a searing kiss to my lips, he replies, "Let them see how I take my girl."

My girl. I guess I am now and that thought pools between my thighs.

Standing off the bed, Jon pushes his jeans all the way down, his boxer briefs following closely behind.

His huge, hard cock is perfectly straight and thick, jutting up and resting just below his navel.

Wow.

"Oh. My. God."

He pumps his cock slowly, dragging his fist from base to tip as he stares down at me. I'm topless and lying across my bed. "Not God, Angel. Just me."

"You are, um, you're huge." My mouth feels dry, a complete contrast to my throbbing center.

He smirks as he stares down at me with blazing intensity. "Stroke a man's ego."

But there's no other way to describe him. I have very little experience to compare, but I know when a man is well endowed, and Jon is top of the class.

Still standing over me, his fist wrapped around his cock, he rasps, "What do you have on under those illegal shorts?"

"A thong," I reply, thumbs tucked under my waistband, teasing him just a little more.

He throws his head back and growls, the sound reverberating off the walls. "Let me see."

Pushing my thumbs down further, I peel the Lycra shorts away from my body, arching my back off the bed as I do. I'm laid bare other than my baby pink thong as I look up at Jon, who continues to hover.

"Take that off, too." He's pumping himself faster as beads of pre-cum emerge.

Pinning my bottom lip between my teeth, I'm loving the way his eyes make me feel. Sexy, wanted, alive. I drop my thong to the floor and return my arms above my head, waiting for my next instruction.

"Christ, Felicity. My dreams could never do you justice."

Our lips connect as he crawls over my body, both of us naked and on top of the cover.

"Are you cold?"

"No, burning up." And I am. I'm on fire, lit with need.

"Spread your legs for me, Angel. I want to feel your sweet pussy in my mouth."

I inch my legs apart, trying to hide my hesitancy but Jon notices, his blown pupils constricting at my unease.

"I've never done this before."

He lifts his head from between my breasts where he was kissing a moment earlier. "No one's ever gone down on you before?"

I shake my head.

He smiles and there's a slight smugness to his grin, but I can tell he's shocked at my admission. "So I'll be your first?"

"Elliott never did that for me. The other way around, yes. But never for me."

"Then he's even more of an asshole and a fool than I thought. This body, Angel, deserves to be devoured. And by the time I'm finished with you, that perfect halo of yours will be crooked."

"What are you going to do with me?" I play to his need to dominate.

Can smiles be filthy? Well clearly, they can because his lips pull into a wicked grin, his right hand coming between my thighs. "Don't be shy and spread these properly for me, baby, and you'll find out."

As I part my legs, my hands still pinned above my head, Jon trails his fingers up the inside of my thigh. "What am I going to find up here?" he rasps into the shell of my ear.

I can't find it in me to reply, my voice overpowered with need.

"Use your words, Angel. Tell me what I'm going to find up here?"

I gulp, hard. "M-my pussy."

His mouth makes its way back to my collarbone as he starts placing open mouth kisses where he's quickly learned my body responds most. Truth is, I respond to everything he does; it's like we're in perfect synchronization, and he knows what I want more than I do. "That's right, and do you know what I'm going to do to your pussy tonight?"

I shake my head, already feeling the unbearable ache building. "No."

"I'm going to taste it."

"Please," I beg, the intensity of his words and touch proving too much.

"Please what?"

"Please t-taste me."

No sooner have the words left my mouth than I feel the pressure of two thick fingers against my entrance. I'm so wet, he enters with ease, his fingers scissoring as he pumps them for the first time.

"Oh fuck, you're so wet for me." He curls his fingers on the second pump, finding that spot I've always struggled to reach myself. My hips shoot off the bed in response. I've lost total control of my body and mind.

"You like that, Angel? Do you like my fingers in that tight, wet cunt of yours? Because I love it." My wetness is audible in an otherwise silent room. "That noise, the sound of your tight wet pussy taking my fingers, I've imagined it every time I've fantasized about you, but nothing could compare to the real thing. Now tell me, are you close?"

My toes curl and when he releases my wrists and my arms fly down, fisting the bed sheets. "I'm going t-to come."

I crash over the edge. It's the most powerful orgasm I've ever had. I've never been noisy in bed but tonight, I scream Jon's name as his thumb slowly rubs circles over my sensitive clit. Drawing his fingers out, he sits up on his knees. "Eyes on me, Angel. I want you to watch the first time I taste you." He brings his fingers to his mouth, dripping with my arousal, and as he sucks on each one in turn, he never takes his eyes from mine, and I swear I come again at that sight alone. "You're so sweet, baby, I think you should taste too." He leans down and traces the only finger he's yet to suck across my lips and I part, taking it into my mouth and tasting myself. "Good girl."

"On your knees for me, Felicity. I'm not done with my meal." The use of my name melts my bones. I'm a puddle, fighting to obey his commands. Desperate for him to touch me again.

Once on all fours, I push away feelings of self-consciousness. He can see every part of me, but somehow, I've never felt more at ease. I trust him, and I want this. I want him.

"Jesus, I wish you could see yourself right now. This glistening pussy." He swipes his fingers through my heat and brings one to his mouth again. "I'm starving and you taste. So. Fucking. Good."

I cry out, sensitive from my last high and desperate for more. "Ohmygod, Jon. More."

"Do you know how fucking amazing it feels to hear my name on your lips as you come apart for me? Do you know how many times I've gripped and stroked myself thinking about the way my name would tumble from your lips?"

"Me, too." I gasp.

In response he unleashes an almighty growl as he places a hand on each of my ass cheeks, parting me wider. "Oh, baby, you are so beautiful."

He eats me out like I'm the last thing he'll ever taste, his tongue flat as it swipes from my clit all the way to the tight hole no one has ever touched. He pierces my pussy with his tongue. "I could feast on you for hours, but I want you to come for me. Explode in my mouth, baby."

He continues to devour me in long skillful strokes, sucking on my clit as he passes over it. He knows exactly what I want and when I need it. "Argh, Jon!" I come undone at the seams, my face buried in the bed, my hands gripping onto something, anything to steady myself.

As I ride my orgasm, I feel his finger press slightly against my ass. "That's a good girl for me, Angel, and one day I'll take you here if you want me to."

I want him to take me any way he wants. Any last shred of willpower to resist has long left the building. "Yes," I reply. "But I want you to fuck me."

He turns me back over, so we're face to face with his hands on my waist and when I set eyes on him, he's shaking his head. "Not tonight, Felicity."

My heart drops. Why not tonight? He had no problem fucking other women he'd never see again. So why not me? What's wrong with me? "Why not?" I ask, rejection creeping up my spine.

Pulling me to his body, I'm now straddling him in the same way we did last night, Jon on his knees, my legs wrapped around his hips. "Because I can't stay tonight." My heart drops further at the thought of the loss. "I need to leave my place at five in the morning, and there's no way I'm fucking you to then just leave you. I couldn't help but have a taste of you tonight." He tucks a strand of hair behind my ear and kisses my cheek softly. "I can't fuck you and then disappear for two weeks. The first time I take you, I want to do it again and again and again, and then I want to hold you all night and have you again in the morning."

My heart catches in my throat. I can't be pissed or disappointed. As much as I want him, I know he's right. "Let me do something for you then," I offer.

Jon pulls back, putting some space between us as he grips my shoulders. "I don't expect anything from you, Angel. What I did tonight was as much for me as it was for you. Watching you fall apart was heaven for me." He glances at my nightstand, my alarm clock reading eleven p.m. "I have to go. I need to pack and grab at least a few hours before I head out for the flight."

I shake my head. "It's so late, you have barely any time to sleep."

With a smile that reaches his eyes, his face looks lighter than ever. "I'll catch up on the plane and trust me, it was worth it. Because tonight, I got to see my girl come apart for me, and I got to call her mine."

He places a gentle kiss on my lips and reaches down to his jeans, tugging at the pocket. "Take this and use it while I'm away."

I blink a couple of times, my eyes barely registering the black fob in his hand. "What's this?"

"A key to my place."

I shake my head, pointing at the key. "I can't take this."

"Take it, Felicity. Stay when you want, sleep in my bed, eat my food. I've stocked the fridge and cupboards with everything you like, including those disgusting black olives." He shudders.

I laugh and throw my arms around his neck. "You didn't have to do that for me."

Summoning his best British accent, he replies, "Oh, but I do, Your Highness." Besides, this place is cold and unsafe. It was easy for me to get past the entrance and to your door tonight. I don't like being anywhere let alone across the country knowing you aren't sleeping somewhere secure."

I roll my eyes. "I've lived here for eight months without an issue."

"Until your ex showed up at your door. No one will get past security at my place. They're expecting you. Just take the damn key, baby. Please."

The last thing I want is for Elliott to show up unannounced again. I take the key from his palm and smile. "Okay, I'll think about it."

He kisses me gently on the edge of my jaw, and my body lights up. "My place isn't far from your work and my private driver, Gerard, will take you wherever you need to go."

With one last kiss pressed to my lips, he eases out from underneath me and reaches for his clothes. "This isn't about me owning or trying to tell you what to do. I just want to protect and care for my girlfriend. I've spent too long chasing you to blow it. I want to give you everything you deserve."

My stomach fully flips. "You, Jon, you are everything I deserve."

CHAPTER TWENTY-SIX

JON

There was a time when I loved away games.

The longer we were on the road the better. A time to play, party, and hook up with gorgeous women. But things have changed and being away from Felicity raises my blood pressure in ways I never expected.

We've been on the road for five days now. We played and beat Cincinnati by three goals. I played okay, but my mind has been elsewhere. Felicity has yet to stay at my place despite my pleading with her to use my apartment as if it were her own. When I gave her that fob on Sunday night, I told her it was for while I'm away but truthfully, I want her to keep it indefinitely. If I had my way she'd be moved in by now. Her skincare on my bathroom counter, her tote bags cluttering my otherwise tidy apartment. On my visits to her place, I've noticed she's a bit messy, jackets thrown over her couch, bags and endless shoes tossed by the door. By nature, I'm neat and organized and everything has its place, but I'll happily sacrifice my obsessive ways to have Felicity's chaos greet me as I walk through the door each night. She is my calm in the chaos.

I pull out my phone and type a text to the woman I can't stop pining over.

ME

Are you at my place?

ANGEL

Nope, I'm still at work.

I look at the time. It's half past nine here, making it half past seven in Seattle. Why is she still at work?

It's half past seven there. Aren't you heading home?

Yep, just finishing up on a case for Monday morning.

I'm going to stay at your apartment for the weekend. I'm heading there now.

Relief floods my veins. Finally, she'll be out of that place and in the safety of mine. My cock hardens at the thought of her in my bed, hair cast across my pillow. If only I were in there with her.

Good. How are you getting there?

I know she won't have Martha with her as she walks the short distance to work each day. Old habits die hard with Felicity and as much as she drives me crazy worrying over her, I love her strength and independence, it's sexy as hell.

Several minutes pass and I drum my fingers on the hotel lobby bar. Taking another sip of my beer, I grow impatient and type out another message.

Gerard can come and get you.

It's fine—I can get the bus.

Fuck, no.

Too late. Gerard's on his way ;)

I ping a text across to Gerard asking him to pick Felicity up from her office and take her to my apartment with a stop along the way.

You're incorrigible.

You love it.

Silence.

Shit.

Was it the use of the L-word? My knee bobs up and down on the bar stool as I grip my phone waiting for her response. It must be ten minutes before she begins typing again.

Gerard's here. I gotta go.

Message me when you get home so I know you're safe.

ANGEL

So, on the way, Gerard said we needed to make a stop. Next thing I know I'm in some swanky spa.

I SMILE down at my phone. I'm back in the hotel room I'm sharing with Zach.

"You look mighty pleased with yourself," Zach comments, looking up from his laptop.

"Just treating my girl," I reply.

> **ME**
> Did you enjoy it?

How could I not? Hot stone massage, facial, and a manicure. Did you have this whole thing planned out?

No. I called in a few favors last minute. I've helped promote their skincare range on more than a few occasions, so a last-minute twilight package wasn't difficult to pull off.

> I'm glad you enjoyed it. I miss you.

I did. I miss you too. Just got my chamomile tea (yes, I'm a grandma) and got into bed, which by the way, is like a bloody cloud.

> You'd be more comfortable with me underneath you.

The thought of Felicity climbing into my bed in her silky sleep shorts sends pressure straight to my cock. Jesus.

Hmmm...no, I still think the mattress wins.

> Keep talking like that and I'll have to punish you when I get home.

I wonder if Felicity likes to be spanked. Fuck me, I hope so.

I'm a good girl. I don't need to be punished.

> We'll see about that. Are you warm?

I am, but where is your TV? I thought you'd have one in your bedroom.

Laughing to myself, knowing she'll have no clue, I pull up

Felicity's contact and hit dial. After a couple of rings she answers.

"Is it just your big TV in the living room?"

I laugh. "Look up for me. Do you see it?"

"Look at wh- Oh, that?"

"Yes, that. If you look above the nightstand, you'll see some controls to lower the projector. That's your TV. It'll come right down above the fireplace. Which is worked by the remote set in the holder by my side of the bed."

"Wait, your bedroom TV is a projector?"

"Yes."

"Could you be anymore extra?"

A smile traces my lips. "I could try."

I hear a ruffling of sheets.

"Jesus, Jon. It's huge."

My smile grows wider. "You've already told me that, Angel."

"I'm rolling my eyes right now."

"Yes, I know it is, but I use it to watch game footage and movies. I need my movies."

"Oh yeah, what do you have loaded on this thing?"

"It's all Netflix."

A few more beats pass.

"Hang on. This is all chick flicks. *Bridesmaids, Pretty Woman, Bridget Jones*...Jon, are you a rom-com man?"

"*Bridesmaids* is one of the finest movies of our time." I look over at Zach. He's not moved or batted an eyelid. He knows me.

"Aw, you old softie. Well, I wish you were here with me. I'm heading straight into *Bridesmaids*."

My mind immediately takes me to images of Felicity in my bed, in one of her tiny sleep sets, curled up watching Bridesmaids.

Jesus.

My voice is low and gruff, "You don't know how much it's killing me knowing you're in my bed, and I can't touch you."

Out of the corner of my eye, I see Zach put his headphones

on. He knows the score, something I've done for him many times.

"Is that so?" she replies in a teasing tone, and I hear more sheets rustling like she's adjusting herself under the covers.

I low groan, needing to be there with her so badly. So, I go for the next best thing. "Forget the film, Angel; let me entertain you."

"Oh yeah? And how do you plan on doing that?"

"Are you wearing those cute silky sleep shorts I love?"

I hear soft giggles and my dick goes from a semi to a full-on rock. "Yes, why do you ask?"

"Hang on." I stand from my bed and head for the bathroom, needing total privacy.

Once inside I prop my phone between my ear and shoulder and lean on the counter. "Take them off for me."

More rustling.

"I'm just slipping them down my legs now."

I squeeze my eyes shut, determined not to blow straight in my pants. "And that cami too if you have it on. I want you totally naked in my bed tonight. Because that's the only way you'll ever sleep in there."

"Okay, it's all off."

"Are you wet for me, Angel? Are you turned on knowing how hard I am for you right now?"

She gasps, "Yes."

"Tell me how wet you feel."

"So wet, Jon."

"Are you touching that pretty pussy of yours?"

"Not yet."

"Good. Because you're going to touch yourself exactly as I would if I were right next to you. Can you do that for me?"

She whimpers in response to my words, "Okay."

"Good girl. I want you to slide one of those pretty fingers through that gorgeous cunt of yours until you find your swollen aching clit."

"Mmm-hmm, yes."

"Is it aching for me, Angel?"

She gasps, "Yes."

I palm my cock through my pants and reach for the zipper, desperate to free myself and search for a release.

"I want you to rub and circle your clit until your legs shake, until you can't take it anymore."

I step out of my pants and push down my boxer briefs immediately fisting my cock. Christ, it's so fucking hard. I've never been this hard for a girl before. I begin to pump slowly.

"Are you touching yourself too?" she asks in a breathless voice.

I low chuckle. "How can I not? My girl's in my bed getting herself off."

"And it's so good, Jon."

I swipe my palm over the head, pre-cum leaking out. "Are you nearly there?"

"Nearly."

"I want you to press two fingers inside your tight pussy and imagine that's my tongue, eating you out."

"Ohmygod."

"Oh, baby, I can taste you right now, how sweet you are as you squirt on my tongue. God, I want you to soak my face. I want you dripping from my mouth."

All I can hear are more whimpers and quick gasps. "I want your mouth on me."

"And it will be. As soon as I walk through that door, I'm going to sit you on my kitchen counter, rip your clothes off, and eat you until you beg me to stop."

"Jon, I'm going to come."

"I'm almost there too, Angel. I want us to come together."

I'm bent over the counter, barely able to keep my phone from crashing to the floor as I continue to pump my cock. Images of my girl right there, the look on her pretty face as she comes undone in my bed, pushes me right to the edge.

"I can't hold on any longer."

"Me neither." On the next pump, I growl and jets of cum release into my hand.

"Oh shit, I'm coming, I'm, this—"

It's the sexiest undoing I've ever heard.

A couple of beats pass as we try to catch our breath, my head spinning out from the power of my orgasm.

Felicity's voice is lazy and satiated, "Shit, I think I've made a mess of your sheets."

My softening cock twitches again. "The thought of you squirting all over my bed is enough to have me chartering a flight back to Seattle in the next hour so I can make sure you fully soak it through."

"I wish you could because that was amazing."

A smile pulls at my lips. "If you think that was amazing, wait until I get my hands on you."

ANGEL

I just got back to your place and there's a decadently dressed floor-to-ceiling Christmas tree that's appeared in your lounge. Do you know anything about this?

I'm glad the home furnishings company I hired last night managed to get everything sorted before she got home from watching Jack's game. I only wish I could've done it all myself, but there's no way I'm having my girlfriend stay at my apartment just before Christmas with the place looking like Scrooge's lair. Even if it does every other year, I'm making an effort for my girl.

ME

No idea what you're talking about?

OMG the garland over the kitchen archway. It's gorgeous!

I wish I was there to see your face right now.

And the fairy lights across the ceilings? Jon, it's a winter wonderland here.

I'm so sorry I can't be there with you, but I wanted the place to at least feel festive.

You have decorations all around your apartment, so I kind of guessed you'd miss them.

Why are you so sweet?

Only to you.

Do you like the color theme?

Emerald? Yeah, it's gorgeous. But I thought your favorite color is blue.

It used to be.

Can you do me a favor actually?

Yeah, sure.

I think I left my toothbrush charger in the bathroom, should be on the counter. Can you check?

I haven't left my charger; it's here and tucked in my suitcase.

What. In. The. World?

My phone starts buzzing. I'm in the locker room with about ten minutes before we head out for pre-game warm-up, but Coach Burrows can ream me out; I'm taking the call.

"Hi," I say, trying to sound casual.

"There's no charger here, but there is the entire range of La Mer sitting on your bathroom counter. No wait, there's two of everything. Shit, there's thousands of dollars' worth here."

I tuck the phone between my ear and shoulder, lacing up my skates.

"Is it the same stuff they used last night at the spa?"

There's a pause. "Wait, this is for me?"

I chuckle. "Of course it is. Apparently, you loved it, so I just thought, you know, early Christmas present."

"Jon, I can't accept this. You've spent way too much money you don't need to spend on me."

"Just accept the gift, Felicity. I know you don't care about money but honestly, it's not about that for me either. Just let me treat you, spoil my girlfriend. Make you smile."

Another pause. "I honestly don't know what to say."

"You don't need to say anything," I reply, shifting my phone across as I start on my other skate.

"Well, thank you. Hey, wait, don't you have a game in like five minutes?"

I check the clock above the locker room door.

"Four minutes to warm-up but yeah, I gotta head off."

I then remember Jack's game earlier today. They were playing Washington, the league leaders. "How did Jack's game go?"

"Two a piece, not a bad result against Washington, I guess."

I'll say. I thought it might be a loss but glad they held out. "How did he play? Did he start?"

"Nah, but he did get much more ice time. Got an assist for the second and his overall game was strong."

Amazing. "Perfect. He's making progress. It'll take time to break into the starting line. He's a freshman."

"Yeah, true. I'm so freakin' proud. He was buzzing after the game. I grabbed a late lunch with him."

My heart warms at the thought of her spending time with her son. "What are you up to now?" I ask as the guys start heading out of the locker room and to the ice.

"Just gonna chill I think, might make a dent in your freezer."

I laugh, thoughts of Felicity curled up on my couch with a tub of ice cream leave me a pining mess. Fucking away series. I don't like to think of her alone.

It's then that an idea pops into my head. "Hey, why don't you head over to my mom and dad's again tomorrow? I can let them know you're coming. Gerard can drive you."

"Hmmm. I don't know. I love them but visiting on my own without you? Seems a bit weird."

I shake my head, casting my mind back to the way she was with Adam. Felicity is meant to be a part of my family. "It won't, and besides, I think Adam's back for the weekend again. You made an impression on him; he hasn't stopped asking when you'll visit next."

"Yeah, I guess we did kind of hit it off. I think it was our love for gardening that did it."

"MORGAN. ICE. NOW!" Coach Burrows's voice booms down the hallway into the locker room.

Grabbing my stick, I stand. "Give me two minutes, Coach!"

Silence. He's clearly gone back to the rink. I'm going to be up shit creek with him if I play like crap tonight.

"Jon, you have to go." She clearly heard his boom too.

I do need to go, but more than that I need to know about this gardening passion of hers. "It's fine. How did I not know you love gardening?"

Felicity sighs. "Well, I don't know if you've noticed but there aren't many backyards in Seattle. Plus, it's more of a past love. I used to care for my mum and dad's garden back in Oxford. They had this amazing acre of land." I can hear the sunny tone appear in her voice; she's clearly recalling their house. "It was a real English country garden, with peonies, Avalanche roses, hyacinths, ah, you name it that garden had it. So, I guess speaking to Adam brought back happy memories. That is until—"

The hairs on the back of my neck bristle, knowing exactly where this is going. "Until what?"

"Until he sold the house, saying the garden was too much upkeep. Especially with me insisting on working full time."

He really is a piece of shit.

"Go to Mom and Dad's tomorrow, yeah? Even if just for Adam; he's been having a rough time, and the way he transformed last week...trust me that it had nothing to do with me, Mom, or Dad." I kind of feel like a dick for putting that last part on her, but something tells me Adam's bond isn't unrequited.

She doesn't take much convincing. "Okay, if you're sure."

"I'll let them know. Look, I really do have to go now, but I'll call you after the game."

"Good luck, baby. Play well. Me and my little chocolate fudge brownie here will be watching."

Baby. Well, shit. Now I'm going to have the best game of my life.

CHAPTER TWENTY-SEVEN

FELICITY

I t's a good thing I don't suffer from allergies.

Since Jon discovered my love of flowers, he's sent me a daily delivery of my favorite blooms, alternating between pink English peonies, pink and white Avalanche roses, and today he's changed it up with an elaborate display of pink, purple, and yellow hyacinths. Each bouquet has arrived tied with an emerald bow. At this point, I'm finding it near impossible to understand how he hasn't dated before. I mean, come on, if I dreamt up my perfect man, he wouldn't be a patch on Jon Morgan.

ME

Sends picture of latest flower arrangement.

Oh, hello hyacinths. I'm running out of room on my desk. Thank you, baby.

It takes less than a minute to receive a reply.

JON

Take them back to my apartment with you.

> I don't want to clutter your tidy living space.

> Take them back. That's an order, Felicity.

> So bossy.

> Be a good girl, and I'll boss you around again tonight.

I cross my legs, squeezing them together under the table as I remember the way Jon got me off over the phone last night.

> What if I don't want to be a good girl anymore?

The dots indicating he's typing a message appear and then disappear but then appear again, and a delicious shudder racks through me as I read his response.

> Then I'll finally be able to have my way with you.

I can feel the heat pooling in my core. I'm surrounded by colleagues, making the whole experience of sexting feel even more intense.

> I'm sorry, you'll have to clarify.

> I don't think you can handle it, Angel.

> Handle what?

> What I want to do to you.

> I'm fisting my cock right now thinking about it.

Oh, Jesus.

> I'm sitting at my desk...surrounded by people.

I'd love to eat you out under your desk.

On my knees between your gorgeous thighs.

You're a bad boy, Jon Morgan.

Yes, yes, I am.

Are you wet for me?

Yes, my knickers are soaking.

Uncontrollably.

Best you take them off then.

Now?

Are you wearing a skirt?

Yes.

Take them off, I want to think of you bare. I feel it'll give me added motivation in practice.

I slowly check around the room to see that no one is watching and then gently tug my thong down from under my pencil skirt, shoving it in my bag. I've never done anything like this before, but the thrill of following his commands sends my need into overdrive. The way I trust him makes me feel sexy in all the right ways.

Sends picture of red thong in my bag.

Good girl, nice and ready for me. When I get home, I'm going to devour that tight wet pussy.

I could double over and melt into a puddle, I'm so horny for him.

> What are you doing right now?

Just then my phone lights up with a picture message.

He's standing in his hotel room bathroom, completely naked and fisting his thick hard cock. His dark, wavy hair tumbles over his eyes as he smiles at me in the reflection. It's by far the hottest thing I've ever seen.

> Yeah, not bad.

> Would you rather I flexed for you, Angel?

> Hmmm, I could take it or leave it.

> I'd rather you took it.

> That can be arranged.

I wish I was anywhere but in this office, and he was anywhere but in Nashville. I miss him.

"Is the sex with him as amazing as they say?" Kate shocks me from my daydream.

Gathering myself quickly, I pinch my fingers, drag them across my closed mouth, and throw away the imaginary key. "My lips are sealed. A girl doesn't kiss and tell."

"Well, I think you're doing womankind a disservice by not sharing the wonders of Jon Morgan in bed with us," Kate responds, picking up her coffee mug to take a sip. "Wait, you look a little flushed, babe." She smiles knowingly at my phone still in my hand. "Were you just texting him?"

"Nope," I say, popping the p and desperately trying to look unaffected.

"Oh my god, you were, weren't you? You were just sexting him in the middle of the office."

I roll my eyes as if that's the most preposterous thing I've ever heard. "Walk with me?" I say, motioning to the kitchenette with my head. I pick up my empty cup and make my way over and away from the eavesdroppers. Discussing my sex life in the middle of the office is not top of my priority list, even if sexting is.

Once safely inside the private kitchenette, I flip the coffee maker on and turn to Kate. "So, we haven't actually slept together yet."

Kate fights, really hard, to swallow her coffee and save me from wearing it. "I'm sorry, I don't think I heard you correctly. You say he hasn't fucked you yet?"

I roll my eyes, glancing through the archway to the main office. "Speak up a little, babe; I don't think Mark heard you on the tenth floor."

"Eh heh," she mocks, "but seriously, you haven't done anything with him yet? Jesus, woman, you've been seeing him for months."

Her assumption about our relationship timeline isn't exactly true, but I let that slide. "We've...done things."

"Thank God for that. I thought you were trying to tell me you hadn't touched him yet or something equally crazy."

I flush slightly, bringing the steaming cup to my lips and burning them. "Technically he's touched me, but I've yet to touch him." *But boy does he have a dirty mouth.*

"I have no words other than to say this is a travesty on behalf of all women. Have you seen your boyfriend's body?"

Yes, multiple times, the last time being around three minutes ago in a hotel mirror, palming his rock-hard cock.

I flip my mind back to her question. "Every time I try to touch him or return the favor, he tells me no and that it's all about me."

"Is he for real? Like, did you discover some magic formula to make book boyfriends a reality or something? Damn, girl." Kate drains the rest of her coffee and shakes her head. "Don't let this one go."

I have no plans of letting him go. But it doesn't matter how much Jon shows me what I mean to him; I still find myself waiting for it to go wrong. For him to wake up and realize he could have so much more—a supermodel, famous actress, hell, even Taylor Swift would probably date him in a heartbeat. It all seems too good to be true. Yet somehow, I can't help but ride this blissful wave, even if I know at the end that my heart will likely drown.

JON

It's eleven at night when our team plane finally touches down in Seattle.

Two weeks of grueling games ended with a three-to-nothing win over the Nashville Storm. Overall, I played well. Four wins out of five leaves us second in the league, and although the season is still far from over, we're in a strong position to challenge for a playoff spot. It's a big turnaround from a few weeks ago when I was hauled into Coach's office and told to take a step away and get my head screwed on straight. Since then, my game has improved. I'm not at my best, but the GM seems satisfied, meaning I'm not likely to be traded anytime soon.

Since Felicity and I officially became a thing, my head has been firmly in the right place. Anxiety no longer gnaws at me as I go about my everyday routine. She's shone her light into the darkest parts of my life and brings me peace. She doesn't see me as some piece of ass on skates; with her I could be anyone—have a regular job and modest bank balance, and she'd still want me.

Looking over at Zach on the spare seat across the aisle, I feel like our lives have had a complete role reversal. When I went over to his place the night Felicity and I finally started dating, he practically poured his heart out, telling me he still loved Amie, and he was having his doubts over whether she actually did him dirty. Schneider is denying anything happened between them and so are his teammates who were there on the night the question-able photos of him and Amie were taken.

Whether she cheated or not, she still sat on another man's knee looking all too comfortable for the picture. She knew they would get back to Zach. Surely, she knew it would hurt him.

Bottom line, Zach could do so much better than Amie despite her groveling for him to take her back. That night at his place, I told him I thought he should move on, that no chick was worth the anguish and embarrassment she's put him through. Zach has never been an emotional guy, always level-headed and clear, but these past two weeks, I've seen a shift in him. He's withdrawn, and when he does speak, it's mostly out of anger or frustration.

During our stay in Nashville, we didn't share rooms, and I'm pretty sure Amie joined him for one or two nights. I'm also ninety-nine percent sure they're back sleeping together, and I'm equally sure she's going to tear him up again. But what can I say to the guy? He won't listen. He's head over heels for the wrong girl, and it cuts me to watch him accept being treated like this.

Since Zach knows my opinion on him rekindling with Amie, the animosity between us has cranked up a notch, and I feel like a shit friend for not supporting his relationship when all he's done since I've known him is pick me up and stand by me as I self-destructed and battled with my mental health. He picked me up from bars in an inebriated state with women hanging off me. He's wiped up my puke when I've been so pissed, I couldn't make it to the bathroom. He's been tough on me when neces-sary, telling me how it is, and he's put an arm around me when I needed it most. And what am I doing for him in return? I'm doing anything but support his feelings for the woman he loves but somehow, I can't find it in me to encourage something I know is toxic. Watching what Elliott did to Felicity, the damage he inflicted on her confidence? I can't stop that from happening to Zach. He seems hell-bent on taking this road, but I'm sure as shit not supporting it. They say love is blind and right now Zach could be its poster boy.

I step into my apartment a little after midnight. Body aching, I gently close the door, letting it shut with a light click. I fully expect Felicity to be sound asleep and curled up in my bed. Warmth floods my chest at the thought.

The arrangements I sent her have been carefully separated into vases and spread throughout the kitchen and living room, and I can't help but smile as I notice she's removed the emerald bows from each one and wrapped them around the vases. It's the little things my girl does that steal my breath, knocking me on my ass every time I see her. She's fucking stunning to look at but on the inside...yeah, she's the most beautiful woman I know. If she wasn't, Adam would've worked that out quickly. He's always had a gift for reading people, and I wonder what he'd make of Amie? He'd probably tell Zach to head for the hills.

I leave my suitcase just outside my bedroom and crack the door ajar. Light still glows from a small bedside lamp set up on my dresser, one that wasn't there when I left—it's cozy. As I look up, I see that the twinkling lights I had installed along the beams of my apartment ceiling are still on and it's kind of beautiful.

It's then I cast my eyes across to the bed and lock eyes on my girlfriend.

My breath catches in my throat when I take her in. Lying on her side, her head propped up on one arm, her gorgeous curvy legs crossed over at the ankle, she smiles at me in a way I don't think I've seen before. It takes everything just to remain upright as I take in what she's wearing. A black, lacy one-piece that cuts high on her hips, showing me the perfect curve of her luscious thighs and leaving very little to the imagination when it comes to her pussy. Through the sheer fabric, I can just about make out the small strip of hair she keeps rather than going totally bare, which I fucking love.

My mouth waters and my dick instantly jumps to attention as I drag my eyes up her body and fuck me, the lace bodice hugs the small of her waist and fights to keep her voluptuous breasts from spilling out and over the low-cut neckline. Thin black straps draw together as they reach her shoulders, and I wonder if they cross over and down her back. Fucking hell, I need to see the back of her because if it's anything like the front, I'm done for. Felicity wears her chocolate hair just as I love it, wavy and around her shoulders. Her full lips shine with her signature peachy gloss, and those emerald eyes cut deep into my soul as she stares heatedly at me through thick black lashes.

"Welcome home," is all she says as she rises to her knees and sits back on her heels, spreading her thighs slightly.

Yep, gone. Totally done for.

This is a side to her I've never seen before. Sure, we've had dirty talk, but Jesus fucking Christ, the woman before me is otherworldly, on a plane of sexy I've never witnessed, a level I never thought possible.

Transfixed, I shrug off my jacket and let it fall to the floor. I reach behind my back and with one smooth action, my black long-sleeved shirt is up and over my head, and my hands fall to my belt.

Before I can begin unlooping, Felicity is across my king-size bed, her hands grasping the buckle. "Let me take care of you tonight."

Placing my palm over hers, I use my other hand to tip her chin up to look at me. "You don't have to, Angel; I'd be happy to cuddle and just be with you. I've missed you so fucking much." More than I thought possible. I haven't been able to stop thinking about her, her scent, her touch, the feel of her lips on mine, her smile and laugh and how it rings around the room, captivating everyone who's lucky enough to hear it.

"I have too. I never knew two weeks could feel so long." Moving her hand to unloop my belt once more, she places a gentle kiss on my lips, and my body illuminates like the Christmas tree in the front room. "It's your turn to be looked after tonight."

Who am I to argue?

I've fantasized about Felicity sucking my dick, her plump lips taking me in so many times I can't believe it's finally happening. "Okay, Angel," I say, as I bring my hands to my sides, granting her full access to take me out. "But with you looking like this, on my bed, having not been able to touch you in two weeks, I'm not going to last long."

That earns me a wicked grin. "Oh, I'm not going to suck it just yet. I have another treat for you first."

Is it possible to come from thoughts alone? Because I'm thinking it is. I'm almost certainly leaking pre-cum.

Felicity unzips my pants, and they pool at my ankles. I step out of them until I'm left in only my gray boxer briefs which are failing to keep me contained as my hard cock pokes out from above the waistband, the tip glistening with my arousal. I feel her heated gaze travel down my body as she takes her bottom lip between her teeth. I lift my hand and gently tug to release that fucking lip. "Keep looking at me like that and I'll go off before you've even touched me."

"Best we get started then." She climbs off the bed and grabs a large towel and a bottle of intimate massage oil. Popping the cap, she kneels back on the bed, straddling the towel which is laid lengthwise across my white comforter. "Come lie here. I want to give you a massage but first, it's best you remove those." She points to my boxers.

I waste no time slipping them off, all the while keeping my eyes fixed on Felicity. I was right. Her lace bodice does cross over at the back, but her ass is completely exposed as it's a thong on the bottom half. Fuck, I'm so horny. I want to rail her into next week.

"Where did you get that little outfit from?" I ask, as I crawl across the bed toward her and lie face down.

Moving over my body and straddling my hips, Felicity seats herself on my ass and then begins squirting massage oil into her palms, rubbing them together to warm them up.

"I picked it up last week from a boutique lingerie store a few blocks away. I saw it and thought you'd like it." She begins kneading my sore deltoids, working her way down to my lats.

"You look so fucking hot." I groan as she continues to work my aching muscles, her touch soothing and effective. She's good at this, and I wonder if she's had practice. The longer she massages, the more my muscles relax until I'm in a semi-conscious state, caught in a blissful world of my girlfriend's hands on my body mixed with the burning need to touch her in return.

A few more minutes pass where we don't speak, instead enjoying the sweet aroma of the oil and the sexually charged atmosphere that's been growing between us since I entered the room.

"Flip over," Felicity finally says.

My cock is impossibly hard from the anticipation of what's to come. I smile up at my gorgeous girl as she straddles my hips and replenishes the oil, bringing her hands to the top of my shoulders, gliding them across my pecs and down my torso.

"Your abs are something else. They're like stone, chiseled to perfection but somehow still soft." She moans as she trails her light-pink fingernails along the dips and curves of my body. Her moan stiffens my cock further as her eyes drop down to where it's sitting just below my navel. I can feel how turned on she is, the heat radiating from where she's now sitting at the top of my thighs.

Without hesitation, she takes my cock in her right hand, gripping the base with a pressure that has my hips jolting off the bed.

"Oh, baby," I gasp on an exhale, squeezing my eyes shut as I try not to go off like a rocket. I'm so turned on I could come on the first stroke.

She giggles, clearly enjoying the torturous pleasure she's putting me through, and then swipes her thumb over the tip of my cock, twisting her hand around the shaft and pumping me slowly. I'm about three seconds from losing it completely.

"You like that?" she asks, her tone sultry and low. Her normally bright-green eyes have turned several shades darker, and her pupils are filled with lust. She's loving having the control tonight.

Continuing to grip my shaft, she slowly drags her center down my thigh as she inches her mouth toward me. I can't only feel her arousal as she moves down my body, but I can smell her sweet scent too, overpowering the final traces of fragrance from the oil. Fuck me, this is the hottest experience of my life. Ever.

"I need to have you in my mouth." No sooner have the words left her lips is her tongue swiping over the crown of my cock.

I let out a guttural groan, unable to contain the searing white heat coursing through my veins.

One.

Two.

She gives three swipes of her pink tongue over the tip before she swirls it around the head, finding that sensitive spot and placing pressure on it. "Fucking hell, Angel," I grind out. Every nerve in my body is on fire as I start to feel the pressure build in my lower spine. "I'm going to come any second."

"You're huge, Jon. I don't know if I can take you fully, but I'll try."

I reach out and cup her cheek, ensuring her eyes are on me. "There's no pressure, Felicity. You don't have to do any of this, but fuck me it's amazing."

A look of determination casts across her face as she slowly lowers her mouth onto my cock once again, this time taking me deeper than before. She takes several inches before she gags, and I want to remind her that she doesn't need to go any further, but I don't. I sense she wants this as much as I do. She takes me as far as she can, which is further than any woman has gone before, and fuck does it feel good.

Lifting back up, she releases me with a pop, and then...holy shit. She spits on my dick, using it as lubrication as she rolls her hand up and down my shaft, gripping me with just the right amount of pressure. "Is that good? Do you like it?"

I've always been a talker in bed but tonight, I'm speechless. Words have left the building as I manage to choke out, "Fuck, yes."

A sexy smile pulls at her swollen lips as she takes me down her throat again, her hair falling forward and over my stomach. I gather it in my fist and tug, indicating I need her to stop. "I'm going to come, Angel, right here, right now, in your mouth." My words are breathy, and my body's coiled like a spring ready to fire off.

"I want to taste you." She leans forward and kisses me passionately, our tongues stroking over and over.

On hearing those words, my last shred of control snaps. "Then open up, Angel, and take me. I want to watch as I brand your throat and mark you as mine."

She does, gripping my hips as she relaxes her throat and takes me fully, moving her head up and down my shaft. Her cheeks hollow out as she sucks my cock expertly, bringing me all the way to the precipice of pleasure. Taking her hair back into my fist so I can see her lips work without obstruction, I begin thrusting my hips in sync with her motions.

"Fuuuck, I'm coming. That's it, greedy girl, take all that cum, suck me dry. It's all for you." I release on a growl that reverberates around the bedroom.

She looks me straight in the eyes as jets of my cum squirt into her mouth and down her throat, and I watch her swallow as she takes everything I have. Her eyes are watery, her mascara slightly smeared, and I *swear to God,* she's the hottest thing I have ever seen.

This woman is a fucking goddess, and she's all mine.

CHAPTER TWENTY-EIGHT

FELICITY

"You taste so sweet; I could die right here and be a happy man."

My toes curl and I fist the sheets, practically tearing them right off the bed as Jon repeatedly drives his tongue inside me. The scruff of his jawline brushes the inside of my thighs as he continues to eat my pussy. He kisses, licks, and devours me like a starved animal. Pulling on the strands of his thick dark hair, my legs begin to shake as an explosion like no other threatens to rip through my body. "I'm going to come."

"Not until I say, Angel. I'm not finished with you."

I cry out in desperation. He's been edging me for the last thirty minutes, which was when I woke up and found him kissing his way up my inner thighs, and I can definitely recommend being woken up this way. I love it, the way he knows what I need. When he reached my apex, he simply shifted my sleep shorts to the side with one hand and began going down on me.

His hands grip the tops of my thighs, holding me down as I writhe beneath him. "I can't hold out, I-I, I can't."

He lifts his head looking me straight in the eyes, his chin dripping with my arousal. "Yes. You can. Just hold on, okay?"

I nod, unsure of what he means, but I trust him completely. Shifting his hands under my ass he flips me over. "On all fours, Angel, but don't bury that beautiful face in the comforter. Turn your head and watch me. Eyes on me, always."

On shaky legs, I do as he commands, loving this feeling of being dominated by the only man I've ever trusted. "Can I taste all of you?"

"Yes."

That's all the permission he needs. Kneeling behind me, he passes his tongue over my pussy once again but this time it continues to travel until he begins circling over my ass. I cry out, having never been touched there before. It feels dirty in all the right ways.

"Relax for me, baby. I've got you; don't worry."

I let my shoulders drop and exhale a steady breath. "You're such a good girl for me. Are you ready for my fingers?"

I cry out so loud I'm pretty sure everyone in his apartment complex can hear what he's doing to me, the pleasure that's rippling through every nerve ending in my body.

Jon slowly replaces his circling tongue with a finger, lightly placing pressure on my entrance. "Are you there, Angel?"

I move my head, attempting to nod but every bone in my body has turned to jelly. "Right there."

"Then come for me. I want you to squirt on my tongue." Jon's finger dips gently into my ass as his mouth finds my pussy. His strokes mirror each other, and within seconds I fall over the edge, his name leaving my lips over and over again until everything goes black.

I'm not sure how much time passes when I hear Jon's voice, "Let's get you cleaned up." He rises from the bed and holds a hand for me to take.

"I'm ready." I've never been so certain of anything in my life.

"I want you. I care about you so much. I want to go all the way with you."

His face softens as he climbs back onto the bed. Turning me on my back, he hovers over me, my head bracketed by his thick corded arms. He kisses my nose, cheeks, and then the corner of my mouth before looking at me, an intense meaning behind his irises. "I want you so badly, Felicity. I have for so long. Since the moment I met you." He drops his face to the crook of my neck and exhales a deep breath like this is truly killing him. "But the first time I take you, it will be as I make love to you. I want to savor your body. I want to worship you all night and then once we're done, I'll fuck you. Hard. I'll make you cry out my name so the whole world knows who makes you feel this way. I want our first time to be special because that will be a first time for me too, to make love, to share an emotional connection with the woman I care so deeply for. This morning isn't the right time. I need to be out for an appointment with my agent in an hour and I told you, there's no way I'm sleeping with you to then leave straight after."

Initially, I want to argue, but as I soak in his words and the genuine meaning behind them, I get it. When we finally have sex, I know Jon wants it to be like no other time he's spent with a woman.

"I understand," I reply simply as I stroke the hair at the nape of his neck, his chin is resting on my chest as he looks into my eyes.

"I don't want to wait long though, Felicity. I can't hold out much longer."

"Well, I head back to Oxford in four days, so..." I shrug my shoulder playfully but immediately regret raising the subject.

Jon lifts his head, his eyebrows knitting together as he stares down at me. "You fly out on Thursday?"

I nod, feeling sure I'd told him I leave for the UK on Christmas Eve.

Lifting from the bed, he thrusts a hand through his messy

bed hair. He looks agitated and worried as he starts pacing the bedroom. "I don't like this. I know that you want to see your family, and I totally get that, but I don't trust him. He's a self-entitled prick and will take any opportunity to cut you down."

I bring my knees up under my chin and look down as I stroke the soft blankets. "I thought we'd already discussed this. I have to go, and I have to stay with my family. Darcy wants us to be together over Christmas, and I must put her first. He won't try anything."

Jon scoffs, his annoyance clearly bubbling, "Yeah, like hell he will. I'll break his fucking neck if he comes anywhere near my girl."

"Look," I say calmly, but I understand why he's concerned. Elliott has given Jon no reason to trust him. "I'm gone until New Year's Eve. It's a few days and then I'll be back. We can have a late Christmas and exchange gifts then; I want to see you open what I got you."

Jon's face softens and he comes back to sit next to me, pulling a shirt over his head as he does. "I hope you get where I'm coming from." He strokes my arm with the back of his hand. "He's an unpredictable asshole who thinks he can treat you badly and say what he wants. It's my job to protect you."

"I know, and I don't want to argue. I just don't have any choice."

Shaking his head, he replies, "You always have a choice, Felicity. Just know this isn't about me; this is about me trying to look out for you. I've got a really bad feeling about this and when you're five thousand miles away, it scares the shit out of me. I'm just asking you to rethink things. I'll pay for a room for you. Hell, I'll buy the fucking hotel if I know it'll keep you safe."

He stands from the bed and pulls on some jeans. "I need to head out, but I'll call you later, okay?"

As he finishes getting dressed and leans down to place a kiss against my lips, I can tell his mind is awash with swirling thoughts and fears about Elliott and me staying in his house. It's clear Jon needs space to cool off and process and so do I. I know he's trying to understand it from my point of view but there's no doubt he's struggling to accept that Elliott will always be a feature in my life, and the facts remain that I have to put my children first.

I gather my things and get dressed, intending to take a shower back at my apartment before I head to the office. I leave Jon a note explaining I've gone to work and pray everything between us will be okay.

"WHAT TIME DO YOU FLY?" Kate comes to stand next to me as we wait for the elevator.

"Tomorrow evening," I reply. My tone is as flat as my mood. It's the day before Christmas Eve, and since I left Jon's apartment on Monday morning, we've barely had a chance to see each other. Between my work and his training and PR obligations, we've been like ships that barely cross in the night. We've exchanged a few messages and the odd call, but everything feels awkward between us. Like there's an elephant in the room that neither of us wants to address. He had a home game last night, but I didn't go. Not because I didn't want to see him, but Mark was snowed under in the pre-Christmas rush, so I had no choice but to work overtime.

"Just call him," Kate says as we both step into the elevator and she punches the button to take us down to the lobby.

"Call him and say what, exactly? Because I've no idea what to say. I have to go back to Oxford to see my daughter and she wants me there. They've been through enough with the divorce, which was driven by me."

Kate raises a hand as she backs out into the lobby. "I'm going to stop you there. You left him because he's a selfish bastard and for the record, he's a narcissist who plays manipulative games. So don't you ever think that you're to blame for the demise of your marriage. That's on him and his toxic ways."

We make our way outside, and I can't help but recall the day Jon was standing propped against his car and waiting to take me back to "the finest restaurant in town." My chest deflates. I miss him so much.

"Just call me when you land, okay babe?"

I pull Kate into a hug and rest my head on her shoulder. "I will, just don't worry about me."

She quirks a brow. "For what it's worth, I think Jon has good reason to be concerned about Elliott. He's an asshole, and I don't trust him. Never have, never will."

What Jon or Kate think of my ex-husband is irrelevant. "There's nothing I can do about it. It'll be fine. It'll maybe be a little awkward at times, but I'll be back in Seattle in a few days."

With one final embrace, we part ways, and I make my way back to my apartment to pack my suitcase and pray this trip will be plain sailing.

JON
Be safe, and call me when you land, okay?

ME
I will. Are you out with the boys tonight?

Nah, the bars will be packed and next to impossible to have a quiet drink, so they're coming to my place for a few beers.

Give your mum, dad, and Adam a hug from me tomorrow.

Apparently Adam keeps asking when you'll be back over.

> When I get back, I promise.

> Do I have competition?

> Definitely ;)

> Can't say as I blame him.

> Just take care, Angel x

I SWITCH my phone to airplane mode and begin flipping through the in-flight entertainment system. Things between us are still tricky, but last night he turned up with a pizza, complete with black olives, and we cuddled, made out, and watched *Sex and the City*, so I feel like we're at least some way to being on track.

"I still can't believe you're dating Jon Morgan," Jack says as he positions his headphones over his ears, ready to get comfortable for the eleven-hour flight. Jon insisted on paying for us to fly first class. I tried to put up a fight, but looking at how little legroom Jack has even in these seats, I can see why he said Jack would need it. He's grown so much in the last two years and hasn't been on a plane since we arrived in Seattle all that time ago.

I've barely spoken to Jack or Darcy about us, but they're aware we're dating and seem cool with it, especially Jack funnily enough. I shrug. "It's just like any other relationship."

He wags his fingers and shakes his head. "I beg to differ. He's one of the greatest hockey players to walk the earth, and I'm not complaining. I'm benefitting from this deal just fine." He smiles with pride.

"I'm confused," I say, turning to face him fully. "How exactly are you benefitting from this *deal?*"

Jack's eyebrows pinch together like I should know exactly what he's alluding to. "With all the technical pointers he's been giving me, stick handling, checking. He's even helped me up my speed across the ice."

I hold up a hand and shake my head. "What?"

He chuckles. "You mean you didn't know?"

I continue to shake my head and blow out a semi-exasperated breath. "Know what?"

"For the last few weeks, he's been coming to help the team with some coaching. After all, we are the local division one side. He's been paying special attention to my training needs though, walking me through plays, etc." Jack stares off in awe. "Playing with him is something else; it's like the stick is an extension of his arm or something."

"That's, um, that's really good of him," I squeak out, totally dumbfounded by what I've just heard.

Jon has been traveling to Seattle University to help my son improve his game and pursue his dream. My mind travels back to that evening at his apartment, when I was sitting at his kitchen counter as he made me a Cosmo, something he'd gone out and got the ingredients especially for. He listened to me talk about Jack's hockey career and how his stickhandling was behind his skating and footwork. He listened, took it all in, and then he acted on it, taking it upon himself to help. He wasn't looking for praise or recognition; he just went about helping Jack be the best player he can be.

Emotion threatens to overwhelm me, and I turn to stare out of the window as we take off and head into the night sky. All I want to do is get off this plane, race to Jon's apartment, and tell him how incredible he really is, even if I know he'll never believe it.

CHAPTER TWENTY-NINE

JON

> Merry Christmas, Angel. Just woke up, so I'm
> guessing it's like three p.m. there.

It's a lie, I haven't just woken up. I've barely slept all night, my palms cold and sweaty, my heart pounding in my throat as I try to keep my breaths steady and relaxed. I haven't had an anxiety attack in months, but the thought of Felicity in that house with *him*. It's triggered me, and my mind has been spiraling for hours as I struggle to decipher what could be realistic concerns about what Elliott is capable of versus what my brain is catastrophizing. As Ben has always said to me, don't act on emotion; try to regulate them first. But if she doesn't reply to my text in the next minute, I'm likely to do something rash.

Thirty seconds later I'm scrolling through my contacts to find Jack's name. We exchanged numbers when I started turning up at his college to help him with technical drills, and just in case he wanted to ask me anything.

But thankfully my phone pings with a notification.

ANGEL

> Merry Christmas. Yeah, we just had lunch and
> I'm clearing up. Why is Christmas so messy?
> Off to your parents shortly?

Jealousy races through me. Oh, so he's playing house with her now. She's not your fucking wife anymore, you prick. She's mine. We should be clearing up the kitchen together. I imagine her slaving over the stove and then clearing up after his sorry ass all while he sits doing nothing or worse still, talking to his finance buddies.

Breathe Jon, breathe.

My fingers fly over my phone's keyboard as I try to type out an indifferent response.

> It's chaos at my parents every year. I'll be
> heading over for lunch at about twelve and I'm
> going to stay over. They're having some family
> and friends over for an evening buffet, which is
> what they do every year.

> Yeah, your mum mentioned she was putting
> that on—I helped her prepare and freeze the
> sausage rolls when I was over the other week.

Thoughts of my mom and Felicity in the kitchen preparing food together flush me with warmth, taking the edge off the crippling anxiety, if only momentarily.

> I've got to go, but I'll call you later, okay? Have
> an amazing day, baby! I hope you get spoiled,
> and I'll be back really soon.

Fuck, I really don't like this, not one fucking bit. The only modicum of comfort I have is knowing Jack and Darcy are there with them, but I'm not foolish enough to think Darcy won't head over to Liam's at some stage and Jack will likely go out since he's a social guy.

> We'll definitely speak later. I'll have my phone on me all day, just call if you need anything. I miss you so much.

I miss you too.

It's seven-thirty and I've got four and a half hours to kill before I need to be at my parents'. So, I throw on some navy athletic shorts, foregoing a shirt, grab a Gatorade from the fridge, and make my way to the gym. I need to burn away the nausea.

FELICITY

"Felicity, forget the dishes for a moment, please. Come open the presents with the kids before they head out."

I set my phone on the kitchen counter and make my way into the lounge as Elliott has asked. These last twenty-four hours have been like taking a step back in time, a window into my former life. Elliott calling the shots, what time we eat, sleep, and unwrap presents. He can't help but need to control every aspect of this family.

On entering the room, I set my wine glass on the side table and walk over to where Darcy, Jack, and Elliott are gathered around and distributing presents into piles.

Elliott smiles at me as I take a seat next to Darcy and place my hand over hers. "I think you'll like what I got you, but if it's not the right color then tell me, and I'll exchange it."

Without hesitation, she rips open the pink wrap. "Oh, Mum, it's perfect! I love it!" She stares down at the mauve Mulberry clutch bag I got her. Normally, I wouldn't spend so much at Christmas, but I remember Darcy seeing one very similar last time we went shopping, and with me buying such an expensive gift for Jack's birthday, I wanted to treat her, especially since she's had a rough year. "Thank you, thank you, thank you!" She wraps her arms around me and squeezes me tight, and I savor this moment of being reunited with my daughter.

I look up to find Elliott scowling at the gift. "That's rather extravagant, Darcy. Your mother went all out this year, didn't she?" He leans across to take a closer look. "Mulberry. Mark must be paying well. Labels like those are normally only seen on celebrities or wives of rich men." I flush at his suggestion. It's subtle enough to bypass both Darcy and Jack but sufficiently cutting to hit me straight where he intended—to have a cheap snipe at my relationship with Jon and that I'm in the money now that I'm a kept woman.

"Earning as you are, you'll be able to quit work soon," he tags on.

Another blow and the tears fight to break free as his snide comments invite back an onslaught of memories from our marriage. He's been on his best behavior since I arrived, controlling yet at least pleasant enough, but now the mask is slipping, and Elliott's true colors are being revealed once again.

I stand up from where I'm sitting and grab my wine glass. "I'm going to grab a refill; anyone need anything?" I ask in the chirpiest voice I can muster.

"No, I'm good, Mum," Jack replies as he begins ripping into gifts from his dad. I don't bother to stay for a moment longer as I make my way back to the kitchen to gather myself before I head back into Elliott's snake pit for round two.

"You didn't open your present from me." Elliott comes to stand beside me as I wait for the kettle to boil for my chamomile tea.

"I was embarrassed you got me anything, I didn't think we were buying gifts for each other anymore." I begin stirring the tea bag through the hot water, not lifting my eyes to his. The entire afternoon has been laced with passive-aggressive comments from Elliott toward me and Jon. And now Darcy and Jack have left for the evening. Darcy has gone to Liam's and Jack over to his friend's, and we're all alone. The part of my visit I've been dreading the most.

Even though Elliott has never hurt me physically, I can't help but flinch at the way he places his hand on my shoulder. "I will always care for you, Felicity, and I wanted to treat you, so please, open my gift?"

Tea in hand, I follow him back to the living room and kneel in front of the tree.

He passes me his gift and with trepidation I begin tearing at the paper. Red wrap gives way to duck egg blue as it slowly dawns on me that, shit, he's bought me jewelry. I freeze, staring at the small box in my hands.

"Well, aren't you going to open it?" Elliott eyes me expectantly.

I pop the lid on the box. It's a rose gold heart pendant with a pretty diamond set in the center. It must've cost a fortune. "Elliott," I say, shaking my head. "This is, well, it wasn't necessary."

"Here, let me put it on you."

"Oh, okay," I reply on a panicked breath, the moment feeling far too intimate on his behalf. Something I categorically do not want to accept.

My phone buzzes in my pocket, but I ignore it since Elliott is standing right behind me, clasping the pendant around my neck.

Taking a step back, he smiles proudly. "It suits you."

I lift my hand to the chain knowing full well this isn't the sort of gift an ex-husband gives his former wife. It's far too personal. Discomfort rising within me, I press my lips together and look at him. "This is too much."

He's exasperated, I can tell. Eighteen years of marriage

means I don't miss a beat when it comes to his moods. "Too much for whom exactly, you or *him*?"

"Him?" If he's going to start a fight, he can at least use his name.

"Oh, come on, you know precisely who I'm talking about. Jon fucking Morgan."

I rise to my feet and make to leave the room. I came back to Oxford for my children, not to argue with Elliott over who I do or don't date. "I'm done with this conversation, Elliott."

He scoffs. "You think he loves you? That he'll still be around in a few years?" At his words, I stop in my tracks and turn around. "Because if you truly think that, then you're more stupid than I first thought."

Anger swells within me. He doesn't know a damn thing. "How could you possibly know what Jon wants? He cares about me, and I care about him. It's that simple."

"So, what, you think he's going to marry you? Settle down and live happily ever after," Elliott mocks. "Get real, Felicity."

I race to boiling point in record time, the red mist descending. "Oh, yes, because that *must* be what I want. Get married, settle down, and have children. Neither Jon nor I could *possibly* want anything else. Unlike our marriage, I'm fifty percent of our relationship and Jon sees me. He knows who I am and that I have dreams. You..." My voice cracks and I fight to maintain my composure as I point at him, my entire arm shaking. "You just kept me under your thumb, to be who *you* wanted me to be. So go fuck yourself, Elliott."

Even after only a few short weeks of being with Jon, I see that relationships can be two-way and healthy, not the dictatorship Elliott ruled.

He looks down at the whiskey glass in his hand, swirling the amber liquid around. He's clearly had a few drinks; his eyes are slightly glazed. "Don't come crawling back to me when that playboy boyfriend of yours does the dirty on you. I mean, are you even exclusive? What happens when he wants children? You're a little old to be giving him a family, don't you think?"

My face drops, and I can feel the blood drain from my features. Shit. What if that is what Jon wants...a family, children. I've been so caught up in the present I haven't stopped to consider what I may be capable of giving him, and exclusive? I think we are. We've never set boundaries, but I assumed we were.

Capitalizing on my uncertainty, Elliott continues to follow me into the kitchen and edges toward me as I stand with my back to the counter. He's about three feet from me, and I can smell the liquor on his breath. A satisfied smile pulls at his lips as he tips his glass toward me. "He could be anywhere right now, with anyone. Your rich and famous boyfriend could have anyone he wanted. I'm sorry, Felicity, but what makes you think you're special to him?" He reaches out and places a hand on my waist and my body reacts, but not like it does to Jon. I recoil. My stomach revolting. "I told you I still care for you and that won't change. You're special to me." His tone is much softer now as he inches even closer, our noses barely apart. I look to the side, uncomfortable with where this is heading and his proximity. "I'm sorry about what happened between us, and I meant what I said that night at your apartment. I want to try again. For us, for Darcy and Jack."

I want to run; I want to get out of this house. My heart rate picks up as I begin to panic and look for a way out of his grasp, but he has me cornered. "Elliott," I say as calmly as I can. "I'm with Jon. I'm happy with Jon. I also meant what I said that night at my apartment. Our marriage is over. It's not what I want anymore."

A few beats of silence pass between us as he goes back to swirling his whiskey and then brings the glass to his lips and downs the remaining drink in one gulp. He bangs the glass down on the counter so hard I'm shocked it doesn't break in his hand. Turning back to me, he narrows his eyes and purses his lips together with rage. "Then I want you out of my house by morning. Get your things and fuck off back to Seattle and to *your man.*"

Intimidated and shaking, I push past him and make for the stairs. It's Christmas Day evening; there's nowhere for me to go, but I can't be within fifty feet of him. Placing one foot on the stairs, I turn back to him. There's a direct view through the hallway and into the kitchen at the back of the house, and I can still see Elliott's back as he faces the counter and pours himself another drink. "Don't worry, I'm gone!" I shout back. "But *you* can tell Darcy why I couldn't stay here as she wanted, why we can't all be together for Christmas."

Elliott spins around, his face contorted with amusement. "Oh, Felicity, you really are that gullible. Jon Morgan's going to have a field day with you."

Realization dawns on me. Oh, holy shit. He lied to me. Darcy never told him she wanted us all to be together and under the same roof. This was his way of getting me here and to his house. Jon was right. Kate was right. Embarrassment rocks my body as I race up the stairs and to the spare room. Why did I just believe him? Why do I always believe him? He saw the mum-guilt within me, knowing I'd want to please my daughter without question, and he capitalized on it.

What the fuck am I going to do?

Opening the door to my bedroom, I shut it quickly behind me and slowly fall to the floor, dragging my back down the wood until I collapse in a heap. Where do I go? Swiping under my eyes, I shakily take my phone out of my pocket to find several unanswered texts from Jon, which must've been the buzzing I felt earlier.

Not bothering to open them, my fingers shaking in panic, I bring up his name and hit dial.

He answers on the second ring. "Jesus, I've been going out of my mind."

On hearing his voice, the walls I built around my heart that were there to protect me from showing vulnerability to anyone ever again come crashing down, and I sob. I sob and wail, drawing in shaky breaths as I desperately try to find the words to tell him what's happened and how stupid I've been.

"Felicity." Jon's voice is calm and kind but equally demanding. "Please tell me, what's happened? Are you hurt? Please tell me he didn't touch you."

I draw in another shaky, uneven breath. "You were right," I say. "He told me he wanted to try again and when I refused, he kicked me out, and now it's Christmas fucking day and I've got nowhere to go."

CHAPTER THIRTY

JON

I'm going to fucking murder him.

I swear to God, if he has laid one finger on my girl, he won't have any left to count the money in his precious investment funds.

I'm in my Porsche doing ninety-five on the freeway and headed for the airport. I don't recall saying bye to Mom and Dad, but Adam caught me as I rushed out of the house.

"It's Felicity, isn't it?" he asked, concern etched into lines across his face. He passed me his phone, which showed there was a flight to London Heathrow leaving in ninety minutes, and I still have an outside chance of making it, provided there are available seats. "Go," was the last thing he said to me as I flew out the door.

I'm grateful I have an overnight bag with me because I haven't had the time to stop anywhere to get supplies. I'm also grateful I had the forethought to pack my passport just in case. Anxiety can be a bitch at times, but when you repeatedly run through every scenario in your head, you are at least prepared for the worst.

I dump my car in the drop-off zone—they can bill me—and race into departures.

"Ticket. Heathrow. Now. Please." At this point I'm unable to form coherent sentences, the bile in my throat impossible to swallow down.

"There are only first-class seats available, sir."

I look myself up and down. "I don't fit into economy seats, ma'am."

I notice her eyes widen just slightly as awareness of who I am sinks in, but she maintains her professional exterior, thank Christ. I can't risk being delayed signing autographs and taking pictures, so I flip my backward cap around to face forward and pull the peak as low as it can go over my eyes.

"That'll be—"

"It isn't an issue," I reply quickly and hand my black AMEX over with shaky hands as she swipes it, checks my passport, and passes me my boarding pass.

Racing through security, which thank fuck is quiet, I pull out my phone and type Felicity a text.

ME

> I land in London at seven a.m. GMT. I'll have my phone on WIFI the entire time. Be there soon, Angel.

Hearing her broken voice on the phone earlier cracked my heart straight down the center, a feeling which left me without any doubts that I am totally in love with my girlfriend. I pause my fingers over the text I'm typing. I want to tell her, my heart pleading with me to admit to her what I've likely known for months. But it's not the right time. So instead, I hit send and swallow the words down even though I'm not sure how much longer I can hold them in.

I HAVEN'T SLEPT in over forty-eight hours, and by the time I pull up to the black iron gates in front of Felicity's former house, my eyes are raw, my head is banging, but my body is thrumming with adrenaline. I've never been this wired, even for the playoff finals.

I'm relieved when the gates open without a code, and I pull into the gravel courtyard. The house is nice. It has that typical English country feel to it. It's double-fronted with a stone porch and a thick black wooden door with a brass knocker set in the center.

Pleading with myself not to hit him but knowing all too well I'm likely to knock him out at first sight, I fling my door open and jog to the entrance.

The door swings open before I reach it, and Felicity stands there, her tiny frame dressed in plaid red and green pajamas and those ridiculous bunny slippers. I smile, amused by her outfit but mostly relieved to find her safe.

I wrap her in my arms, pull her off the ground, and plant a kiss on her forehead. Fuck, she's gorgeous. Setting her back down on her feet, I cast a glance over her shoulder. "Where is he?"

"He went out. I haven't spoken to him since last night, so I don't know when he'll be back."

I scan my eyes over her face and then down her body. "Did he hurt you, touch you?"

She shakes her head but keeps her eyes pinned on me like she's begging me to believe her. "No, he was just an asshole."

"Grab your things. I'm guessing Darcy and Jack are still out?" The driveway is totally clear.

"Yes, they haven't got home yet."

Packed up and making our way to the car, Felicity stops dead in her tracks. The iron gates begin opening, and a white Jaguar F-Type pulls alongside my red Mercedes rental car. I feel Felicity stand closer to me, her breath unsteady, and her intimidated response instantly ignites my rage. I'm grinding my molars so hard, they could snap under the pressure.

Elliott's already striding toward me as I look up at him with a shit eating grin. "Get off my fucking property before I call the pol—"

He doesn't get a chance to finish his threat. Instead, the end of his sentence is met with the force of my fist. Bones crunch in his nose and blood sprays across his pristine Jag. Shame.

"Jesus, I think you broke my nose!" he screams, clutching his face and buckling over.

I grab Felicity's hand, and we make our way to my car. Popping the trunk, I fling her bag in next to mine and open the passenger door. Buckling her seatbelt, I close her door and make my way back to the piece of shit still wailing in his driveway.

Crouching down in front of him so he can see my eyes, blood still pouring from his nose, I talk very clearly and slowly. "Let me make one thing perfectly clear, Elliott. Come within a hundred feet of my girlfriend again and your nose will be the least of your worries. I'll take your fucking head off."

With that, I casually make my way back to the car but stop and turn on my heel. He's still bent over, clutching his face. Perhaps he's never been punched before and that thought alone surprises me. "She told me what you said last night," I say, my shit eating grin making a return. "And I wouldn't be concerned over our exclusivity. I plan to make her my wife."

FELICITY

We twist and turn around country lanes, Jon's bloody knuckles gripping the steering wheel so tightly it could crush under the pressure.

The navigation system is on, but he's ignoring it. The robotic voice has been asking us to "make a U-turn" for the last ten minutes.

"Do you know where you're going?" I'm not sure he does.

"I'm just driving as quickly as I can away from that house. The further I get, the less likely I am to turn back and gouge his eyes out so he can never look at you again."

He's raging. I've never seen him this upset. His knees bounce with adrenaline; his hands squeeze and tremble.

"Pull over."

"What?"

"Just pull over. Here, in this lay-by." I point to an area set to the side of the road.

Jon pulls in and puts the car in park. Immediately I undo my seatbelt and cross the center console, flipping a leg over one side of him so I'm straddling his lap. Seating myself, I immediately feel him start to harden.

He pushes his head back into the seat and stares into my eyes. His are puffy and slightly red, a sure sign he's had very little sleep. He looks exhausted. Pushing a strand of hair that's come loose from my messy bun, he tucks it behind my ear.

Desire surges through me. I want him so much. I want all of him. To me, every part of him is beautiful. The imperfections others may see are nothing but perfect to me.

I run my hands through his thick and disheveled dark hair. It's a bit longer than usual, and there's more than a couple of days' worth of scruff on his chin. "Thank you for coming to me. I'm sorry I didn't listen to you," I whisper, as entranced by his steely eyes as I was the day I collided with him in that hallway.

"You were just doing what you thought was right, and I'd burn the fucking world before I let anything happen to you." He tilts his hips slightly, so his hard cock grinds against my already throbbing core. A low moan escapes me as I imagine what it would be like to have him inside me.

His hips stop rocking. "Where did you get that from?"

"Get what?"

His hand flies to my neck. "That."

Shit. I must've forgotten to remove it.

I can't lie, even if I know it will upset him even more. "Him. He made me wear it, and I must've forgotten to take it off last night."

Jon's jaw ticks as he leans forward and inspects the pendant. "He's still in love with you. In his own fucked up way."

"It doesn't matter what he is."

I reach behind my neck to unclasp the necklace, but Jon beats me to it. He dangles it in front of him with a look of disdain. Next thing I know, he opens his window and casts it out into the gravel.

Returning his eyes to mine, a deep feral need in them, Jon grips my hips and begins kissing my neck and slowly, he grinds into me again. "We need to get out of here, or I'm going to fuck you right here in this car."

"Then do it," I gasp, as he grinds on me harder. I rest my head on his chest, and I notice the trembles wracking his body previously have now subsided under my touch. I'm so horny I can feel my wetness begin to seep through my underwear.

"Not here." Jon lifts my chin and kisses me passionately, his tongue swiping across my lips and when I open for him, he devours me as I writhe on his lap, desperate for more friction.

His hands drop to my jean-covered ass and he moves me over and over his impossibly hard erection. He's so big I have no idea how my tiny five-three frame will take him when the time comes. We continue to make out in the car. Several others drive by, but honestly, I couldn't give a shit. It's all about me and my man.

A few more minutes pass before we break apart and Jon starts the engine. "Let's get to the hotel," he says in a breathy voice as he punches a name into the navigation.

"Where are we staying?" I'm pretty sure I can guide us to wherever we need to go.

"Nous restons à la Chateau," Jon replies, *in freakin' French*. My eyes bug out at his near-perfect accent and the fact we're staying at one of the most exclusive hotels in Oxfordshire on Boxing

Day. I don't bother asking how he managed to reserve a room at such late notice. Nothing surprises me anymore when it comes to my boyfriend.

I reluctantly climb back over to the passenger seat as he shifts into first. "You speak French?"

With his hand resting on the steering wheel, he throws me a wink. "Linguistics graduate in college. I majored in French." With that sexy-as-hell bombshell, he checks over his shoulder and pulls out of the lay-by, and all the while I mentally calculate how many pairs of spare knickers I packed on this trip.

"THIS PLACE IS REALLY BEAUTIFUL." We make our way down the mahogany-paneled corridor away from our luxury suite overlooking the beautifully manicured gardens. Even in the winter, it's beautiful with layers of stunning roses, snowdrops, Cyclamen, and crocuses to name a few. The hotel itself is a mixture of English country cottage and opulence, and it works perfectly.

Hand in hand, we enter the dining room, and I feel underdressed in my emerald A-line dress and black pumps. I hadn't planned on going out for dinner, so this is the best I could do being so far from the nearest shops.

"You look so fucking stunning I can barely breathe." His breath and cologne envelop me as we make our way to the table and take a seat.

The waiter takes our drink order, and I opt for the Italian dry Pinot Grigio, but Jon sticks with mineral water since he's tightened up on his dietary schedule as the Scorpions continue to push for the playoffs.

"It's nice being able to take you out without having every pair of eyes on us in the room." He takes my hand across the table but then decides he's too far away and pulls his chair around, so we sit next to each other. "Kind of nice not to be as recognized."

He leans across and kisses me softly on the corner of my lips. "I'm obsessed with you; fuck knows what I'd have done if he hurt you."

My heart thunders against my rib cage. I can feel my pulse in my ears as he pops his dimples and smiles brightly. "I have to head home tomorrow evening, and I want you to come back with me. I can't leave you here. Your home is with me, in Seattle at my apartment."

My mouth pops open on instinct as I process his words. "Are you asking me to move in with you?"

"I don't want you to live in that apartment any longer. You belong with me, by my side, in my bed, and in my arms."

I know what my answer is because I'm in love with him. Christ, how have I gone from being a woman determined not to enter another relationship for many years to being so sure of moving in with my boyfriend of a month?

"Okay," I say, squeezing his hand.

Jon blinks at me as his dimple-popping smile returns. "As in okay, okay?"

"As in okay, okay," I say, an excited giggle bubbling out of me.

"I'd pick you up and spin you around if this wasn't such a refined establishment."

I snort a laugh. "I dare you."

Pushing back his seat he says, "Oh, Angel, you should know by now I'm not a guy who shies away from anything."

All at once, I'm seeing the grand dining room from six-feet-four as it spins around me, Jon balancing me on his shoulder. I've never heard his laugh so carefree and hearty, and I grip onto his waist, savoring what is definitely one of the best moments of my life.

"GIVE ME A BITE THEN." His spoon goes into my chocolate torte, *again*, but I quickly bat it away with mine.

"Um no. If you wanted some pudding, then you should've ordered it."

"Spot the only child." He tries once more, but I'm quicker at blocking his path.

"I'll let that one slide but think of it this way: I'm keeping your dietician happy."

Jon quirks a playful brow and leans forward until his lips lightly graze my ear. "You finish your dessert, Angel. I'm going to feast on something far sweeter when we get back to our room."

I press my thighs together under the white linen tablecloth and almost drop my spoon on my nearly empty plate.

He angles his head, so our lips are almost touching. "Do you think the walls are thick in this place?"

I gather the final piece of torte on my spoon, offering it to him, and he casually takes it in one bite. The way his tongue peeks out and licks the underside sends shockwaves to my pussy, and I feel my nipples tighten. "Maybe, it is quite old. Why?"

"Because I want to rock your world tonight."

Oh. God.

CHAPTER THIRTY-ONE

FELICITY

We can't get into our hotel room quickly enough as we practically fall through the doorway, laughing and grabbing at each other. His lips are all over my neck as he presses open mouth kisses down to my exposed collar bone. My skin erupts at his touch, every part of my body so responsive to him.

Lifting me into his arms, he carries me through the all-white and mahogany styled suite and past the lit fireplace in the lounge area. We get to the four-poster bed draped in ivory bedding, and I'm certain this is the most romantic setting I could ever imagine.

Jon sits on the edge of the bed and lifts me onto him, so I straddle his thighs, and we continue to make out until my lips are swollen and my cheeks, jawline, and neck are deliciously sensitive from the roughness of his stubble. I can't wait to feel that same sensitivity between my legs.

"Tonight is all about you, Angel. I'll show you what it's like to be with a real man who worships every inch of this flawless body."

He continues to kiss down my shoulders and over the straps

of my emerald dress as he slowly begins to pull at the bows tied at the top. My dress falls from around me until it pools in my lap, leaving my breasts exposed and my peaked, tight nipples on full display for him.

"You aren't wearing a bra." His eyes are heavy, filled with lust.

Taking my left nipple into his mouth he begins to lightly bite and suck on me, and I moan with pleasure, throwing my head back and gripping onto his shoulders for dear life. "Are you bare for me?"

"Just a thong."

He groans around my sensitive breast, the vibrations intensifying the pleasure. "Best we get it off then."

His calloused palms trail up my smooth legs, and I inwardly thank myself for shaving this morning. "Your skin is so fucking smooth, like silk," and his hands dip beneath the hem and travel over my hips until they find my black lacy thong. Hooking his thumb under the straps, he tugs it down, and I slowly lift off, planting my tiptoes on the floor. I come to a full stand and step out of them, but instead of casting them to one side, Jon pockets them. "These are for me." A cheeky grin pulls at his lips.

"Will I be allowed them back?"

"Probably not. I hope you packed some spares." Tapping his chin in thought he moans, "On second thought, no, I hope you didn't. I'll just steal the rest. My girlfriend bare is my idea of paradise." Grabbing me by the waist, he pulls me to him. He's still sitting on the edge of the bed, so I step between his legs. I'm so small, his face is level with the underside of my breasts.

He begins kissing his way down to my navel, and my whole body tightens in response. I'm so desperate for release it's almost painful as my pussy throbs in need.

As if reading my mind, Jon picks me up and switches us around until I'm sitting on the edge of the bed, bare and ready for him. "Spread your legs for me, baby. I want to see that perfect pink pussy and how it glistens for me."

I open my legs slightly, but he pushes them further apart. "Lie back and bring your feet onto the bed."

I shuffle back and do as he asks. I'm so exposed, he can see every inch of me, yet I've never been so comfortable in my own skin.

Jon pins his eyes on me, his lids hooded as he starts unbuttoning his white dress shirt, the sleeves rolled up past his forearms. He pulls them off and over his hands, dropping the shirt to the floor. Next, he unbuttons his gray pantsuit trousers, leaving them hanging open before he drops to his knees in front of me.

Propped up on my elbows, I watch him run a finger over my soaking pussy. "Ohmygod," I cry out, my knees already beginning to shake.

"It's time for my dessert."

Moving between my thighs, he sucks and swipes his tongue over my entrance as he applies just the right amount of pressure to my clit. I won't last long, not like this. My hand automatically falls to the top of his head as he continues to work me into a frenzy. He groans in pleasure and the vibrations shoot straight up my spine.

"I'm not going to last long," I shriek.

"Then come for me, baby. This won't be the last orgasm you have tonight. The next one will be on my cock."

"Oh Jesus, *yes!*" I scream as I come undone. I come so hard I swear I feel my release in his mouth as he continues to nip, suck, and swipe at me until I'm so sensitive I can't bear it any longer.

My legs shake and my body feels sated and relaxed when Jon rises to his feet above me. He pushes his trousers all the way down and his abs ripple as he steps out of them. Through dazed eyes, I watch as my sculpted boyfriend lowers his briefs, his straight hard cock glistening with pre-cum.

His tanned body climbs over me as I scoot back up the bed until my head rests on the pillows. Leaning back on his heels and between my thighs, he bites down on his bottom lip as he watches me intently, pumping his cock from base to tip.

"Are you ready for me, Angel? Because I'm so fucking ready for you. I'm going to make love to you all night and then once I'm done being gentle, I'm going to fuck you until that pretty little voice of yours fails from screaming my name."

Oh, his mouth, his deliciously dirty mouth. "I'm so ready."

My eyes drop to his cock, and I wonder once again how the hell I'm going to take him. I've only ever had sex with Elliott, and he was nowhere near Jon's size. It's not just his length but his girth too—he's enormous in every way.

"Will it hurt?"

He begins to crawl over me, but he doesn't crush me under his weight, instead hovering on one forearm, his hand brushing a strand of hair from my eyes. "You're going to fit around me perfectly."

He lines himself up at my entrance but stops just as he begins to slowly press inside. "Are you on birth control? You know I haven't slept with anyone since the moment I laid eyes on you. You're all I've wanted, and I've never been bare with anyone else."

"I have an IUD, and I trust you."

He smiles against my lips and then slowly starts to ease himself inside once more. I open my legs wider as my body stretches to accommodate him. He's so big it burns as his head drops to my shoulder and he continues to guide himself inside.

I gasp. "I feel so full."

Chuckling he looks down at where we're connected. "I'm only about halfway there."

My eyes widen in shock, and I shake my head. "I can't take anymore, like seriously, you're too big."

"This cock was made for only you, Angel. Just relax and let me look after you."

I bring my legs around his waist and cross my ankles at the small of his back while he continues to kiss me and slowly ease his way inside. When he bottoms out, the slight sting gives way to a feeling of total fullness and the pleasure begins to build.

"You feel amazing," I sigh, and I begin to writhe and mentally beg for him to start moving.

Jon's head remains in the crook of my neck. "Wait, baby, or I'm going to blow myself right inside you. Fuck, you feel so fucking awesome. You're like my fucking blueprint."

A couple more minutes pass as we kiss, and then he begins rocking his hips slowly, moving himself in and out with gentle thrusts.

"You're so wet for me, I can hear it. Can you hear yourself taking me like the good girl you are?"

My body ignites, threatening to burn an inferno with every deeper stroke he takes inside me.

After a couple more minutes of torturous bliss, Jon sits up on his knees and brings one of my legs over his shoulder, placing open mouth kisses from my ankle up the inside of my calf, knee, and inner thigh, all the while moving inside me. The change of angle allows him to thrust deeper, and his hard cock begins caressing a spot so deep it's never been touched. I cry out as white-hot pleasure races up my spine.

"Has anyone ever touched you there?"

I shake my head at him. "No."

He smiles and then gathers my other leg up and places it over the same shoulder, so my body crosses over his diagonally. "How's this?" he adds, intensifying his thrusts as he bends over me slightly to deepen once again. "You're so fucking flexible. I've been desperate to find out how I can bend you around my dick."

I'm starting to come undone again. Watching Jon's gorgeous body make love to mine is proving all too much. "I'm going to come again. Yeah, I'm com—"

He slams into me hard, the bed shaking beneath us as his hips move over mine. His cock touches that spot over and over, and I fully unravel, throwing my arms over my eyes.

"Eyes on me, Angel, always on me. I want you to watch me fuck you because there will never be another man taking this sweet little pussy. It's mine. All fucking mine. Tell me, who's pussy is it?"

"It's y-yours," I scream. "It's all fucking yours."

As soon as I come, Jon pulls me up and back across the bed. I'm on all fours now with my ass over the edge as he stands behind me at the foot of the bed. "Now I'm going to fuck you so hard I'll have to carry you to the airport tomorrow."

I instantly feel his cock slam into me from behind, the movement alone almost sending me over the edge once again.

"How hard do you want it, Felicity?" His tone is serious, and I don't miss the way he uses my name.

"Hard," I moan.

"Best you hold onto that comforter with everything you have then."

I grip it until my knuckles turn white, and he pounds into me in delicious strokes, my name tumbling from his lips. I turn around to see his head thrown back, his arm on my right hip as he grips the overhead bar on the four-poster bed. His muscles bulge and contract as he continues to give it to me from behind. But his thrusts aren't rash; they're smooth and expertly placed, sending wave after blissful wave through me.

"I'm getting close, Angel." His arm above his head falls to my waist as he continues to drive into me.

"Come inside me, baby—fill me with your cum," I say, knowing full well he'll love the possessive talk.

"You'll be so fucking full of me; it's still going to be dripping down your thighs as we board that plane tomorrow."

"Do it."

On a roar he does, his hips moving at a more erratic pace, and I feel his cock pulse as he unloads inside me. He chants my name as his face falls to the nape of my neck, placing soft, gentle kisses.

After a few beats of us catching our breath, Jon finally pulls out and drops to his knees, taking me by surprise. "Don't move, Angel. I want to make sure every bit of me stays inside you."

I'm still on all fours as he presses his fingers inside me, pushing his leaking cum back into my pussy. "That's right you greedy girl, keep all of it to yourself. It's all yours now, and I'm going to fill this sweet little pussy full of me every damn day."

"Do you have a breeding kink, Mr. Morgan?" I tease.

His tongue swipes across his bottom lip. "I do now."

THE WALK-IN RAINFALL shower feels incredible in this place, and it takes up the entire back wall of the bathroom. Jon walks in a few minutes later, completely naked and his cock is still semi-hard.

After he fucked me again, I headed for the shower, and it seems like he's going to join me here too. At the sight of his beautiful physique, my already sated body still finds a way of responding and telling me it wants more.

He steps in behind me and starts massaging the shower gel I was using into my shoulders. "That was fucking incredible. I'll never forget it."

I peer back at him over my shoulder and smile. "Yeah, you're not bad."

Arching a brow in amusement, he throws his arms around my waist, his chin resting on my shoulder. "Admit it, I rocked your world just as I promised I would."

I laugh. "Yeah, you did."

He begins working shampoo through my hair. "I've been waiting to do this for ages."

"What?"

"Wash your hair with this fucking amazing shampoo. The moment I met you I was hit with this coconut scent, and I couldn't wrap my head around what it was. Turns out it's this, and it drives me fucking wild."

"It's nothing mind-blowing or expensive, just a drugstore brand."

"Everything about you is mind-blowing, Angel." He brings his lips to my ear. "You are an amazing woman and a kick-ass mom—strong, powerful, and so fucking beautiful. It kills me to think he kept you from living out your dreams. Promise me you'll always chase them from now on."

I don't know where that came from but I feel its sincerity deep in my bones. Since my parents passed, no one has ever encouraged me to follow my dreams and believe in myself.

I swipe under my eyes, knowing full well it's not moisture from the shower. "Thank you," I whisper. "You are the most amazing man I've ever met. You need to believe me when I tell you that you're everything. You're so worthy. What you've done for me, for my son, and the kindness you put out into the world. Don't ever believe you're anything other than perfect."

Clearing his throat, he places a chaste kiss on my shoulder and then grabs the shower gel and begins scrubbing himself.

The entire bathroom is filled with steam as we continue to rinse ourselves and each other, the experience arguably just as erotic as the way he took me in the bedroom earlier.

"I have a game on Tuesday in New York. Are you still off work?" Jon asks.

"I am."

"Can I fly you out to come watch me? We can stay in New York for a couple of days and have an extended Christmas."

Smiling up at him, I throw my arms around his neck and kiss him softly on the lips. "Sounds amazing."

"Good. Maybe I'll finally get you in my jersey too."

I tap my finger on my lips and look to the side. "Um, I don't know about that. Isn't that some sort of declaration to the world? Like it's serious," I jest, unable to help myself from winding him up.

"Oh, we're way past jersey-wearing declarations, Angel."

I pull back slightly, still smiling from ear to ear. "Define *way past jersey-wearing declarations*."

Keeping his gorgeous gray eyes trained on mine, I see an emotion pass through them I've not seen before. He turns his head to face the misted glass wall as he brings his hand up and begins...writing something.

In a state of confusion, I watch his finger write the letter "I" and then move to another word, "love," and finally he writes "you."

My breath catches in my throat, and I fight to swallow the lump forming. Realization hits me hard as it begins to sink in.

"Is that defined enough for you, Felicity? I'm completely in love with you."

CHAPTER THIRTY-TWO

JON

"Just wondering if there was a bigger suite available?" Felicity asks. Her cheeky, sarcastic tongue is in full flow these days, and I love it.

"Would you prefer something a little more elaborate, Ms. Thompson?" I ask, dumping my suitcase on the king-size bed and wrapping my arms around her waist from behind.

"Well, it is a tad on the small side. I expected more of you."

"I do apologize, Your Royal Highness."

"For a linguistics graduate, your British accent needs some work." Felicity pats me on the shoulder and saunters off toward the bathroom, leaving a trail of clothes behind her as she strips down to her red bra and lacy thong. At the doorway, she glances back at me and winks, and I can say with absolute certainty I've never moved so quickly, not even on the ice.

"By the way, Kate said she can help with the move. I mean, I don't have much in the way of personal items, since my apartment came fully furnished, but I do have a few knick-knacks to clutter your apartment with. Sorry." Felicity looks up at me from her phone.

I pause on packing my training bag. "That's kind of her, but she doesn't need to worry about the move and neither do you." I glance at my watch and hope I haven't gone too far this time. "The removal guys are arriving at your place in about an hour so by the time we get home, it'll be done. I arranged it all with your landlord, and he's agreed to release you early from the lease."

I cast a tentative glance in her direction, but her expression is unreadable. "I should probably be mad at you for wading in like a bull in a china shop."

"But?" I press.

"Honestly? I'm kind of too excited to be mad. Although it's always nice to be kept in the loop you know."

I puff out a breath and lean across to kiss her, smiling against her lips. "Me, too, Angel, and I know. I was hoping to keep it a surprise, but you kind of forced my hand here."

I pull away reluctantly and stride into the bathroom to gather my wash gear. A couple of minutes later, I return to the main room but stop dead in my tracks at the sight of my girl wearing my name and number—every hockey player's holy grail.

"What do you think?" she asks, giving me a little twirl.

I bring my fist to my mouth and bite down on a groan. God damn, my name looks like it was made for her.

"I think if you prance around in that much longer then I'm going to be *really* late for my morning skate." I've just fucked her twice against the tiles in the shower, but my dick twitches for more, and I stride over, debating whether to miss the session altogether.

Giggling, she steps away from me and pulls on some jeans. "I think I'm going to check out the shops while you're out this morning. I'll be at the rink for six." She kisses my cheek, pulling on her black winter jacket, emerald scarf, and cute Scorpions hat, and makes for the door. "Have a good skate, baby."

Oh no, she doesn't. I grab her by the waist and pull her to me. "Or...you could stay here with me, and I'll make sure my name on the back of that jersey isn't the only way I claim you as mine."

She smiles but instead spins my cap so it's facing backward. "Better. But seriously, you're going to be late. However, if you play your cards right, I promise I'll be wearing this and only this for you later."

I drop my face to the crook of her neck and drag my hands down her sides, tempted to lift her and throw her onto the bed. Her petite size is perfect for doing just that. But I resist at the thought of Coach's unbearable wrath if I were to be late. I pull on the bobble of her hat. "What's on your shopping list, Angel?" *Please let it be lacy lingerie.*

"Nothing in particular. I just heard it's great here for retail therapy, so I'm going to explore, maybe grab a few bits for Darcy's birthday, although it's still a few months away."

"Was she okay with you coming back to Seattle early?" I ask, knowing Jack was more than fine with it as he joined us in first class from Heathrow. He's a good kid and we're starting to form a friendship; I see a lot of Felicity in Jack.

"I didn't tell her what happened with her dad. I'll leave him to explain why he has a broken nose. But yeah, she understood why I couldn't stay. To be honest, I don't even think she's left Liam's since Christmas Day."

Reaching into my back pocket I pull out my wallet and hand her my credit card. "Anything you want, just put it on this."

She shakes her head vigorously. "Jon, no. I can't take this."

"Are we really having this conversation again? Let me spoil my girlfriend."

She tentatively takes the card, but I have my doubts that she'll use it.

"When you arrive at the stadium later, just head for the family suite."

"Will anyone I know be there?"

"Jensen's parents are visiting from Alberta, so they'll be there, and then there's Amie, Zach's girlfriend. They recently got back together."

Felicity stiffens. "Based on my last experience, I'll be avoiding any interaction with her."

My brows knit together. "Clue me in here."

"Let's just say I can see why Zach has had trouble with her in the past. She made it pretty clear to me that night at Riley's that I was the *flavor of the month,* and you were basically just using me for sex."

My blood boils. How am I only hearing about this now? I knew something went down that night when she wanted to leave. "She's so full of bullshit," I snap.

"I gathered that, but if I was in any doubt, she pointed me toward her friends Bryony and Sarah, I think they were called. Apparently, they could 'vouch for your antics,'" she mocks.

Turns out Amie isn't totally full of bullshit. I've fucked them both. I think. Possibly together.

"I put her straight though, baby." Felicity folds her hand around the nape of my neck, pulling my head toward hers, so our eyes meet. "I don't give a shit about your past, only your future. I'm just not that keen on being Amie's new bestie."

Fuck me, this woman.

What have I done to deserve her?

I inwardly work to control my anger at the blatant way Amie tried to sabotage my relationship. "Yeah, keep away from her. She's bad news." I kiss the corner of her mouth and rest my forehead against hers. "I love you, so fucking much." I'm yet to hear those words in return, but I know they'll come. I've always been ahead in my feelings and that's okay, as long as she gets there eventually.

Her thumb strokes my cheek as our noses brush. "I'll see you on the ice. I'll be the one wearing number twenty-two."

"Evans, what the fuck is wrong with you?" Coach Burrows yells from the side.

We've been going over some light drills. Zach's game has been off for weeks, and his head has been everywhere but on the ice. The team has been carrying him, but against the New York Blades, we need our enforcer and at six-five and two hundred and thirty pounds, Zach has always been our guy.

I skate over to him; he's barely spoken with the team since he got here, but he hasn't even looked at me. "Yo, man, what's going on?" I take a gulp of my Gatorade and lean against the side.

"Nothing," he snaps.

"Well, clearly there is. You haven't been at it for the past few weeks." I'm desperately trying to toe the line between best friend and captain responsibilities. He of all people should get that as my AC. "Coach is riding you because your head hasn't been in it for weeks. I need you; we need you at your best tonight. So, tell me, what can I do to help?"

He turns to look at me for the first time all session. "You can help me by fucking off."

The fuck? This isn't the Zach Evans I know, my bro on and off the ice. His words piss me off, but his tone slices straight through me.

"Yeah, well, no can do. So, get your shit together or we're toast out there tonight."

I shake my head and begin to skate away. "You think you're untouchable now you have the girl? Jesus, you stroll around here like you're God's gift. You've been so wrapped up in your own perfect world you can't see anything other than her. Not even your *so-called bro* and the shit I've got going on." He skates up to me and shoves his hand at my chest. He's got an inch and at least ten pounds on me but more than that, Zach might be a pussycat off the ice, but he was born to fight on it.

"What?"

He blows out a humorless laugh. "Yeah, I thought so. No fucking idea what's going on around you."

"Well, I won't if you don't fucking tell me!" I shout, bringing the rest of practice to a halt.

He lurches forward getting right in my face, his anger bubbling over. "I shouldn't fucking have to. I've always been there for you man, and where are you when I need you? Knee deep in pussy, as fucking always."

My stomach rolls, and I want to hurl. He's right. I don't know what's sent him into this downward spiral, but I do know I should've been there to protect him. My heart rate begins to pick up, and all I can hear is the throbbing pound of my pulse in my ears and a sharp pain in my chest. "It's Amie, isn't it? She's been giving Felicity shit too."

Zach drags a gloved hand over his face. "Yeah, something like that." Bitterness is still clear in his voice. "The whole situation is fucked. My fucking life is totally fucked." His last two words shake as his voice cracks. I've never seen my stoic best friend break, but he's on the edge of losing it now, I can tell.

"Okay, you're worrying me now, just tell me what's—"

"She's fucking pregnant, alright? She told me three days ago that she's pregnant. At first, I was scared but excited, and now... Now there's doubt over whether it's mine."

What the fuck.

My mouth opens but the words die on my tongue.

Finally, he continues. "The news hasn't broken yet, but it will. This is Amie. Of course it will break. She called me last night telling me she'd been sleeping with Schneider after all, and he's claiming it to be his. He wants her to take a paternity test as soon as possible, but she's saying it can only be mine." His laugh is dark. "Apparently, she loves me."

I'm dead on my feet, unresponsive. Zach's revelation swirls in my head, but nothing seems to be registering other than this is bad. *Really* fucking bad. And the kicker? He's about to play the other potential father in only a few hours. I have to tell Coach that he needs to be benched; it's not safe for him to play in this headspace.

My best friend drops his head between his shoulders and pulls off his helmet, running a hand through his sweat-soaked mousy brown hair. "No one knows, not even my parents, and I'm desperate to keep it this way." He looks up at me then, his blue eyes glassy but fierce. "I'm playing tonight. Do not tell Coach. At this rate, I'm one bad game away from the farm team, so please, just keep it quiet."

I shake my head. "You know I can't let you go out there when you're in the place you are."

He pokes me hard in the chest with his gloved hand. "And how many times have I kept my mouth shut when you played still half-cooked? How many times did I cover for you when I dragged you out of bars just hours before practice? I've got this handled, but tell Coach, and you and me..." he motions between us. "We're done."

"HE'S A LIABILITY OUT THERE." Coach Burrows turns to me on the bench. It's the start of the third period and we're down three to nothing. The entire team is crumbling, but Zach is playing in slow motion. He and Schneider have been eating at each other all game, the tension palpable and bordering on lethal.

My game isn't much better. I've barely made a clean pass, and my defensive support in the slot and behind the net has been non-existent. My legs feel like weights. My body's thrumming with adrenaline, but I feel like I'm skating through molasses.

I've barely looked up at Felicity. She can probably already tell something's not right, but I can't tell her. I trust her implicitly, but this is Zach's business to tell, and I've let him down way too many times already to risk his confidence, our friendship already hanging by a thread.

"Get out there, Morgan, and for fuck's sake, get it together."

I replace my mouthguard and jump the boards. "Got it, Coach."

The small Scorpions away crowd cheers as I take back to the ice. I pick up a loose puck from behind our net and begin an offensive move. It's a rare turnover and I'm determined to make something of it. I sell their center with a fake pass and slip it to Jessie instead, who's flying down my right-hand side. He takes the puck and sinks it with a wrist shot. The buzzer goes and we've pulled something back. I look up to see Felicity going wild, pumping her fist in the air and a wry smile pulls at my lips.

Five minutes to go and we're playing better, but Schneider is out for blood. He's checked three of our players in this period alone and earned himself a penalty. He contests it with the ref, but he's having none of it. The small section of Scorpions fans cheer as he makes his way to his second home. It's then I see Zach skate past the penalty box, turn his head, tap the glass, and say something. Schneider is on his feet banging his stick and screaming, but Zach simply waves and smiles, only riling him up further. I've played with and against Schneider for years and he's a piece of work, but I've never seen him look like this. He's unhinged.

"Let's get this finished," Zach says to me as he skates past, getting in position for the restart of play.

It's three-two by the time Schneider returns to the ice. His eyes zeroed in on my best friend. The game has descended into chaos as the tension between them both has infiltrated the other players. There are only three minutes left on the clock, but barely any hockey is being played. The crowd feeds into the fighting frenzy, loving the brutality on display.

I chance a glance up at Felicity, who has her head down and buried in her hands. She can't watch, and I hate this for her. I hate myself for not taking Zach off the ice tonight, too.

The puck comes loose from a tussle against the boards and Jessie breaks with it. He's so quick there's no way I'll catch up to him, but he doesn't get far as he's checked by one of their defensemen who sends it back up for a counter.

His pass to Schneider is loose, and he narrowly misses it as it sails past him and toward Zach, who picks it up in the far corner.

And that's when it happens. Like it's in slow motion, unfolding right before me, and all I can do is stand and watch. Schneider sets his eyes on Zach as he gathers it under control and begins to turn, opening up his body to lay off a pass. The puck leaves Zach's stick, but Schneider isn't interested in the offensive. He's only got one form of attack on his mind.

He collides with his body just as I see Zach's helmet turn and register the onslaught, but it's too late. He wasn't prepared. Normally he'd be expecting a potential check but not tonight, not with the way he's been MIA in this match.

On impact, Zach's body snaps backward, his head the first to make contact with the boards, but it's not the crack of the splintering glass I hear. It's the kind of crack only bones can make, and I swear that's all I can hear even over the roaring crowd. It's the hardest hit I've ever seen in my career.

Zach lies crumpled on the ice, the force of the hit having sent his helmet flying from his head, his stick is lying several feet from his lifeless body.

Registering the seriousness of the situation, the crowd falls silent, but Schneider continues to rage on. "Fuck you, Evans!" he spits, as his captain drags him away and the ref rushes to intervene when three of our players, Jensen included, begin beating down on Schneider.

A few beats pass and my instincts take over, my adrenaline finally surging me forward. I know I'm screaming, but I can't hear anything other than the ringing in my ears as it grows louder. I know my pads are soaking through as I kneel next to my best friend. I see the doctors rushing around him, checking his state of consciousness. I recognize that his right leg shouldn't be at that angle, and I register the blood beginning to pour from his face and over his jersey, staining his number sixty-six.

But all I can think at this moment is this is all my fault.

This is all on me, and I'll never forgive myself.

CHAPTER THIRTY-THREE

JON

"It's too early to say anything at this stage," the neurosurgeon treating Zach confirms. "We're currently scanning Mr. Evans to ascertain if he has a fracture or dislocation of the cervical vertebrae; a spinal concussion is also possible, and we of course hope for the latter. As soon as we know more, we will be informing his medical team and family. I can confirm that Mr. Evans has two broken ribs, a fractured tibia, several deep lacerations to his face, and a broken jaw."

My phone buzzes in the back pocket of my pants but I ignore it. I can't think of anything other than my best friend right now.

Coach turns to me. "Head back to the hotel, Morgan. There's nothing more you can do. I'll call you when I hear from the medical team."

I shake my head. "I'm staying right here." There's no way he would leave me. He never has. Zach's words at practice earlier repeat in my head. *"I've always been there for you, man, and where were you when I needed you?"*

Walking into the restrooms, I lean my hands on the counter.

My thoughts are spiraling out of control and for all the therapy I've had over the years, I've always had Zach to lean on, support me, and tell me it'll be okay. But now that person thinks I've let him down, that I'm not worth his time, and you know what? From his position in a hospital bed, I'd say he's probably right.

"Fuck!" I twist my fist and punch the paper towel dispenser over and over until my knuckles are bleeding and raw, the physical pain providing a brief distraction from the mental anguish.

My phone buzzes again and this time I check it.

ANGEL

> I'm still at the stadium with Jensen's mum and dad, but I'm heading back to the hotel soon. I'm praying Zach is okay and please, baby, let me know you are too.

I go to pocket my phone but figure she won't stop until she hears from me. Right now, I just need to be away from her. She can't see me like this.

ME

> Ask them to make sure you get back to the hotel okay. I don't know when I'll be back.

I repocket my phone and head back outside to join Coach.

"Any word?" Jensen comes to sit next to me; it's been hours since we last saw the neurosurgeon and still no update.

"Nope," I reply, disinterested in conversation but I do note the absence of Amie. We haven't heard from her at all and have no idea where she is. In love with Zach? Give me a break. If anything happened to Felicity, I'd be glued to her bedside from the minute she arrived.

"My parents made sure Felicity got back to the hotel okay."

I nod, bending down to face the floor, my forearms resting on my knees. "Thanks."

"She's worried about you, man; says she's barely heard from you since you tore out of the stadium."

"I'm worried about my best friend. She'll understand I've got to prioritize him."

"Yeah, that's understandable, buddy, but at least text her back."

"I fucking did!" I snap. I've barely made contact because my headspace is so fucked up right now, in this state, I'm enough to drive anyone away. I just need to be on my own.

"Barely."

"You know what, Jensen, if you haven't got anything useful to add then fuck off. I'm not in the mood."

"Don't do this, Jon." He's witnessed me at my worst, and I know he can sense what's coming, the road I'm on. I can too. I know my behavior is erratic and my emotions are spiraling, but I'm powerless to stop it. With every passing minute, I feel my grip on rational thought slipping and the voice telling me I'm not enough getting louder. The temptation to give in and let it pull me under is getting stronger.

I don't reply. I just sit back and put my hood up, blocking everyone around me out while we wait for someone, any fucking one at this stage, to tell me if my friend will walk again.

FELICITY

I lie in our hotel room, staring absentmindedly at the episode of *Friends* I have on the TV.

I know something is very wrong with Jon. Aside from the fact his best friend is lying in a hospital bed and we're uncertain what spinal damage he's sustained, the look in his eyes when he left the rink scares me, like something inside him had died. His only text reply to me tonight was cold at best and while I totally get this is hard for him, I can't help the gnawing concern that this is all to do with a decline in Jon's mental health. His lack of self-esteem leads to anxiety and possibly depression. I know little about his medical history other than he has been seeing his therapist, Ben, long-term but seeing him tonight tells me he's in a dark place.

I pull up my phone again, desperate to know what's going on, and thankfully Jensen gave me his number earlier. I get the feeling he's not just concerned over Zach's well-being, too.

ME

What's happening? I'm going out of my mind here.

Three dots appear quickly, and a reply comes through.

JENSEN

He hasn't told you?

I haven't heard a thing. He's gone dark on me.

For fuck's sake. It's good news. It's a spinal concussion. Docs hope the feeling in Zach's legs and arms will return in a few days. He has a broken tibia, two broken ribs, a broken jaw, and he needed stitches to his eyebrow, cheek, and lip due to the impact with the boards.

I don't know what to feel. There's relief that Zach's spine isn't seriously injured, but he's looking at a long time out of the game. At least the rest of the season, even I can tell that.

Schneider has a broken jaw, broken nose, three missing teeth (courtesy of me), and a concussion.

I hope they throw the book at him.

We'll have to wait to hear an official ruling, but he's looking at a twenty-five-game suspension and a heavy fine. With a pre-meditated hit like that, he should never play again. He could've fucking killed him.

How's Jon?

When we heard the news that Zach would be under strong pain medication all night, he left the hospital. I tried to talk to him, but I don't know...he doesn't seem good. Like he's blaming himself for what happened.

I'm beginning to panic, wondering what state my boyfriend is in right now.

Where is he?

He wouldn't talk to anyone. Just sit tight. He'll come back, probably once he's cleared his head.

I want to call him, but I stop myself. My gut tells me he needs this time alone, and I'll give him that space. Even if it's killing me not to go out into the night and search every building until I find him.

IT'S GONE four in the morning when the door to our suite opens, and I hear a thud and then...laughter?

Pulling back the covers, I fly out of bed. "Jon, is that you?"

I find him leaning over a console table, half-conscious and reeking of booze. There are broken shards from a vase he must've knocked over and his light gray hoodie is ripped and covered in stains like he's fallen over several times, his trousers in a similar state.

But it's when I see his eyes that my heart cracks clean down the middle. Puffy, red, and totally vacant. He's sure done a number on himself, drinking into total oblivion.

"Jon, baby, what have you done to yourself?" I try to pull him onto my shoulder, but he's a dead weight.

On hearing my voice, he turns his head in my direction and a tiny smile traces his lips. "Doooooo yyyou lorve me, Annngel?" His voice is a slurry mess, but I can just about make out the words.

"Let's not talk about this now, okay?" I reply. "Let's just get you into bed."

"Yoooou mmmmean eferythinnng to mmeee."

"I know, baby. You do, too. Can you walk with me?"

I try to haul Jon's huge body from the console table but as soon as we try, I collapse to the ground and Jon tumbles forward and onto me. I feel a sharp shoot of pain in my left wrist as I try to break my fall. "Ow, shit."

I look across to find him fully passed out. I'm almost certain he's going to hurl at some point, so I shrug off the pain and move him onto his side, then fetch some spare blankets and pillows and place them on the floor. I roll one underneath Jon and prop him up with a pillow, then wrap us in another blanket as I cuddle his huge body from behind.

A few minutes pass and his breathing begins to even out. Taking one of his hands in mine, I intertwine our fingers, as Jon has done with me so many times before. I know he won't remember my words tomorrow but as I whisper them into his ear, I hope on some subconscious level they'll resonate with him. "You are worthy Jon, and you mean everything to so many people, especially to me. You've changed my life, and I love you." I drift off to sleep, in the comfort that I know he's here and safe with me.

ONE WEEK LATER

"We can figure it all out closer to Easter break, but I can't wait to see you, Mum. Oh, maybe we can finally make it across to Vancouver Island. That's if Liam's stomach can take the ferry. He wants to puke just at the sight of open water." Darcy giggles.

I laugh down the phone while chopping vegetables for the traditional British Sunday lunch I'm making for Jon's parents and Adam. I'm running behind schedule, and Jon still isn't back home. He's over an hour late with no word from him.

"He's never had a strong stomach. Remember when Jack got sick that Christmas, and he turned whiter than a sheet."

She giggles harder. "Yeah, I do. Probably wise that he studies architecture and not medicine."

"Too right."

"How're things with Jon? All fully moved in and settled?"

I pause my chopping and squeeze my eyes shut. *Keep it together.*

"Yeah, it's great. I'm just prepping traditional Sunday dinner; we have his parents and Adam coming over in..." I look down at my Apple watch and see the emerald strap Jon bought me, another reminder of the man I fell in love with yet who's been absent from my life for the past week. "Oh shoot, in like thirty minutes. Honey, I need to go, but I'll call you later, okay? Love you."

We hang up the call, and I hit panic mode. I've not even made a start on the batter for the Yorkshire puddings and the entire kitchen is a mess.

Where the fuck is he?

I grab my phone and send him yet another text.

ME

> Your parents and Adam will be here in half an
> hour. Please tell me you're on your way.

Nothing. A further ten minutes pass and he hasn't even read my message.

Trying to stay calm, I fly around the apartment and finish up the food, then clean, lay the table, and throw on Jon's favorite dress. I'm trying everything to catch even a flicker of reassurance that my boyfriend is still in there somewhere. We still cuddle in bed, but the sex has completely gone. He's either had too much to drink or he's too exhausted from overworking in the gym and collapses as soon as nighttime comes. When he realized I'd sprained my wrist trying to help him into bed that night in New York, he was devastated that "he'd hurt me" as he said. It was an accident, but he didn't see it that way, using it as another reason to hate himself.

Jon loves those closest to him unconditionally. He's the most generous person I know when it comes to his heart and what he has, but I'm still struggling to find a way through to him when it comes to turning that love on himself, and I'm starting to question if I'll ever achieve it. His mental health issues are clearly deeply ingrained and other than his therapy, he's only ever used temporary "fixes" to continue functioning. Ways to numb the pain and distract his mind.

The direct elevator to our apartment pings, indicating that we have guests. Right on time, and he's still not here.

I stare in the mirror and fix my hair once more.

You can do this.

"You can definitely cook for us again, Felicity. You clearly know your way around the kitchen. Although, I don't think I'll be eating another thing for the next week!" Jennie compliments me with her usual bright smile, but the mood this afternoon has been anything but. Jon's family has been here and eating for the past hour, but there's still no sign or word from Jon. I covered for him by saying he was held up at practice, and I really hope he was.

I stand from the table and begin collecting the dishes. "The pavlova recipe was my mum's; I can send it to you if you like?"

"That would be wonderful, honey. Do you need some help with the dishes?"

"No," I reply, still plastering on my façade. "Just relax; I've got it."

I balance the dishes in both hands, thankful my wrist healed quickly, and blow out a deep breath when I reach the kitchen. I check my texts, but there's still no word from Jon.

I lock my phone just as a hand reaches to place a glass on the counter and I look up to find Adam. Like the rest of us, he knows something isn't right and while he prefers not to verbalize too often, I can tell he wants to talk.

"He's having a hard time again, isn't he?" Adam asks, hands in his pockets and looking down at the floor.

I choose not to sugarcoat the situation. Adam is one of the most honest and direct people I've met. "Yes. Since Zach's accident, he's gone downhill, over training and drinking. He won't talk to me, but I can tell he blames himself for what happened."

Adam nods in understanding. "He's always been like this. He takes on the world and achieves so much yet thinks he'll never be good enough."

"I know," I say on a soft exhale.

"You won't give up on him, will you? He's a good person, and so are you." Adam raises his head but doesn't make eye contact with me, though I can see the anguish written all over his face as he stares at the kitchen cabinet in front of him. He's hurting for his brother.

I place my hand on Adam's forearm. "No, I won't give up on him. I'll make sure he sees just how wanted he is."

My eyes are blurry with unshed tears as I turn back to the sink and begin clearing the dishes.

"You love him."

My tears spill over, and I turn back around to face Adam. "With all my heart."

CHAPTER THIRTY-FOUR

JON - ONE WEEK LATER

My life feels like a version of Groundhog Day.

But it's the only way I can keep myself from losing complete control. When I'm not on the ice, I'm in the gym, lifting weights and pushing myself to the limit on the cardio machines.

I barely see Felicity as she comes and goes to work, and I feel like an asshole. From the moment we returned from New York, I've driven her away on a clear path to self-destruction. I'm waiting for her to wake up and realize I'm not worth it, because it's going to happen. If I can't protect my best friend and make the right decisions on the ice, how can I possibly be the man to protect her for life?

Yet despite it all, I can't bring myself to end it with her. Through the overwhelming noise in my mind, my heart screams to hold onto what we've got, no matter how broken it feels right now. She tries to touch me, but I push her away, and when she invites my family over for a traditional British Sunday lunch, what do I do? I hide in the gym, pussying out and not wanting to face my reality.

I lift the Olympic bar for a fifteenth rep and replace it with a bang, sweat pouring from me as I snatch up my bottle and towel and head for the locker room.

Practice finished hours ago, and Zach is the last person I expect to see sitting on my bench when I push through the door, his crutches set to the side. He looks like hell, his face is swollen, bruised, and marred with stitches.

His head swings around when I come into view.

"How'd you know where to find me?" I ask, wiping the back of my neck with my towel, sweat still dripping from me.

"You've lost weight." He doesn't bother responding to my question. When times are tough, I'll be here or at a bar, and he's not wrong to guess the gym. He's also not wrong that I've shed a few pounds over the last couple of weeks; overtraining and undereating will do that to an athlete.

I take a seat on the bench opposite but say nothing, instead choosing to hear Zach out.

He runs a hand up the back of his neck before it comes down and smacks his thigh. "What happened in New York, it wasn't your fault. My head was up my ass, and I put you in an impossible position, and for that, I'm sorry. What I said to you that morning, I shouldn't have taken it out on you." He purses his lips together and shakes his head. "I thought she fucking loved me, but she didn't, and then I see you wrapped up in Felicity and that's all I wanted, you know. You've spent your whole life fucking around with women, and I've been searching for the one, and yet all I get is a woman intent on emotionally breaking me and sleeping around behind my back. You literally bump into the first woman you've ever been seriously interested in, and she turns out to be your soulmate. I was hurting, and I was out of order and what happened with Schneider, that was on me and him. Not you."

"You were right the first time, man. I have been a shitty friend. I should've stopped you from—"

"Stopped me from what exactly?" Zach's tone is sharper, and

I can detect a tinge of frustration. "Stopped me from meeting Amie? Stopped me from dating her? Stopped me from going back to her and sleeping with her in Nashville? Or did you plan on stopping me from telling Schneider the baby's mine when he was in the penalty box? You can't take everything on as your responsibility, and you can't blame yourself when things go wrong. Do you know how hard it is to stand by and watch you crucify yourself?"

He looks up and blows out a harsh breath. "Let me tell you something. The very thing you've always wanted, you're pushing away. You're pushing her out of your life before you've even gotten started. She's the sort of woman dreams are made of, man. The sort of woman I've been searching for all these years, and she's chosen you. Women like her don't date just anyone, and that's all you need to know about yourself, Jon. You have her, so for fuck's sake, don't throw her away. You'll spend the rest of your life regretting it."

Zach gathers his crutches and stands from the bench. "You've never let me down, Jon, but you're on the brink of sabotaging and letting yourself down in the most catastrophic way possible."

I HEARD everything Zach said and to be honest, I knew it all deep down, how lucky I am to have her. How much I care for and love her has never been in question. But as I pull up in my apartment parking lot, I'm afraid it's too late, that the damage has been done.

I chased her for months, trying to convince her to date me and to give me a shot. I worked to build her trust, and in the blink of an eye, I feel like I've destroyed it all. She's stood by me through everything, but I wouldn't blame her if she decides it's over. For weeks I've buried every emotion and hidden behind coping strategies, frozen and numb to everything. My best friend is right; I'm in destruct mode and I'm teetering on the edge of making my worst nightmares a reality.

Walking into my apartment, I half expect to find her things gone. I don't. Instead, I find my brother perched on the end of the couch, watching a rerun of last year's playoffs.

"Felicity's at work; she gave me the code."

"That's cool. It's good to see you, bro," I reply, setting my keys on the side. Adam's never been to my apartment unannounced, let alone on his own.

"I'm here to talk with you."

"I'm all ears." Knowing whatever he has to say is important. He's here for good reason and my stomach clenches at what he might have to say.

"She loves you." My head shoots up.

What?

"She loves you, Jon." He points his finger at me, frustration twisting his face. "And you're going to throw it all away."

How does he even know what she feels?

"She told me, at the dinner you never showed up to. She cried, and she told me."

I take a seat on the couch opposite him and press mute on the TV.

Adam looks down and scuffs the floor with one of his feet. "We know you've struggled, but I want to tell you that you're the best brother. You've stood by me, cared for me, defended me at school, you even bought a house for me."

Tears spill from my eyes, and I quickly wipe at them with the backs of my hands.

"If you let her go, I'll lose her, too. She's special."

My heart rate soars as it threatens to beat clean through my chest. The ringing in my ears makes a return, and I wipe at my neck, feeling sure I had showered after the gym, but sweat pours down my back. "I think I might've already blown it."

"I told you; she loves you. She told me. Don't lose her."

She fucking loves me. Even after what I've put her through. She still wants me.

"I need to drop you back home," I tell him, rising from my seat.

FELICITY

"Yeah, they're tough but you absolutely aced your bachelors; there's no way you won't get through the bar exams."

"Hmmm, I think your confidence in me might be a little misplaced, Kate."

"A little like the lack of faith in yourself," she responds, pushing off my desk.

"It kills me to think he kept you from living out your dreams. Promise me, you'll always chase them from now on."

Jon is the reason I decided to take Mark up on his offer and take the plunge and sit for the bar exams to become a human rights lawyer. I need to be with him, but no matter what happens, I know without a doubt the impact he's had on me, my confidence, and my outlook on life. I want to make him proud, but I also owe it to myself, having abandoned my dreams for someone else's all those years ago.

I grab my jacket from the back of the chair and my bag from the desk. Pretty much everyone has left the office as I head to the elevator and down to the lobby. Bright lights blind my vision as I push the doors open and head out into the night sky.

"Hey, Angel."

Jon's standing a few feet away, clad in black jeans, a gray sweater, white Nikes, and a backward cap. He looks delicious—no, better than delicious. Utterly beautiful. It's neither what he's wearing that picks up my pulse nor the white muscle car he's leaning against. It's the sight of his wide dimple-popping smile. A sight my heart has been craving.

I lurch forward and into his arms, his spicy cologne enveloping me in warmth against the frigid night air. "It's just like that night you picked me up," I whisper against his chest.

"Fancy some fried chicken?"

I snort-laugh, and it's definitely attractive. "Fancy? Going all British on me, are you?"

Jon throws his head back and laughs. "Watch it, Mary."

"You know what I fancy? Heading home and getting cozy."

He smiles sweetly, his expression lighter than I've seen in a while, and relief washes over me in waves. "Me too, Angel."

CHAPTER THIRTY-FIVE

JON

I lay the woman I love down on our bed and slowly unbutton her blouse.

It's taken thirty minutes to get from my apartment complex parking lot to our bedroom since we made out in my car for a good twenty and then in our private elevator for another ten. I feel like I'm floating, my body is thrumming with the need for her touch, the trace of her pale pink fingernails, and the caress of her warmth.

I need to be inside her, fast. But much more than that, I need her to know how much I appreciate everything she is. Her loyalty and resilience to walk with me even through the darkest tunnels of my existence.

"I'm so fucking sorry. Forgive me," I whisper against her stomach. I nip and kiss around her navel before I travel lower and drag her skirt and panties down and over her hips.

"There's nothing to forgive, Jon. I just want you to know, I'll always be a safe place for you."

"You make me feel everything that's worth feeling."

"Show me how that feels," she says on a breathless whisper.

I lean across to dim the lighting in the room. I flick a second switch, uncertain of where I am in my playlist when Khalid's "Better" starts playing through the speakers. Perfect.

"Lie back, Angel." I'm not sure how much time passes, but I know for certain every minute is spent serenading my girlfriend. She comes undone beneath me as I nip and suck at her inner thighs and pussy, enjoying her sweet taste on my tongue.

"Jon," she cries, and I continue to eat her out as her orgasm begins to overtake her body.

"What do you want?" I ask, licking the last of her off my lips.

"Everything. I want it all."

I stand from the bed and push my pants and boxer briefs to the floor. I pull my sweater over my head and unbutton my shirt but leave it hanging open, too eager to get her back in my arms.

She's on her knees over the other side of the bed, her emerald eyes admiring me as I undress.

"Crawl to me."

When she reaches me, I lie down beside her, grab her by the waist, and lift her on top. "Ride my cock, baby. I want to watch you bounce on my dick."

The tight throb of her pussy is overwhelming when she lowers herself, taking every inch of me as she moans and throws her head back.

"Jesus. You squeeze me so good."

Slowly rocking her hips over me, she begins to find a rhythm that sends us both into orbit. "I've missed this so much." She gasps.

"Me too, being this close to you, my soulmate. I never knew how to breathe before I met you, it's like my body has been starved of what it needs." I grasp her hips and sink my fingertips into her soft, curvy body as she continues to take what she wants from me. And I give her everything I have.

"You're it for me. This is everything I want."

"I love you, Jon." Her head falls forward as she comes again and lazily kisses my lips, her body totally sated.

My heart squeezes, hearing those words from her. Words I never thought I'd hear never mind feel worthy of. But I do. Being here, in this moment, feeling everything she is deep in my bones. I know I'm enough.

But I'll never get enough of my dream girl.

"You said you want all of me? I want all of you too, I want to take every part of you. Is that okay?"

She looks down at me through hooded eyes. "Yes."

"Turn around."

Once she's on her hands and knees with her back to me, I push her legs apart and palm my cock. It's already aching in anticipation of taking Felicity in a way I've fantasized about for months. Reaching into drawer of my nightstand I pull out a bottle of lube and squeeze an amount over her ass.

Rubbing it over her with my fingers, she gasps in pleasure. "Deep breaths and relax for me, Angel."

I swipe my fingers through her soaking pussy and as she moans, I use it to massage her. Slowly pushing my finger inside, she begins to buckle under the intense pleasure, so I support her, wrapping my arm around her waist.

"How does this feel?"

"A-Amazing."

"I'm so fucking hard for you."

"I'm ready."

Her green light given, I rise to one knee and slowly begin to ease myself inside her ass. I've never felt anything as tight as the way my girlfriend grips my dick. She moans and gasps as I continue to bury myself deep inside her until I'm seated all the way.

"I love you so fucking much, Felicity." I'm taking her in the most intimate way possible, and my heart swells knowing the total trust she's placing in me in this moment.

Once I'm happy she's comfortable, I begin to stroke into her as I keep a firm grip on her hips. I feel dizzy as the familiar feeling of an orgasm builds at the base of my spine and pressure rises in my balls.

"I never knew it could be like this," she gasps, and I can tell she's close too.

Me neither, Angel.

"I'm right there. I won't last much longer, not with the way you're wrapped around my cock."

"Me too, I'm right...ohmygod. I-I...I'm com—"

I come on a roar and empty myself inside her as my hips begin to slow their movements against hers.

I'm still fully inside as I pull her gently to my chest, sitting back on my heels. We're chest to back as I place open mouth kisses along her neck and collarbone.

After a few minutes, I pull out and lay her back on the bed. "Wait here, Angel."

She hasn't moved at all when I return a few moments later with a warm cloth to clean her up. "That was fucking amazing, baby."

She rolls onto her side, hands tucked under her head, and a satisfied glaze sheens her eyes. "Possibly mind-blowing."

"Yeah?" I chuckle and kiss her forehead. "So, you wouldn't object to a repeat performance of that sometime."

She checks the non-existent watch on her wrist. "Hm, give me about thirty minutes to recover, yeah?"

Half an hour later, I'm not inside her again, much to my disappointment. Instead, Felicity's sitting at the kitchen counter dressed in my jersey and nothing else. I'm making waffles because she said she wanted them, and I'm so whipped for her I slipped out in the middle of the night to grab fresh eggs and syrup.

Watching with fascination, she proceeds to take the biggest bite I've ever seen, and my dick rises when her tongue peeks out and sweeps the trailing syrup from her bottom lip.

"Keep doing that, Angel, and those waffles will be cold

before you even have time to finish them," I say as I walk around to where she's seated and scoot her up, sitting her back down on my lap. I take a bite of food directly from her fork and smile at her around my mouthful. The way she brings me to life.

After these past couple of weeks, I just want to be close to her. Especially as I leave the day after next for another away series. "How was work?"

There's a proud look in her eyes. "I made a decision today."

I kiss her jaw. "Oh yeah?"

"Mm-hmm, I've decided to sit for the bar exams to give myself a shot at becoming a lawyer."

"Are you kidding me? Felicity, that's fucking amazing. God damn, I'm so fucking proud of you." And I am. I've never been so proud of anything or anyone in my life.

"It's the first step in a long process, but I figure I have to start sometime, right?"

"Does this mean I get to see you in suits, heels, and curly wigs?"

She belly laughs. "That's kind of old-fashioned now, but if you insist, I'm sure I can wear one around the apartment."

I reach down and lightly squeeze her ass. "That's an order, Ms. Thompson." Each time I say her surname it makes me want to change it to mine as soon as possible.

A few beats pass before Felicity turns to me; a sobering look across her face. "Will you start seeing Ben again? I know you've straightened things out with Zach, and you have me and your family, but I really think talking everything through with him would be good."

Placing a kiss to her shoulder, I reassure her. "I see him tomorrow afternoon right after practice, and I need to start being totally open with him. I've held a lot back from you and everyone else about the way I sought the comfort of women, buried myself in the gym, and at times drank myself stupid to numb the pain, but I know I won't go back there now. Adam came to talk to me earlier, and he told me how much I've done for him." My voice cracks, thick with emotion.

Offering me her last piece of waffle, I lean forward and take it. "He's proud of you. We all are."

"I'm so lucky to have you."

"Not lucky, Jon. This, everything you have, the people around you. You deserve it." She pauses and strokes my cheek with her thumb, swallowing me whole with her bright-emerald eyes. "And I'm one of those people who loves you. I love you so much. You've shown me what relationships can be like, shown me that I can follow my dreams, and that a love like this isn't limited to fiction. You are my living and breathing fairytale."

I slant my mouth across hers, and I kiss her. I kiss her with every part of me. I kiss her like she's my life source and I'm hers, and I don't stop until we break apart, both of our chests heaving as we gasp for air. "You're it for me, Angel. Beyond you, there's nothing else."

"Even if I can't give you children? I mean, technically I could, but at thirty-nine, I'm not sure I could do it again."

Tucking away a lock of hair from her messy bun, I lean closer until my lips brush her ear and I smile as I watch her skin react to the caress of my breath. "Just in case you didn't hear me the first time, I'll say it again. You're it for me, Angel. Beyond you, there's nothing else."

EPILOGUE

FELICITY - FOUR MONTHS LATER

"For the hundredth time, I'm not telling you. These lips are firmly sealed." Jon makes a zipping motion across his mouth.

I sit back in my seat, considerably annoyed I haven't managed to break him over the last twenty-four hours since he told me I wouldn't be going to work for the next week. Apparently, no amount of blow jobs, sex, private dances, or even promising to allow Miley Cyrus on in the car for the rest of time will crack this man.

Since then, I've tried to break Kate, Darcy, Jack, Adam, Zach, Jensen, and the rest of the team, but they're all traitors, refusing to budge an inch. They're all Team Jon, and that has been duly noted by me. I thought at least Adam would be on my side. He's giving Kate competition for best friend status, and over the last few months, I have seen more and more of him as he attends games with us in the box. He even comes over for dinner at our apartment at least once a week. Adam's doing great, and this has helped Jon so much. Seeing happiness flood their lives is nothing short of what both these amazing men deserve.

I stretch out and yawn in the passenger seat. Jon woke me at the crack of dawn this morning, told me to dress comfortably, and then our doorman proceeded to roll two suitcases out to his G-Wagon, so clearly, he's in on it, too.

"Just a little clue then."

"No."

"I'll sneak olives into your dinner."

"And I'll happily eat them," Jon says, eyes on the road and keeping a straight face.

"Liar."

"You're around eleven hours away from finding out where we're going, and I'm so proud of you for being patient." He delivers the last part of that sentence in a mock patronizing tone while patting my knee.

I pull out my phone.

ME

This is your final warning.

KATE

Girl, I'm warned. But I'm still not giving you shit.

Dammit.

It's around twenty minutes later when Jon pulls into the terminal that I recognize the team uses to fly out for away games since I've been dropping him off here for the past few months.

My heart trips out slightly. "We're getting on a plane?"

Pulling up in the private parking lot, he leans across and undoes my seat belt, kissing me on the bridge of my nose. That shit eating, dimple-popping, annoyingly-does-me-every-time grin is still on full display.

He takes my hand and leads me to the private jet while the ground staff take our bags and load them onto the plane.

"I've never been on a private jet before," I say in awe as we

290

board, and I take in the plush leather interior and elaborate decor.

We take our seats, and the captain announces how long the flight will be but again, no destination. The usual safety procedures are announced and before I know it, I'm thirty-thousand feet in the air and sipping on a Cosmo at six in the morning.

"We're a half hour from landing, Angel. Are you ready to find out where we're going?" Jon whispers in my ear, waking me from my sleep.

I yawn. "Born ready."

He laughs and gives the cabin crew member a nod.

"Good afternoon Mr. Morgan and Ms. Thompson, I hope you enjoyed a pleasant flight with us today. I'm pleased to confirm we will very shortly begin our descent into Tromsø Airport, and from there you will be collected by your chauffeur and taken straight to your destination."

My breath hitches in my throat as tears begin to prick in my eyes. "Y-You brought me to Norway."

Raising my hand to his mouth, he kisses my knuckles gently. "I hope your dad won't mind me stealing his idea."

I don't know what to say as the tears spill over and down my cheeks. I miss my parents every day, and Elliott forcing me to sell their house and then moving to Seattle has made them feel even further from reach. But as the wheels touch down at Tromsø Airport, I feel a part of my dad deep within my soul, almost like he's been waiting for me to meet him here.

JON BOOKED us a cabin right on the water and in the middle of nowhere. It's the perfect place to watch the aurora.

"Oh my god, look at the size of that hot tub. I could take a swim in that thing."

"Why don't you get in and try it out?"

"Aren't you coming in with me?" I stick my bottom lip out like the thirty-nine-year-old child I can be.

"Let me think about this..." He leans against the marble counter. "You, me, a huge hot tub, and the northern lights? Yeah. I think I'll be joining you."

I make my way to the master bedroom. "Well, give me a few; I need to get my bikini on."

"Good luck with that."

I turn on my heel. "What do you mean?"

"I didn't pack one. Guess you'll just have to go in naked."

I quirk a mischievous brow. "Oh, really?"

Two can play at that game, Mr. Morgan.

Standing only a few feet away, I slowly walk back toward him and unzip my hoodie. I only have a cami top underneath, and given I was told to dress comfortably, I skipped the bra.

The moment Jon sees my peaked nipples he groans, a deep rumble from his chest. "I want you fully naked and in that tub in the next thirty seconds."

Our cabin is totally secluded as I slip into the warm bubbling water. I'm still waiting on Jon, who's been messing around in the bedroom for the past five minutes.

It's a beautiful clear night, perfect for watching the auroras dance in the sky.

Grabbing my hair tie from my wrist, I throw my unwashed hair up into a messy bun. I'm makeup-free and feeling less than attractive but what the hell.

Two hands fall to my shoulders as they nudge me forward and then a sculpted naked body slides in behind me until my back is to his chest and his arms are around me.

"I'm sorry you didn't make the playoffs." With Zach out for the rest of the season, it was an uphill battle, and the Scorpions narrowly missed out.

Jon's lips fall to the soft flesh of my neck. "Sitting here with you in this tub, I'm not all that disappointed."

I throw my head back and bask in the way his lips move

across my pebbled skin. His touch affects me even more than the day we met.

"It's starting, Angel."

I look up to see the sky illuminate with green. Greens turn to pinks as the most beautiful show unfolds above us. A lump forms in my throat. "This is perfect, everything about this."

Jon clears his throat. "There's only one other thing that could make this night more perfect," he whispers from behind me, his voice barely audible above the hum of the hot tub.

I cast my fingers over the surface of the water, loving the way the bubbles tickle my skin. "What's that, baby?"

I turn around to see him leaning over the tub, his back on full display. I pull my hand from the bubbles and trace my fingers over the large angel wings he had tattooed. I'll never forget the day he showed me the beautiful art he had carved into his skin, he told me it was in my honor and how I set him free from the demons in his mind and breathed life into his world. "It's so beautiful."

He turns around to face me, and I straddle his thighs, my core clenching at the position and us both being naked, skin on skin. A finger comes under my chin. "This way I'll always have you with me. No matter where I am." He kisses me softly on the lips. "You aren't just everything I want, Felicity; you're everything I need."

I place my hand on his sculpted chest, and he brings his forehead to mine.

"Marry me."

I pull back slightly and search his face.

Did he...?

"Marry me, Felicity." His voice is shaky with trepidation, waiting for my response. One hand drops from my chin to my waist, holding me gently as he brings his other hand into view, and there in the center of his palm is a small black velvet box. With one hand, Jon skillfully pops the lid to reveal an oval-cut emerald ring. The huge stone is set on a thin white gold band, simple yet insanely elegant. "Adam helped me choose it. We both agreed that emerald is your color. I also figured that asking you here, under these lights, was the closest I could get to asking your dad for his permission."

Reaching out, I pluck the ring from its box and look up at my fiancé.

"Okay."

His dimples pop. "As in okay, okay?"

I laugh and squeak out, "As in definitely, one hundred percent yes."

It's there, with a stunning emerald engagement ring on my left hand, telling me one day I'll be Mrs. Morgan, that the man I almost discounted as a cocky, only-up-for-a-good-time playboy, makes sweet love to me under the northern light sky.

"HAVE YOU HEARD FROM ZACH?" I ask, walking into the bedroom. Jon is sitting on the edge of the king-size bed, staring down at his phone.

"Yeah, he's just taken the test, and we now wait for the results." He blows out a breath. "I'm glad it's being done now, so he knows where he is before the baby's born."

I nod, feeling every range of emotions on Zach's behalf. "Yeah, he'll step up no matter what though. He's just that sort of guy."

"He's one of the best guys I know. He sends his congrats, by the way." Jon holds his phone up. "Let me take a picture to send to him."

I plaster on my best cheesy grin and hold my hand out like the giddy teenager I am.

"Do you think he'll be okay, you know, while you're away?"

Jon nods assuredly. "He'll be fine, plus I'll keep checking in with him."

He returns his attention back to his phone. "Mom is going crazy. She wants to know if she has a daughter-in-law yet."

I look down at my ring for the hundredth time. "Just put her out of her misery."

Typing out a quick message, he tosses his phone to the side. "Come here."

I stand between his legs as he rubs up and down the backs of my thighs, palming my ass and squeezing it gently. "I think we should get married in England."

I balk at this suggestion, assuming he'd want to get married near to his mum and dad. "Really? I assumed you'd want to get married in Seattle."

His shrug is indifferent. "It's tradition to get married where the bride's from, isn't it?"

"I guess so, but where would we hold it? Oh, maybe the place we stayed at on Boxing Day." I can't pronounce the name and my French accent is atrocious.

Jon smiles up at me, kissing along my jaw. "J'ai une meilleure idée."

"Hang on, I think I remember this phrase from high school." I tap my chin, deep in thought. "I have a...better idea?"

"C'est exact."

I clap my hands, far too excited by my small triumph.

"Qu'en est-il de vingt-deux Kennington Voie?"

"Hm, this one might be a bit above my pay grade. So, I think the first part is 'what about' and I know what Kennington is, that's my par—"

I pause and attempt to process what I think he just said.

"That's my parents' old house," I whisper. "We can't marry there." I chuckle at the outrageous notion. "Not unless the current owners allow us to hold a ceremony and grant us a license."

"No, you're right, that would be a bit far-fetched."

"Just a little." I laugh, staring down at my ring, *again*.

"It *would* be a little far-fetched if the owner wasn't standing right in front of me."

I inhale with a gasp and my head whips up to meet Jon's steely-gray eyes, his trademark dimple-popping grin curving up to meet them.

"So, what do you say, Angel? How about marrying me in that gorgeous English garden of yours?"

THE END.

Zach's story is coming July 2024. Preorder his book to find out what happens next!

ACKNOWLEDGMENTS

My Husband: Jon Morgan encourages Felicity to chase her dreams and you are absolutely the inspiration behind this. Your willingness to do the heavy lifting and day to day tasks while I retreat upstairs to write. You've held my hand through the darkest of times and celebrated in the brightest. You are truly the best person I know and I'm so lucky to call you mine.

My Dad: Firstly, thank you for following me on social media but never once reading or watching any of my posts, and if you did, thank you for never telling me. In all seriousness, you've always been my greatest cheerleader. From the moment I was born to the present day, you have always been in my corner, guiding and encouraging me to be the best person possible. Our bond is and always will be unbreakable.

My little boy: At seven years old, I think you've taught me more about life than anyone ever has. One day, I hope we will be able to exchange words and you will be able to tell me just how annoying I am when I smother you with kisses. Truly though my LB, I love you from the very depths of my soul. What a special and wonderful boy you are.

Kate: I must tell you chick, I'm not sure writing this book was good for project stay young, but at least it kept me busy and away from leaving you ten-minute-long voice notes. I don't think you'll ever realize how much of an inspiration you are to me. But you are. I carry you with me everywhere I go. Thank you for being such a wonderful friend.

Abby: It seems like a long time ago when we went on our

walks, and I bent your ear about this mad idea I had for a spicy hockey romance. It was in fact almost a year ago and I want to thank you for putting up with my neurotic messages and voice notes through this entire time. You are truly an amazing friend and I'm so glad we met. Flip flop next summer?

Sam: What is life? I know we've said it a thousand times, but I'll say it again. We did the thing, and where would I have been without you? You're always the first person I go to when I have some news, or I need to cry, vent or share ridiculous ideas with. I'm so glad I messaged you that November night and told you all about my idea for a reformed playboy reverse age gap hockey romance. From the first moment, you took me under your wing and helped me navigate the bookstagram world. You are one of my greatest friends and I'm honored that you consider me to be yours. I hope you're cool with that because newsflash, you're stuck with me forever.

Hannah Gray: Hannah, what a beacon you are in this cutthroat industry. I've gone from reading your books in my garden to calling you a friend. Thank you for all your support and guidance.

Tina: Finally, I've found someone who likes olives as much as me! That should be reason enough to remain friends for a lifetime. Thank you for your help, keen eyes on my manuscript, for Alpha reading book two and generally being an honest, kind and supportive guide.

Sariah: SARIAH! I'm here to tell you that Jon is FINALLY YOURS. ALWAYS. It genuinely fills my heart to think of you kicking and screaming your way through Boarded Hearts and I am here for it all. Thank you for being my biggest fan and for shouting about me from one day. Good girl.

Jessi: Bestie! Always and forever. Best believe when I next visit Florida, I'm hitting you up for that hug and to generally go crazy over every single book boyfriend we share. P.s. you have a great British accent.

Ash: Can we go feral over hockey players forever? Thank you for keeping me sane, well mostly.

My beta team: To everyone on my beta team, Ashley, Tina, Lauren and Sam—THANK YOU! Thank God it wasn't 37,000 words! LOL.

To all at Wordsmith Publicity: Autumn and the whole team at Wordsmith, thank you. I've learned so much and cannot wait to continue working with you as we release the rest of the series. You go above and beyond, and I am forever grateful.

To the Bookstagram community: What an incredible place this is to be. You have welcomed me with open arms and promoted me and Boarded Hearts in a way I can never repay. All I can do is offer you Zach, Jensen and maybe one other...EDGE.

To all my readers: Most importantly, to everyone who has picked up and read Boarded Hearts. THANK YOU. Having the opportunity to write my words and share Jon and Felicity with you has been a true honor and I really hope you'll stick around to follow the rest of the Scorpion boys as they fall in love and find their HEA. I love and appreciate you all.

ABOUT THE AUTHOR

Ruth Stilling is an avid romance reader turned writer. Having spent many years reading about and dreaming of her ideal book boyfriend, she finally decided to create her own, and to share him with the rest of the world.

Living in a small town in Derbyshire, England, Ruth is an introvert by nature and spends much of her time talking with her equally book crazy friends from across the globe.

What started as a dream soon turned into reality as she began piecing together and planning her debut novel, *Boarded Hearts*. In becoming a published author, Ruth is following her dreams and will always encourage her readers to do the same.

When she isn't writing your next book boyfriend, Ruth enjoys watching all kinds of sports and is an Aston Villa and Derby County fan. The outdoors is a real favorite, and if the British weather were kinder, she would spend all her time writing outside.

Ruth is a wife to her best friend and number one cheerleader, whom she married in 2015, and she is a mom to her beautiful son who has shown her a new perspective in life—enjoy and celebrate who you are as a person, and cherish those who are there for you through rain and shine.

Ruth is incredibly excited to share the rest of the Seattle Scorpions Series with you!

You can follow Ruth and keep up to date via Instagram and TikTok by searching @authorruthstilling

Printed in Great Britain
by Amazon

42583850R00179